CHAMPAVERT

Borgo Press Books by PÉTRUS BOREL THE LYCANTHROPE

Champavert: Immoral Tales

CHAMPAVERT

IMMORAL TALES

PÉTRUS BOREL

THE LYCANTHROPE

Translated by Brian Stableford

THE BORGO PRESS

MMXIII

CLASSICS OF
FANTASTIC LITERATURE
NUMBER SIX

CHAMPAVERT

FIRST EDITION

Published by Wildside Press LLC

www.wildsidebooks.com

CHAMPAVERT

CONTENTS

INTRODUCTION

Champavert: Contes Immoraux by "Pétrus Borel, le ly-canthrope," here translated as *Champavert: Immoral Tales* by Pétrus Borel the Lycanthrope, was initially published in Paris by Eugène Renduel in 1833. It was the second book to appear under the signature of Pétrus Borel, having been preceded by a volume of poems entitled *Rhapsodies*, published the previous year. It was not the last such publication, although the later ones were, so to speak, illusory, for reasons explained in the preface to *Champavert*.

The preface in question explains that "Pétrus Borel" was the pseudonym of someone named Champavert, who had recently committed suicide, and that the collection of stories was an initial sampling from the papers he left behind—including the story of Champavert's suicide. Like the narrative voice that describes Champavert's death retrospectively in the final passage of the final item in the collection, someone or something did live on after that alleged suicide, but it was not the same person; the Pétrus Borel who had secretly been "Champavert le lycanthrope" was dead, and had indeed committed suicide, spiritually and artistically. As is obvious to any reader of *Champavert*, the Pétrus Borel who published the novel *Madame Putiphar* [Potiphar's Wife] (1838) and several further stories—including "La Nonne de Penaranda" [The Nun of Penaranda] (1842) and "Le Trésor de la caverne d'Arceuil" [The Trasure of the Cave of Arcueil] (1843) in the *Revue de Paris* and "Miss Hazel" (1844) in the *Revue pittoresque*—was not the same person, and signaled the fact by omitting to add "le lycanthrope" to his signature.

Biographies of Pétrus Borel tend to blur this circumstance, inevitably, because biographies, by their nature, are committed to a world-view that measures continuity in terms of physical presence, and cannot admit the possibility that an artist might commit suicide, although the man in whom he dwelt carries on living, in a purely metaphorical sense—but Pétrus Borel the Lycanthrope was a key member of the French Romantic Movement, and he understood things differently.

The "biographical sketch of Champavert" that begins the collection explains how Borel came to adopt the nickname "lycanthrope" as a consequence of being accused, on the basis of *Rhapsodies*, of being a Republican. If he was a Republican, he replied, then his was the Republicanism of the lynx or the lycanthrope—by which he meant the ultimate social outsider, a wolf in human guise. Had he lived in a later era, no one would have been so foolish as to accuse him of Republicanism; they would have charged him with being an Anarchist, which would have been closer to the mark, but still a trifle wide. An Anarchist is a believer, committed to the faith that the total destruction of the sick civilization in which we live might herald a new and paradisal dawn. Had he ever heard of Anarchism, Pétrus Borel the Lycanthrope would doubtless have been less scornful of it than he was of Christianity, but that would not have altered the fact that, for him, there was no possibility of dawn after disaster, but only of oblivion.

Having said that, it is worth noting that the subsequent literary work that came closest of all to reproducing the violent sensibility of the stories collected in *Champavert* is *Les Microbes humains* (1887; tr. as *The Human Microbes*) by the anarchist Louise Michel—but Louis Michel had to be unjustly imprisoned, not for the first time, and held incommunicado in solitary confinement in order finally to raise her virtuous outrage to the pitch that overflowed furiously into that novel; Pétrus Borel only needed to be in the world, to be alive, to feel the same awful psychological pressure. He was a remarkable man, and a remarkable writer—perhaps the most remarkable of all the members of the Romantic Movement, albeit one of the least successful in commercial terms.

Joseph-Pierre Borel, who subsequently tarted up his preferred forename to make it more distinctive, was born in 1809 in Lyon, the twelfth of fourteen children of an ironmonger. His younger brother André—some of whose poetry is quoted in *Champavert*—was a keen genealogist, who expended a great deal of effort trying to prove that the Borels were of aristocratic descent, and eventually took to calling himself André Borel d'Hauterive, with the result that many biographical sketches of his brother do him the same imaginary favor—very inappropriately, for Pétrus Borel did not care a fig about aristocratic descent. Quite the reverse; he remarked regretfully on the fact that his father had "come down from the Mountains" in order to take up residence, and a civilized occupation, in the city of Lyon. He seems, however, to have been fonder of Lyon than of Paris, to which the family moved in 1820, and where his father set up a business dealing in esparto products.

The "Biographical Sketch of Champavert" notes, contemptuously, that his education was "confided to priests," which only served to give the young Pétrus a powerful appetite for atheistic self-education, and that thereafter, he was apprenticed to the architect Antoine Garnaud—who was presumably a relative, his mother's maiden name being Garnaud. It was during that apprenticeship, which became increasingly theoretical before evaporating completely, that he found his true vocation, when he began attending the *cénacle* hosted by Victor Hugo, and then became the heart and soul of its splinter group, the *petit cénacle*.

The first *cénacle*, which gave its name to subsequent gatherings of writers intent on disrupting the dry dominance of Classicism and infusing new life into French literature under the banner of Romanticism, had been founded and hosted by Charles Nodier, but as Nodier's health had deteriorated and his cantankerousness got worse, while Victor Hugo's reputation had grown apace, the focal point of the movement had changed location. The younger writers drawn into the circle, however, found Hugo and his intimates a trifle intimidating, and soon set up their own meetings, where they could feel more at ease.

Most of what eventually became common knowledge regarding the *petit cénacle* is derived from the fond memories of it recorded by its most successful member, Théophile Gautier, in what he called, inaccurately and immodestly *Histoire de romantisme* (1871; tr. as *The History of Romanticism*). In that account, although its author freely proclaims that Borel was the star and presiding genius of the group, it is Gautier who takes center stage, especially in the elaborate description of the première of *Hernani*, the play by Hugo whose staging in 1830 seemed to the Movement's supporters and opponents alike to be a crucial benchmark in its progress: the moment when the pressurized dam finally burst and the great inundation began. Borel and Gautier organized the claque that was instructed to applaud the play and, if necessary, engage in fisticuffs with its detractors: a claque whose renown is now focused on the emblematic red waistcoat that Gautier commissioned for the occasion. Borel could not afford to order a red waistcoat from a tailor, and turned up in his everyday clothes—a circumstance that serves to symbolize their subsequent careers, in the course of which Gautier, metaphorically speaking, never took off his flamboyant waistcoat, flaunting it as the banner of Romanticism for an entire generation, while Borel faded into the background. Had the battle actually turned physical, however (it did not), we can be sure that it would have been Borel that took the brunt of the enemy assault, and then led the retaliatory charge.

It is difficult now, on reading *Hernani*, to see what all the fuss was about. It includes words that had not been heard on the Parisian stage before, and sentiments that had not been expressed there before, but they rapidly became commonplace, and there is nothing remotely shocking about them now. In a fashion typical of Romantic works, the play pushed the envelope of what was thought to be acceptable at the time, and by so doing, permanently revised the tacit rules of acceptability. Pétrus Borel, however, was not a crafty pusher of envelopes; he wanted to smash the barriers of acceptability to smithereens, rip up the rules, hurl them in the fire and spit on the ashes. He succeeded; *Champavert* is still capable of shocking readers today, and hopefully will, in this very belated translation.

Borel was not alone in this quest for extremes; indeed, he can be retrospectively affiliated to a subsidiary school of Romanticism, usually known as the *roman frénétique* [frenetic fiction], whose archetypal example was provided by Jules Janin's *L'Âne mort et la femme guillotinée* (1829; tr. as *The Dead Donkey and the Guillotined Woman*), a work that had a considerable influence on Honoré de Balzac as well as the members of the *petit cenacle*. Janin never attempted anything as frenetic again, though, and the entire school faded away—as it had to do, because any writer who begins his career by going directly to an extreme has nowhere to go thereafter but backwards.

Borel was no exception to this rule, but he went to a further extreme than anyone else, and had, in consequence, a more distant and precipitate retreat to make. He was not only more extreme than Gautier, who always retained an elegance and style that blunted and polished his occasional mordancy, but more so even than the *petit cénacle*'s other conspicuous *poète maudit*, Gérard de Nerval, who eventually capped his own excess by going mad. Gérard's madness could never quite match the extremism of Borel's sanity, though—or, to be accurate, the sanity of Pétrus Borel the Lycanthrope; for the Pétrus Borel that was still alive when *Champavert* was published, and who remained alive thereafter until 1859—he died of excessive exposure to the sun, after failing to hold on to a job as a colonial administrator in Algeria and being forced into the open as a humble colonist—was no longer possessed of that mortal extremism.

Champavert bears the subtitle "*contes immoraux*," which is generally considered to be sarcastic, because the tales are, in fact, extremely moral. Although one or two of the characters do speak out in favor of vice and injustice, it is only in order that we might loathe their villainy or deplore their cynicism more intensely. All the tales are horror stories, including the one that is blatantly farcical, and what they attempt to horrify their readers with, and call upon their readers to be horrified by, is the violence and corruption of the human world, which they abhor in no uncertain terms. However, Borel did not mean "immoral" in that crudely literal sense, as he points out obliquely in the one farce included in the collection, when he pleads for the necessity of the final chapter on the grounds that the story would be "immoral" without it, because, in fiction, crime has to be punished.

Borel was, in fact, very well aware of the fact that fiction has an inescapable moral order, because a work of fiction, unlike the real world, has a God—the author—who has the power, and therefore the responsibility, to decide the distribution of rewards and punishments within it. Readers know that, and therefore expect, by and large, that omnipotent authors will be benevolent, albeit in mysterious ways, ultimately punishing the characters guilty of the crimes they commit, one way or another. Borel was also well aware, however, of the falseness, absurdity and perversity of such authorial rewards and punishments, and of the fact that it is precisely because of the tacit expectation of some kind of "moral balancing" that the refusal of an author to exercise his omnipotence in saving the innocent and damning the guilty can create in his readers a peculiar sense of outrage and sadness: the sensibility of "tragedy." He knew only too well that arranging "moral" endings in works of fiction is blatant fraud, a kind of artistic false accountancy, and he did not feel—could not feel—that such cooking of books could be justified merely on the grounds that readers yearn to be defrauded, and feel perversely cheated if they are not. Pétrus Borel the Lycanthrope wanted to be an honest accountant, even though he knew full well that, not only would very few readers thank him for it, but that many would be acutely discomfited by it. That was one of the reasons why he committed suicide in advance of the publication of his uncooked book.

Champavert, therefore, is a work of art that hardly anyone liked, and that many people disliked intensely. Borel's friends undoubtedly understood what he was doing, and why, and sympathized, and some of them even took the trouble to compliment it in print, but they did so rather wryly, because they knew what its fate would be. A typical example of such wry praise can be found in the review in the *Revue de Paris*, the chief organ of the Romantic Movement, which was written by one of the writers quoted in *Champavert*, who signed his reviews "P. L." but his other contributions "P. L. Jacob, le bibliophile," although his name was Paul Lacroix. Lacroix appreciated the book, as any true bibliophile would, but he also appreciated the fact that it was doomed in the contemporary literary marketplace, where the demand for lycanthropic fiction was so small as to be hardly measurable.

Champavert was not, however, eternally damned, even to oblivion. The essential method of *roman frénétique* was to be echoed, albeit more subtly, not only by particular writers but by an entire genre: the *conte cruel*. That term was popularized by one of the genre's more enthusiastic practitioners, the Comte de Villiers de l'Isle Adam, and vulgarized when such tales became the standard fare of the Grand Guignol theater. Typically, later *contes cruels* feature a more refined form of cruelty than the one brought into focus by Borel; they deal in foxy twists of a slim knife rather than furious lycanthropic stabs with a broader blade, but their fundamental principle is the same; *Champavert*, much more so than any of Jules Janin's many story collections, remains the great prototype of collections of *contes cruels*, and came to be appreciated as such by connoisseurs of the rogue genre.

More interestingly, perhaps, one particular idiosyncrasy of Borel's literary method was hailed as significant precursor of surrealism. The Surrealist Movement—a lineal descendant of the Romantic Movement, via the Symbolist/Decadent Movement—had a core interest in reducing the mediation of consciousness in literary production, aiming toward an ideal of spontaneity in which the subconscious element of the mind might leak on to the page without overmuch interference by the censorship of rational thought. It is arguable that the appearance of Borel's work is more closely akin to the essentially artificial endeavor of attempting to produce a fictional replica of a "stream of consciousness," but it certainly was spontaneous, arising from the surges of indignation and despair that sometimes carried him away in the process of creation. It was not merely in his vocabulary and the sentiments he expressed that Borel broke through tacit barriers, but also in his syntax and punctuation.

Because of the way in which the typical French punctuation of printed speech operates—with considerably greater ambiguity than the formularistic English usage of quotation marks—it can sometimes be difficult for a reader to distinguish between a character's speech-acts and the narrative voice, and that ambiguity is greatly enhanced when character's thoughts are being represented as well as vocalized speech. In Borel, more than any other author of his time, there is a confusion of representation that sometimes makes it difficult to tell whether a character is speaking or thinking, or whether the narrative voice is intruding upon the business of reportage to address the reader directly. Sometimes, at least, that confusion is deliberate and the blurring strategic, reflecting and creating a calculated confusion between character and narrative voice, which does indeed disrupt the formality of the text to such a degree that the narrative occasionally seems to be an inchoate surge of feeling welling up from somewhere considerably deeper than the rational surface of consciousness, encapsulating not merely real outrage but real anguish.

The stories in *Champavert* are indeed stories, not reportage, and even its preface is a tongue-in-cheek work of fiction, but the fact that they are not autobiographical does not mean that they are not felt, keenly and deeply. That is one of the reasons why *Champavert* is such a remarkable book, which rewards reading even, and particularly, by readers who find the experience profoundly discomfiting, in more ways than one. It is a difficult book to translate, partly because it uses so many exotic, foreign and improvised words, and partly because the routine translation of French syntactical and punctuational devices into English ones inevitably fails to reproduce Borel's idiosyncratic variations, without being able to substitute for them adequately, but I have done my best to retain as much of the flavor of the original as I could.

This translation has been taken from the version of the Renduel edition reproduced on the Bibliothèque Nationale's *gallica* website. Because Borel used so many exotic spellings it is sometimes difficult to identify mere misprints, but there do seem to be quite a few; in many instances where proper names are misrendered, or rendered in an unfamiliar form, in the original, I have replaced them, usually without adding a footnote.

A BIOGRAPHICAL SKETCH
OF CHAMPAVERT

It is always a difficult task to puncture illusions, always a painful duty to relieve the public of its comforting errors, the lies to which it is devoted and has pledged its faith. Nothing is more dangerous than to create a void in the human heart. I would never risk such a scabrous mission. Believe, believe! Abuse yourselves and be abused! Error is almost always pleasant and consoling.

In spite of that reluctance, my religious sincerity gives me the duty today to unmask a deception, fortunately unimportant: a pseudonymy. Please, do not get upset, as you usually do, when you are told that "Clotilde de Surville" does not exist, that her book is apocryphal; that the correspondence of "Ganganelli" and "Carlino" is apocryphal; that "Joseph Delorme" is a pseudograph and his biography a myth.[1] Please, please, I beg you, don't get upset!

Pétrus Borel killed himself last spring. Pray for him, in order that his soul, in which he no longer believed, might find mercy

---

1. "Clotilde de Surville" was the notional fifteenth-century author of a book of poems published in 1803, probably forged by the Marquis de Surville who had died in 1798, after trying to provoke an insurrection against the Directoire in Provence. Carlino was an eighteenth-century actor, famous for playing Arlequino [Harlequin] whose supposed exchange of letters with the contemporary Pope, surnamed Ganganelli, was fraudulent. Joseph Delorme was the subject of *Vie, Poésie et Pensées de Joseph Delorme* (1829) by Charles-Augustin Saint-Beuve; no serious pretence was ever mounted that he was a real person.

before the God that he denied, in order that God will not strike error with the same arm as crime.

Pétrus Borel, the rhapsodist, the lycanthrope—or, to tell the truth, as we have promised, the poor young man who concealed himself under that soubriquet, which he adopted when scarcely emerged from childhood—has killed himself. Thus, few of his comrades knew his real name; none ever knew the cause of that disguise. Did he do it out of necessity or eccentricity? No one knows for sure. The same name was once made illustrious in literature and science by Pétrus Borel de Castres, a learned doctor and antiquary, physician to Louis XIV, the son of the poet Jacques Borel.[2] Was he descended from that family maternally, did he want to resume the name of one of his ancestors? No one knows, and doubtless no one ever will know.

So, as we have reestablished in the title of his book, his real name was Champavert.

There is no sweeter pleasure than that of being accepted into the intimacy of a sensitive—which is to say, superior—individual who is dead; it is a very praiseworthy indiscretion to want to initiated into the secret of the life of a great artist or an unhappy man. One loves the writer who consents to display like tapestries the often-hidden lives of people who are dear to us. Although that of the young and fatal poet with whom we are concerned will not excite any great interest in you, I nevertheless think that you will not find it unwelcome that I have been able to unearth a few details and circumstances of that anomalous life—of which, regrettably, little is known. Champavert rarely talked about himself; he generally came into society like an apparition, without any known antecedents or any presumed future.

There is some reason to believe that he was originally from

---

2. The reference is to Pierre Borel (c1620-1671), an early microscopist, who might have been blurring the truth slightly when he referred to his father Jacques as a "mathematician and poet," as it seems more likely that he was an astrologer, and no examples of his poetry survive.

the Hautes-Alpes, born in ancient Segusia,[3] often having been heard to curse his father for coming down from the Mountains, and proudly to name as his compatriots Philibert-Delorme, Martel-Ange, Servadoni, Audran, Stella, Coisevox, Coustou and Ballanche.[4] He had, however, left his fatherland at a young age.

He represented himself to those who knew him as no older than twenty or twenty-two, but his features, grave at first sight, aged him considerably.

He was rather tall and slim, perhaps even thin; he had a dark complexion, a characteristic profile, large eyes, black and white, and something in his gaze that was exhausting when it was fixed, like the covetous eye of a snake attracting a prey.

Contrary to the habit of our epoch, like Leonardo da Vinci in contrast to his own, he wore his beard long after the age of seventeen; the most insistent pleas could never persuade him to cut it. In that eccentricity, he was four years in advance of the apostles of Henri Saint-Simon.[5] The most accurate way to convey an idea of him is to say that he bore a strong resemblance to Saint Bruno.[6]

His voice and his mannerisms were soft, to the great surprise of anyone seeing him for the first time and who had imagined

---

3. Julius Caesar's account of his wars in Gaul includes mention of a people called the Segusiani, living in the region where the city of Lyon was eventually founded. The name was further popularized by a thirteenth-century religious writer who signed himself Henricus de Segusia.

4. Philibert Delorme, Étienne de Martelange, Jean-Nicolas Servan, alias Servandoni, various members of the Audran family of artists, Jacques Stella, Antoine Coysevox, and Pierre-Simon Ballanche were all born in Lyon, Borel's birthplace.

5. The reference is probably to the Comte de Saint-Simon's sometime secretary Léon Halévy, who wore his beard uncultivated for a while during the period when Borel knew him in Paris; it was not typical of Saint-Simonians in general.

6. The reference is presumably to the cycle of paintings of St. Bruno painted by Eustache Le Sueur and displayed in the Louvre, although only one of them represents the saint with an unkempt beard.

him, on the basis of his poetic writings, to be an ogre or a devil. He was kind, gentle, affable, proud, steadfast, obliging and benevolent; his loving heart—*amoroso con los suyos*, to use the divine Spanish expression—had not yet been spoiled by egotism and gold. When he was deeply wounded, however, his hatred, like his love, became implacable.

When he was dragged into society he brought into it an impression of painful melancholy, like a deer expelled from its thicket.

With regard to details of his childhood, almost none are known; even those he confided to his intimates are unknown. Willfulness was always developed in him to the highest degree; he was bold, headstrong and imperious; scorn for habits and customs was innate in him; he never gave in, even at a very young age. He had a horror of clothes and spent his early years entirely naked; it was only later that anyone succeeded in making him put on the most necessary garments.

There is also a vague suspicion that his education was confided to priests—an opinion to which his irreligion lends adequate support. There is no a hero to a valet, no God to those who live in a temple.

He often took a kind of delight in relating that he had always been exasperating for his masters, always feared by them, without their exactly knowing why; perhaps he often put them in a quandary by his questions *à La Condamine*,[7] and, scenting their crass ignorance, treated them with scorn and disgust! He also said, with pride, that he had been expelled from every school he had attended.

As study was his only passion, and Latin alone did not slake his thirst for knowledge, he was always surrounded by five or six dictionaries of ancient and modern languages, and schol-

---

7. Charles Marie de La Condamine (1701-1774) was a geographer and mathematician who became famous when he supported Isaac Newton's suggestion that the Earth was not a perfect sphere, continually making scrupulous measurements that proved his case, but to which the orthodox supporters of imaginary sphericity steadfastly refused to pay any heed.

arly works that he obtained with difficulty, which his ashamed masters burned in succession.

Already, in those days, he was afflicted by a sadness, and an indefinite, vague and profound chagrin; melancholy was already his "idiosyncrasy." Some of his former schoolfellows recalled having seen him spend entire days weeping bitter tears, without any known or apparent cause; later, he was never able to define these desolations himself. Assuredly, life in forced community had thrown him into that chronic state of suffering, and that suffering, that ennui, excited his sensitive organism and tormented his grievous irritability.

The course of his brief career was similar to that of one of those torrents whose source is unknown, which sometimes flood valleys and sometimes run underground.

That first epoch of his life was followed by a number of years about which we have not been able to obtain the slightest information—except that we have found the following two brief notes among his papers, which give rise to the presumption that his father had placed him, against his will, in apprenticeship to some artist or artisan.

November 1823

Yesterday my father said to me: "You're grown up now, and one needs a profession in this world. Come with me; I'm going to offer you to a master who will treat you well; you'll learn a trade that ought to please you, you who draw on walls, who make poplars, hussars and parrots so well; you'll have a good position." I didn't know what all that meant; I followed my father, and he sold me for two years.

January 1824

So this is what a position is, a master and an apprentice. I don't know whether I really understand, but I'm sad and I think about life; it seems to me to be very short! On this transitory earth, then, why so many cares, so many painful cares—what's the point? Now, I laugh when I see a man who is settled, or in the process of settling. What does a man need, then, to make his life? A bearskin and a few substances. If I've dreamed of a life it isn't this one, Father! If I've dreamed of a life, it's that of a camel-driver in the desert, an Andalusian muleteer, a Tahitian!

* * * * * * * *

It is probable that the man with whom he served his apprenticeship was an architect, for someone recalls having seen him, a few years later, working in the architecture studio of Antoine Garnaud; otherwise, we not been able to discover anything about this phase of his life; doubtless he was engaged in a hand-to-hand struggle with poverty, and in the intervals left to him by his stupid labors and hunger, he abandoned himself to study. Architectural designs and poems have been found among his papers bearing the same dates. His assiduity at the Antoine Garnaud studio gradually became less frequent, and he disappeared entirely therefrom. His aversion for ancient architecture, whose exclusion is well-known, was surely caused by that withdrawal.

He retreated into the shadows in order to devote himself to the studies of which he was fond; he was only seen to reappear at rare intervals, directing a few constructions, or in the studio of some skillful painter whose amity he had obtained.[8] It was also about this time, approximately two years before his death—toward the end of 1829—that he associated himself with a few young and timid artists, in order to be stronger as a bundle, in order not to be broken and knocked down on entering into society. He was even regarded by many as the high priest of that rough-hewn camaraderie, which was considered very

8. Théophile Gautier was a student in an artist's studio when Borel met him, and when they organized the *Hernani* claque, the other students in the studio were recruited along with other friends of the members of the *petit cénacle*.

scandalous, and whose intentions and title were perverted by ignorance and malice. But let us not anticipate; Champavert, in a collective work that will be published shortly, has reestablished the veracity of the facts and enlightened the public that the newspapers have deceived.

His last companions, whose names are cited in the *Rhapsodies*, and who knew him very intimately, would have been able to provide exact and positive information about him; but, as he did not approve this publication, they have closed their doors to us.

It was toward the end of 1831 that Champavert's poetic essays appeared, under the title *Rhapsodies, par Pétrus Borel.* No little book ever caused such a great scandal—a scandal, moreover, such as is always caused by every book written with heart and soul, without politeness for an era, in which art and passion are forged with the head and the hand, beating the breast on every page. We are too favorably disposed to pass judgment on those poems; no one would believe us to be impartial—so we shall only say that they seem to us to be abrupt, suffered, felt, full of fire, and, if we may be forgiven the expression, sometimes "flowery" but more often "cast-iron." It is a book impregnated with venom and pain; it is the prelude to the drama that followed it, and which the most naïve had foreseen. A work of that sort has no second volume; its epilogue is death.

We shall, for the benefit of our readers who are unfamiliar with them, present a few extracts, in support of what I have just said.

This is the piece that opens the collection; we are giving preference to its citation because it is full of dolor of a rare frankness, and contains a few circumstances of his life about which we have been unable to speak; it is addressed to a friend who had given him hospitality, it seems, in a time when, like Metastasio,[9] he had no shelter but the sky and the roadway.

---

9. The pseudonym of the Italian poet and librettist Pietro Trapassi (1698-1782)

When your Pétrus or your Pierre[10]
Had not even a stone
On which to rest, dry-eyed,
Or a nail in a miserly wall
On which to hang his guitar,
You gave me a shelter.

You said: Come, my Rhapsodist,
Come finish your ode in my home,
For your sky is not azure
Like the skies of Homer
Or the Provençal troubadour;
The air is cold, the ground is hard.

Paris has no boscage;
Come then, I'll open the cage,
In which I live, cheerfully poor;
Come, amity unites us,
Together shall share
A few seeds of hemp.

Quietly, my shameful soul
Blessed your soothing voice
Which caressed its misery;
For you alone, at the austere fate
That overwhelmed my solitude,
Shed a tear, Léon.

What! My frankness wounds you?
Would you wish, out of weakness,
One's poverty to be veiled?
No, no, new Malfilâtre,[11]

10. I have translated all the poems in the volume literally, without making any attempt to reproduce their rhyme-scheme of scansion.

11. The poet Jacques Clinchamps de Malfilâtre (1732-1767) was poorly born and unsuited to the salon society that was the principal broker of

I want, in the visible century,
To display my nudity!

I want everyone to know
That I am not a coward,
For I had two portions of dolor
At that banquet of the earth,
For while still young, poverty
Could not break my vigor.

I want everyone to know
That I have only my moustache,
My guitar and my heart
Which laughs at distress;
And that my masterful soul
Always emerges victorious.

I want everyone to know
That, without toga or shield,
Neither chancellor nor baron,
I am no gentleman
Nor a cheap hireling
Parodying Lord Byron.[12]

At the court, in its orgies,
I have made no elegies,
No hymn to the deity;
On the side of some duchess,
Wallowing in wealth
No lay on my poverty.

---

literary fame in his day, but his reputation grew even if his income remained
meager.

  12. Byron had established a stereotypical stance of irreducible world-
weary gloom that attracted many imitators, most of whom were faking it.
Borel wasn't.

Here are a few other verses and a few fragments chosen, so to speak, at random, all similarly full of chagrin and venom, and of the thought mutedly underlying them, and which was to doom him a short while later.

COMPLAINT

Joyful, importunate sound of a melodious keyboard,
Speak—what do you want of me?
Have you come into my attic to heap further insult
Upon this defeated heart?
Joyful sound, come no more; pour intoxication on others;
Their life is a feast
That I have not disturbed; you're troubling my distress,
My clandestine agony!

Imprudent, were do you come from? Doubtless a white hand,
A beautiful finger imprisoned
In rich jewels, has struck your reed
Of ebony and ivory;
Are you accompanying an angelic child
In her timid lesson?
Perhaps the somber rhythm and the melancholy tune
Betray her song to me.

No, I hear the muffled footsteps of a noisy crowd
In a narrow room;
It is whirling around, excited by the waltz,
Shaking the walls and roof.
Outside, confused sounds, cries and whinnying horses,
Flowers, slaves, torches;
The rich spread their joy and the poor moan
Ashamed in their rags!

Around me there is only a palace, indecent joy
Wealth, sumptuous nights,

Future, glory, honors; in the midst of that world
Poor and suffering I am
As if surrounded by the great, the king, the Holy Office
On the *quémandero*,[13]
All in pomp assembled to inhale a sacrifice,
A Jew on the *brazero!*

For everything overwhelms me: oblivion, misery, desire,
Are parceling out my days!
My amours embroidered the crêpe of my life with gold,
No more amours henceforth.
Poor girl! I was the one who dragged you
Along the path of pain;
But with a stronger poison, before it withered you.
You killed unhappiness!

Oh I, no more than a child, timid, weak, force-fed
With that sharpened blade
Have not sliced with this cowardly arm
My ulcerated breast!
I ruminate my disgrace; its shadow is pursued
By a customary regret.
What renders me so spineless and chains me to life?
Poor Job on his dung-heap.

HYMN TO THE SUN

There, in the sunken path, a solitary stroller
In my clandestine disgrace,
I come, suffering, and lie down on the ground
Like a brute beast
I nurse my hunger, head on a stone
Appealing to sleep
To staunch my burning eyelids a little;

13. An adaptation, for rhyming purposes of *quémando* [burning—i.e., of heretics]

I have exhausted my ration of sunlight!

Back there in the city, the sordid avarice
Of the king, over every Champart,[14]
Sunlight and void are sold to the human flock;
I have paid; I have my share!
But over everyone, all equal before you, just sun.
You shed your rays,
Which are no gentler on the face of an august prince
Than the dirty face of a beggar in rags.

Excerpt from a piece entitled
HAPPINESS AND UNHAPPINESS

He is a bird, the bard! He must remain wild;
By night in the branches, he twitters his song;
A muddy duck strutting on the river-bank
Saluting every rising or setting sun.
He is a bird, the bard! He must grow old austere,
Sober, poor, ignored, grim and careworn,
Singing for no one, and having nothing on earth
But a torn cape, a dagger and the skies!
But the bard today is a womanly voice,
A tight-fitting suit, a scrubbed pretty face,
A parrot on a perch, singing for Madame,
In a gilded cage, a pet canary;
He is marvelously fat, weeping warm tears
Over obligatory evils after a long meal,
Carrying an umbrella and swearing by his arms,
And, elixir in hand, invoking death,
Jewels, balls, flowers, horses, châteaux, slender mistresses
Are the materials of his leaden poems:
Nothing for poverty, nothing for the humble in distress;
Always insulting them in his velvet verses.

_____

14. A tax levied on landowners in Medieval France

Please! Spare us your autocratic airs;
Good for you, if you glean wealth by the handful,
But don't dress your verses up like your servants,
Which cause our foreheads, circled in rags, to blush.
Hey you, fluffy perihelion of those suns,
Don't take so much care to hide your tatters,
It's only in their refuge that the mind unwinds;
The bard only grows intoxicated by need!
I have caressed death, laughing at suicide,
Often and gladly, when I was happier;
Now I hate it, and am afraid of it,
Wretched and undermined by homicidal hunger.

POVERTY

By my cheerful expression, laughter on my lips.
You deem me happy, comfortable, unleavened and fever-free,
Living from day to day with no ambition,
Ignorant of remorse, virginal to affliction;
Through the walls of a noble breast,
Can one see the desiccating heat and the undermining fire?
In a dull lamp that is exhaustible,
It is necessary, like the heart, to open it or break it.

When you took your head to the executioners, poor André,[15]
You struck your forehead upon the cart in rage;
Having not done enough for immortality,
For your country, its glory and its liberty.
How many times, on the rock that borders life,
Have I kicked my foot, banged my desirous head,
Crying my long and painful torment to the skies;
I sensed my power, and I felt shackles!

---

15. The poet André Chenier (1762-1794) was one of the precursors of
the Romantic Movement; he was exceedingly unlucky to be arrested by
mistake, and then sent to the guillotine by Robespierre, whom he had once
criticized in a poem, a mere three days before the end of the Terror.

Power...shackles...so what? Nothing! One more poet
Who would make the divine, but his Muse is mute,
His power is in shackles—get away! We no longer believe
In this sighted century in any but accomplished talents;
Work, we no longer believe in marvelous futures.
Work! Oh, the need that howls in my ears
Stifling any thinker that rears up in my bosom!
What reply can I make to the chords of my lute? I'm hungry.

Oh, all of that makes the heart bleed. Let us pass on.

His independent stance and his violent love of liberty had caused him to be labeled a redoubtable Republican. He thought he ought to respond to that accusation in the preface to his *Rhapsodies*, "I am a Republican," he said, "as a lynx would understand it; my Republicanism is that of lycanthropy! If I speak of a republic, it is because that word, to me, represents the broadest independence that association and civilization can permit. I am a Republican because I cannot be a Carib Indian; I need an enormous sum of liberty; will the Republic give that to me? I have no personal experience of it, but when that hope is dashed, like so many others, I shall still have the Missouri!"

Because of that, the newspapers called those verses lycanthropic, him a lycanthrope and his turn of mind lycanthropism. The epithet had a great success in society, and stuck. He was pleased to hear it; so, we have deemed him worthy of our respect for not disowning that characteristic banner.

In the midst of all the hateful criticisms hurled at him, which would have saturated a soul less steeped than his, he did not doubt his strength for an instant, and received in private many gentle consolations, a little sincere applause, and true advice.

Among others, there was a letter and some lines that were addressed to him in this regard, which was found among his manuscripts, and which we shall reproduce here.

Monsieur,

Forgive me for being so long delayed in thanking you for the gift that you were kind enough to make me of your poems. Monsieur Gérard[16] only gave me your address a few days ago.

If molten metal has rejected its scoria, those scoria can be presumed to be metallic, and although it might annoy you to presume too much about your future, I would like to believe that it will be remarkable. I have been young too, Monsieur, young and melancholy, like you, and I have often blamed the social order for the anguish I experienced; I still have a fragment of verse—for I wrote verses when young—in which I expressed a desire to go and live among the wolves. A great confidence in the divinity has often been my sole refuge. My first tolerable verses will attest to that; they are not as good as yours, but, I repeat, they are not without numerous parallels. I tell you that in order that you might judge the sad but profound pleasure that yours gave me. I have all the more sympathy with some of your ideas because, although my destiny has undergone a great transformation, I have neither forgotten my first impressions, nor acquired much taste for the society I cursed at twenty years of age. Although I no longer have any complaint to make on my own account today, I mourn when I encounter its victims. But Monsieur, you were born with talent, you have received a better education than me; you will, I hope, triumph over the obstacles with which the road is strewn. If that happens, as I hope it will, always conserve the fortunate originality of your mind, and you will have cause to bless providence for the ordeals to which it has subjected you in your youth.

You probably do not like eulogies, so I will not add anything to what I have already said. I think, in any case, that you would prefer to know the reflections that your poetry has suggested to me. You will see that it is not out of egotism that I have said so

---

16. Gérard Labrunie, better known as Gérard de Nerval (1808-1855), also cited simply as "Gérard" when his verses are quoted in the headpieces to two of the stories in the collection.

much to you about myself.

Accept, Monsieur, with my sincere thanks, the assurance of my consideration and keenest interest.

Béranger[17]

16 February 1832.

TO PÉTRUS BOREL

Brave Pierre, why the melancholy
That reigns in your verses; why, on the future,
That dolorous gaze, followed by a long sigh,
Why that disgust for life?

It is, however, beautiful; look at the horizon
That is opening before us, bright with light...
Come, we shall cross these feeble barriers
That hold us like a prison.

What does a little pain matter in the morning of life,
Or the dark cloud wandering at our zenith?
The name that one engraves in rude granite
Escapes the fingernail of envy.

And when evening comes, we shall rest,
We shall find the glory at the end of the quarry,[18]
And love will be there, seductive chimera!
Pouring its balm upon our distress.

Look at those immobile masses around us

---

17. The lyric poet Pierre-Jean Béranger (1780-1857) became enormously popular as a popular songwriter.

18. The French *carrière* [quarry] also means "career," so there is an untranslatable double meaning here, related to the previous reference to *granit* [granite]. Borel echoes the double meaning in one of his own stories.

Ignorant of the sweet embraces of love,
Or the fine transports of ambition,
Incomplete and crippled beings!

Do they not have more right than us to denounce
   Heaven,
Those who, thrown naked on this arid road,
Pressing the empty cup to their fiery lips,
Encounter nothing but bile?

And you, you complain, when, full of youth,
You run free and strong, like a brave charger,
Of a few days of mourning that make you forget
The sweet kisses of a mistress.

What more do you ask, then, for your share?
Love, glory, amity will fall due to you in part,
Is that not enough to charm the voyage?
Fortune will only come in time!

Forward, forward! Be brave, Pierre!
Bear your heavy cross along wretched roads,
Without showing to others your hands and keens
Bruised by the edges of stones.

For glory is a bad mother to her poor children!
Bow down before the laureates of the world entire;
But it ought not to see the crown of thorns
That tears their burning foreheads.

Those verses bear the signature of a great artist who honors
France; we would have liked to be able to publish it, but we are
afraid of offending his modesty and of seeming too indiscreet
in revealing the source of a naïve poetry that is utterly and con-
fidentially intimate.

On comparing the two sides, one of abuse and the other of

noble and friendly advice, one will see, in this as in all cases, that vile criticism only emerges from below.

This is all that we have been able to collect regarding the material life of Champavert; as for the history of his soul, its entirety is in his writings; we shall see it again, first in the present volume of stories, and then in the *Rhapsodies*, whose second edition will appear shortly. Finally, for details regarding his disgust for life and his suicide, we shall refer to the story entitled "Champavert," which concludes this volume.

Monsieur Jean-Louis, his inconsolable friend, has been kind enough to confide all of Champavert's manuscripts and papers of which he was the owner to us, in order that we could put them in order, and he has authorized us to publish any that seemed to us to be worthwhile; to begin with, we have selected and collected these unpublished stories from among many others. If the world gives them a good reception, we shall publish them all successively, as well as several novels and plays, which we also have in our hands.

Is the premature death of the young writer a real and regrettable loss for France? We cannot answer that ourselves; it is for France to judge. It is for France to assign his rank, for Lyon, his homeland, to redeem and secure the apotheosis of its young and excessively unfortunate poet. We think it only polite, however, to warn readers who seek out and like "lymphatic"[19] literature to close this book again and go to another. If, however, they desire to have some notion of Champavert's state of mind, they have only to read what follows.

On receipt of the letter in which Champaverrt informed him of his extreme determination, Monsieur Jean-Louis left immediately, hoping to arrive in time to deflect him from his fatal plan; he was too late. As soon as he arrived in Paris he went to Champavert's domicile; he was told that he had gone away on a long voyage. He was unable to obtain any information in the city. That evening, however, while reading the *Tribune* in the

19. In the pseudo-Classical medical theory of the humors a lymphatic temperament is one that lacks energy.

Café Procope he found cruel and positive news. The next day, he collected his friend's cadaver, which had been exposed in the Morgue for three days, and had it buried in Mont-Louis cemetery; close to the grave of Héloïse and Abelard, you can still see a broken mossy stone on which, by leaning over, one can, with difficulty, read these words: To Champavert. Jean-Louis.

Greatly moved by the suicide of that young heart, and touched—tears having escaped me during the tale that Jean-Louis told over coffee—he approached me and said: "Did you know him?"

"No, Monsieur; if I had known him, we would have died together."

I acquired his friendship, and that worthy young man, before returning to Lachapelle in Vaudragon, made me a gift of the portfolio found on Champavert.

This is almost all that it contained: a few whimsical notes, scribbled at random in red pencil, almost totally illegible, and a few verses and letters.

To begin with, I deciphered these pensées on donkey-skin.

* * * * * * *

It is always advisable for men not to do anything futile, of course; but one might as well tell them to kill themselves, for, to be honest, what is the good of living? Is there anything more futile than life? A useful thing is something whose objective is known; a useful thing must be advantageous in itself and in its result, to serve some purpose, at least potentially; in sum, it is a good thing. Does life meet even one of these conditions? Its objective is unknown, it is neither advantages in itself nor in its result; it does not serve, and cannot serve, any purpose; in sum, it is harmful. Let someone prove to me the utility of life, the necessity of life, and I shall live....

For myself, I am convinced of the opposite, and I often repeat, with Petrarch:

Che più giorno é la vita mortale
Nubil'e, brev'e, freddo e pien di noia;
Che pò bella parer, ma nulla vale.[20]

* * * * * * *

The thought that has always pursued me bitterly, and thrown the greatest disgust into my heart, and this: that one only ceases to be an honest man on the day when the crime is discovered; that the vilest scoundrels, whose atrocities remain hidden, are honorable man, greatly enjoying favor and esteem; that men must often be laughing quietly inside when they hear themselves treated as good, just, honest, most serene highnesses!

Oh, that thought is heart-rending!

Thus, I am reluctant to shake the hands of people other than intimate friends; I shiver involuntarily at the idea, which never fails to assail me, that I might perhaps be shaking a faithless, treacherous, parricidal hand!

When I see a man, I look him up and down and sound him out involuntarily, and I ask in my heart whether he is really, in truth, a man of probity, or a fortunate brigand whose assaults, thefts and murders are unknown, and will be so forever. Indignant and nauseated, with scorn on my lips, I am tempted to turn my back on him.

If men were, at least, classified like other animals, if their various forms reflected their penchants, their ferocity and their bounty, like other animals—if there were a form for the ferocious murderer as there is for the tiger and the hyena; if there were one for the thief, the usurer and the avaricious man, as there is for the kite, the wolf and the fox—it would then be easy to know one's society; one could love judiciously and one could avoid the evil, chase them away and expel them, as one flees and expels the panther and the bear, while loving the dog, the deer

---

20. From Francesco Petrarca's *Triumphus Temporis* [The Triumph of Time] Approximately: What more is mortal life than a single day/Cloudy, cold, short and filled with grief/That has no value, fair though it might seem?

and the ewe.

* * * * * * *

"Merchant" and "thief" are synonymous

A poor man who steals the smallest object out of necessity is sent to the penitentiary, but merchants, who are privileged, open shops on the sides of roads in order to rob the passers-by who stray into them. Those thieves have neither skeleton-keys nor pliers, but they have scales, account-books and haberdasheries, and no one can get out of them without telling themselves that they have just been robbed. Those petty thieves eventually get rich and become "property-owners," as they call themselves— insolent property-owners!

At the slightest political disturbance they flock together and take up arms, howling that they are in danger of pillage, and slaughtering with a clear conscience anyone who rises up against tyranny.

Stupid brokers—it's a fine thing for you to talk about property and kill as looters the worthy people impoverished at your counters! Defend your property, then! Unfortunate rustics who, leaving the countryside, have come to fall upon you in the city, like flocks of crows or hungry wolves, to feed on carrion! Defend your property! Dirty dealers, what would you have without your barbaric pillaging? What would you have, if you did not sell brass as gold, dye for wine? Poisoners!

* * * * * * *

I do not believe that one can become rich without being ferocious; a sensitive man never accumulates. In order to be rich it is necessary to have but one idea, one obsession, hard and immutable: the desire to make a heap of gold; and, in order to increase the size that heap of gold, it is necessary to be a usurer, a crook, an inexorable extortionist and murderer, especially maltreating the weak and the small. And when a mountain of gold is made, one can climb it, and from the height of its summit, with a smile on one's lips, contemplate the valley of despair that one has made.

* * * * * * *

The big businessman steals from the wholesaler, the wholesaler steals from the shopkeeper, the shopkeeper steals from the householder, the householder steals from the laborer and the laborer dies of hunger. It is not people who work with their hands who succeed; it is exploiters of humankind.

* * * * * * *

In a notebook these verses were written, which I presume to be his, being unable to recall having seen them anywhere else.

TO A CERTAIN MORALIST

It is as well, at the height of the pulpit where one is enthroned,
At one's ease, with a mocking smile,
Festooning one's utterances and decorating one's sermons
Not to be lying in one's heart!
It is as well when one has just said something new,
To rebuke mores and good taste,
Not to go forth to extract one's parables
From guard-rooms or the gutter!
Above all, it is as well, when a bard puts on
The mantle of the apostolate,
Not to shoot from a balcony of the Louvre
On the populace down below!

But who, then, Brothers, is that rude anchorite?
Who is this surly monk?
This harsh quibbler, this fat man in a biretta,

Who has come to remonstrate with us?
Who, then, is this torturer with the canine muzzle,
Lacerating everything, denying the beautiful,
Sullying art, who says that our age is in decline,
Only good to feed the crows?
Who is he, Brothers? He sings dirty songs,
Drives the people and raises a hue and cry!
On the thresholds of brothels he preaches morality,
Like a drover shouting at his herd!

* * * * * * *

I shall say nothing about the death penalty; enough eloquent voices have condemned it since Beccaria;[21] but I shall rise up and proclaim the infamy of the witness for the prosecution, and cover him with shame. Can one imagine being a witness for the prosecution? What horror! Only humankind offers such examples of monstrosity! Is there a barbarism more refined, more civilized, than evidence for the prosecution?

* * * * * * *

In Paris there are two caverns, one of thieves, the other of murderers; that of thieves is the Bourse, that of murderers the Palais de Justice.

---

21. *Dei delitti e delle pene* (1764; tr. as *On Crimes and Punishments*) by Cesare Beccaria (1738-1794) was the Classic Enlightenment text arguing against the death penalty.

MONSIEUR DE L'ARGENTIÈRE, THE PROSECUTOR

Why seek, therefore, with a thought,
Child! to moralize this Rome, weary
Of its rhetors of Greece, and extracted from them all
Like a morsel of flesh from the teeth of jealous dogs?
Why not let this queen of the world,
Wallow at its pleasure in its filth,
And show it the mud beneath the silvery waves,
And trouble its long slumber with grave words?

Can you not sing of Dametas and Phyllis
And Tityrus mourning the death of Amaryllis?
Or, leaving aside those bucolic tales,
Elevate your genius to noble Georgics
Sing in six-line verses of Aeneas and his ships,
Saved by Neptune from the fury of the seas?
Have you not the voice of your blonde mistress,
And her throat as lax and supple as the waves,
And that Iberian with the large black eyes,
Who sang as one sung in Cordoba by night?

Barthelemy Hauréau.[22]

---

22. Barthelemy Hauréau (1812-1896) was still young when praised by
Théophile Gautier, from "the pulpit of Romanticism" for his journalistic

If they are red with blood, they will be redder still!

André Borel.

ROCOCO

A single candle placed on a small table illuminated a large high-ceilinged room feebly. But for the occasional clink of glass and silverware, and a few outbursts of voices, it would have seemed to be a death-watch. By carefully searching the half-light, as one's gaze searches the etchings of Rembrandt, one deciphered the decoration of a dining-room, of the characteristic era of Louis XV, which the mock-Roman classics maliciously call "Rococo."

It is true that the ledge framing the ceiling was grooved and ridged, in strips and gullets, without the slightest relationship to the entablature of the Erechtheion, the Temple of Antoninus and Faustina or the Arch of Drusus; it is true that it was devoid of projections, coronas, drip-catchers and gutters to expel non-existent rain; it is true that the doors were not surmounted by so-called Attic coronals; it is true that the arcades did not have a height two and a half times their breadth; and it is true that in no respect did it resemble the spiritual models of the illustrious Signor Giacomo Barrozi da Vignola, and that it laughed up its sleeve at the five orders—but it is also true and ought to be said that the interior in question was not an ignoble pastiche of the gross architecture of Paestum, or the architecture of Athens, frozen, bare, constant, and repetitive, or the apish and imitative architecture of Rome; it had its own appearance, style and coquetry, the exact expression of its era, fitting it in every respect. Its physiognomy was so unique that, after a long succession of centuries, one would recognize the Rococo of Louis XIV and Louis XV at a glance—an advantage not possessed by the

endeavors, although he later became a historian of note; this poem does not appear to have been published anywhere else.

dire and ignorant copies of the antique made by contemporary builders, who do not imprint any cachet on their epoch and do not receive any, to the extent that times to come will mistake their works for bad antiques out of place.

The great panels of the wainscot were covered with paintings of dead nature worthy of Venninx,[23] but by an unknown hand; and the transoms by the operatic pastorals, *fêtes galantes* and Camargue shepherdesses of the immortal and delightful Watteau. Their compositions were graceful and delicate, the colors suave and crystalline, following the custom of that grand master, whom ignorant and ingrate France ought to rehabilitate and redeem as one of its finest glories. Glory, then, to Watteau! Glory to Lancret! Glory to Carle Vanloo! Glory to Le Nôtre! Glory to Hyacinthe Rigaud! Glory to Boucher! Glory to Edelinck! Glory to Oudry!

And, if one has to be completely honest, I confess that I experience a sensation almost as dreamlike, and a pleasure as comfortable, in these vast dwellings of the seventeenth and eighteenth centuries, as in a Byzantine capitulary hall or a Roman cloister. Everything that is reminiscent of our forefathers, of our ancestors who died on French soil, casts a religious melancholy into the heart. Shame upon the man who does not shiver, whose breast does not palpitate, on entering an old dwelling, a dilapidated manor or a derelict church!

Two men were sitting at the table on which the candle stood.

The younger had lowered a white face, over which red hair rained; his eyes were cavernous and false, his nose long and pointed; you might have thought that his side-whiskers were cut squarely over his cheeks, like gaiters—which tells you that the scene was taking place under the Empire, somewhere around 1810.

The older man was thickset, the prototype of the natives of the plain of the Franche-Comté. His hair, a thick thatch, was

---

23. A notable painting in the Palazzo Pitti in Florence had been mistakenly attributed to one Jean Venninx, about whom nothing at all is known now that that attribution has been falsified.

suspended, like the gardens of Babylon, over his large, flat owlish face.

They were leaning voraciously over the table, like two wolves disputing a carcass, but their dull interlocutions, muffled by the sonority of the hall, were like the grunting of pigs.

One of them was less than a wolf; he was a Public Prosecutor. The other was more than a pig; he was a Prefect.

The Prefect had just received his appointment to a provincial capital, and was leaving the following day. The prosecutor had been fulfilling that function for some time at the assize court in Paris, and had gladly offered a farewell dinner to his friend.

Both of them, clad in black, like physicians, were wearing the mourning-dress of their murders.

As they were speaking in low voices, often with their mouths full, the negro standing in the doorway—for the young prosecutor de l'Argentière was a slave-owner, and played the returned aristocrat—could only catch a few stray sentences of the following kind.

"My dear Bertholin, what a fine dinner I had yesterday at the home of our friend Arnauld de Royaumont. From his apartment, which overlooks the Grève, I watched the execution of the seven conspirators we condemned a few days ago. What a delicious meal! At every mouthful I saw a head fall!"

"Poor greenhorns! Still believing in the fatherland! Those fellows wanted to be Brutuses or Hampdens!"[24]

"Did they not have the effrontery to want to address the people from the height of the scaffold? How swiftly their words and heads were cut off, damn it! Which didn't prevent them from howling at the top of their voices beforehand 'Long live the Fatherland! Vive la France! Death to the tyrant! Death to the tyrant!' Poor beasts! It's necessary not to trifle with these brigands—peel them! They need to be promptly sent to the executioner; otherwise, damn it, His Majesty won't have a single night's peaceful sleep."

24. John Hampden was the central figure of the "English Revolution" that deposed Charles I and eventually established Cromwell's Commonwealth

To judge by these scraps, the conversation could not have failed to be very edifying, and it is regrettable for the honor of the magistracy that the accursed negro was not able to collect more.

At dessert, however, the Corsican wine having raised the scale of the conversation by a third, which had become noisy and full of laughter, it would have been easy for a stenographer to record the following.

"By the way, my dear l'Argentière, skillful in subterfuges and loopholes as you are, how would you get yourself out of this difficulty? I absolutely have to leave tomorrow morning, but I have a very appetizing rendezvous tomorrow evening."

"The matter is simple, my friend. I would either leave without going to the rendezvous, or go to the rendezvous and not leave."

"A bad joke."

"If you want something more serious, first inform me more fully about the substance. What is this rendezvous? Is it of the masculine or the feminine variety? Is it commercial or lecherous business?"

"Feminine and lecherous."

"*Père Duchesne*'s thunder![25] If you're not committed to the Aristotelian unity of the play, the problem is easy to solve. I'd take the princess with me, and, tomorrow evening, I'd have the rendezvous in Auxerre."

"And what if the prude plays Lucretia?"

"Damn it! I'd play the petty Jupiter and, one way or another, I'd force the beautiful Europa to go with me."

"And what would you do the next day?"

"I wouldn't do anything; I'd leave her in Auxerre, full of my memory!"

"And what would the unfortunate woman do in her turn?"

"Unfortunate? Fortunate, on the contrary, that I've given her

---

25. *Le Père Duchense* was a radical newspaper published from 1790-94, shut down when its editor, Jacques Hébert, was guillotined. It was named after a character featured in fairground burlesques who was always angry about something, especially abuses of power.

a profession! She'd only have to take the coach and come back here to look for nurslings!"

"You're unscrupulous, l'Argentière. No, my friend, no—she's not a woman worthy of such cavalier treatment, she's an unfortunate child!"

"Go on—sensibility! Quickly, where's my handkerchief?"

She has a dazzling glamour—she's a hamadryad, a sprite whose spell is alluring...."

"To the precipice."

"I'd follow her...whoever sees her loves her, whoever has yet to see her will love her."

"A plague on faint-hearted lovers!"

"You can forge yourself a heart of iron, but it would soon be dented."

"In what cemetery, you old bear, did you dig up this fresh flesh? How the devil did you win the favors of this freak?"

"As for her favors, I never boasted about that; I'd be lying. As for the windfall, it's undeserved. For a long time, this poor Apolline has been living in the same house as me; I've known her since childhood; she curtsies to me with so much grace whenever she encounters me; she's always well and neatly dressed. How often the sight of her casts a shadow in my soul! I curse my celibacy and my isolation; I envy all the joy of a father, a possessor of such a beautiful creature; then paternity no longer presents itself, as in my youth, in a comical appearance.

"In those days, under the Consulate, her father had a relatively high position, which poured abundance into that little family, but having been found to be involved, I don't know how, in some plot one morning, some pretended conspiracy, the consul's police were alerted, and he's been locked up ever since, without any trial, as a prisoner of the State. His Majesty the Emperor is vindictive. The opulence of the house fell with the father.

"Apolline grew older every year in poverty and in beauty; having arrived at the age when coquetry and the need for adornment make themselves keenly felt, she no longer had anything to pretty herself up but a few rags, faded gilt and ruined wood-work, but she retained something regal, an imperious residue. Alas, how sad it was to see such a beautiful woman ashamed and shunning the light, enveloped in a tattered shawl with sandals on her feet, going down to buy coarse vegetables at the local market! My heart often bled for her! What could be more poignant and more bitter?

"If you want to laugh, l'Argentière, at least laugh at me, for it would be ferocious to laugh at her."

"I'm laughing, Bertholin, at hearing words so contrary to your custom emerging from your mouth. You, a dogmatic bach-elor, hating women on principle—a man of sound judgment, in sum! You've chosen a bad time to fall in love. Continue your role as Père Cassandre; it's too late to play Arlequin!"[26]

"Are you trying to wound me?"

"More and more ridiculous—you're definitely in love."

"Well, yes. I'm in love, and I won't blush at a sage love, a love engendered by pity, and I bless Heaven...."

"Or you bless nothing!"

"...Which has kept me free until today, in order that I might be the guardian of that orphan."

"You've subscribed to Chateaubriand, haven't you?"

"In order that I might become the guardian angel of that abandoned virgin, whom need would kill or corrupt. She's entirely isolated today; her poor mother, weakened by so many years of privation and further undermined by the sufferings of her daughter, died three months ago. Moved when Apolline's screams told me that she was about to expire. I went up to console her and offer her my services in that horrible circum-stance. I took responsibility for arranging the funeral, and had her buried by the Mairie. For the first time, I spoke to Apolline: imagine the blow that struck me when I went into that bare, untidy room, when that girl, kissing my hands, her voice full of

26. Père Cassandre and Arlequin are stock characters in the French cast adapted from the Italian *commedia dell'arte*, often featured in farces, pantomimes and puppet shows.

tears, thanked me. I was beside myself—I don't know, I don't remember anything, I wept! She, distraught, kneeling beside a camp-bed, was leaning over her mother's body, calling to her....

"That hour took ten years off my life!

"And it is from so much pity that so much love has emerged.

"A few days later I went to visit her; all the time I was chatting with her, I noticed an embarrassed attitude; she always maintained a sitting position, with her hands folded on her lap. When she got up to show me out, I saw that her dress was torn, with a hole in the front, and that her little hands had been trying to hide her poverty.

"After an interval of assiduity, seduced by her sad and gentle spirit, smitten by her rare beauty, as bewildered as a young man, I confessed my passion to her. She replied that she had too much esteem for me to presume that I wanted to exploit her deprivation, and that she believed sincerely in the nobility and purity of my sentiments, but that having resolved to leave the world where she had suffered so much, she was going to write to the Mother Superior of the Convent of Saint Thomas in order to be admitted to the novitiate there. I had a great deal of difficulty dissuading her from that project; I made her see that she would assuredly be killing herself by embracing an austere life after all the comforts that had weakened her. Finally, she gave in.

"I am not sufficiently deluded to think that the sweet Apolline has any strong love for me; she cherishes me like a father; for her, I am a generous guardian, a compassionate friend. She is all the more attached to me because she has encountered none but egotistical and ferocious beings. She is good, sensitive and benevolent, without any hint of foolishness—who could ask for anything more? All the gifts that I have tried to offer her, all the presents I have brought her, she has nobly refused; it is her duty, she says, to act thus, and an honorable young woman cannot accept anything except from her husband. So, I've promised her that we will be married before long; that thought filled her with joy. I therefore asked her for a rendezvous tomorrow evening, at nine o'clock, at her home, in order to discuss the preparations for our marriage, and perhaps....

"I'm not lying, you see—this is the letter she sent in reply:

My dear Bertholin,

I presume that great occupations during the day have caused you to choose such a late hour, but may the will of my husband be done; his servant will await him. I shall extinguish my lamp to prevent any suspicion on the part of my wicked and indiscreet neighbors. Come in secret.

Your friend and wife in heart.

"Fully resolved, I shall leave without informing her, to spare is painful adieux; if I saw her again, I sense that I would no longer have the heart to leave. When I get there, I shall write to her. As soon as I'm installed in my Prefecture I shall come back to marry her clandestinely, and then I shall take her away immediately and introduce her to my administrators as having been my wife for a long time, in order to cut short any witticisms.

"I shall definitely leave tomorrow morning, but it's necessary that I send her some money incognito, in order that the poor girl does not die of starvation in my absence.

"Eleven o'clock already! Adieu, adieu, l'Argentière!"

As he spoke these final words, Bertholin had risen to his feet and retreated toward the door—but the prosecutor, who had listened to the story with cold, bleak and sustained attention, followed him, asking him questions, until the foot of the staircase.

"You say, Bertholin, that this Apolline is beautiful?"

"Oh, my friend; I have lived a long time and seen a great deal, but I have never met a woman so seductive. Imagine Bertin's Eucharis, Parny's Éléonore,[27] a nymph, Egeria, Diana!

27. Antoine Bertin and Évariste de Forges de Parny were eighteenth-century contemporaries; the former disguised a woman with whom he was

She is tall, slender, graceful; she is as pale and melancholy as an invalid; her hair, which she wears in a band over her forehead, completes her virginal appearance, and beneath her thick black eyebrows her great blue eyes languish."

"And you say that she lives in the same house as you?"

"The same, at the end of the corridor above my apartment."

Then l'Argentière threw his arms around Bertholin's neck and embraced him like a paten—a strange politeness on the part of a man so disdainful and cold.

WAS-IS-DAS?

Nine o'clock was chiming at the Carmes, at the Luxembourg, at Saint-Sulpice, at Abbaye-au-Bois, at Saint-Germain-des-Prés, seemingly playing a charivari to the falling night.

At that moment, in the Rue Cassette, a man slipped into a house of rich appearance and stealthily climbed the stairs. At the very top he went into, and paused within, a dark corridor; through the planks of a door a voice was audible; he put his ear to the keyhole; the soft voice was reciting an evening prayer. He knocked gently with his finger.

"Who's there?"

"Open the door, Apolline, it's me."

"Who's that?"

"Bertholin."

Immediately, she opened the accursed door, which creaked like dancing-shoes and whose hinges grated like a weather-vane.

"Bonsoir, my friend."

"Bonsoir, all beauty."

"Forgive me if I receive you so inconveniently, without a light; it's because, poor as I am, I have no curtains on my window, and everything in my home can be distinguished from the room opposite. So why choose so late an hour?"

---

smitten under the name of Eucharis in *Les Amours* (1773) while latter did likewise in the character of Éléonore in *Poèmes érotiques* (1778).

"By day my head is stuffed with business matters and besides, broad daylight is unconducive to effusion. What is love without the night? What is love without mystery?"

"It would be wrong of me to criticize you for that, for I never love God so much as at night, in an exceedingly dark church. Do you have a cough, my friend?"

"Yes, kicking my heels outside the Minister's door, I contracted a cold and a sore throat, which is inconveniencing me considerably."

"That's why your voice seems hoarse and altered. But let's talk seriously; tell me, my dear, what point is there is putting off our marriage any longer? If people were to perceive our liaison, they would speak ill of me."

"Patience, my love, patience! Today, I received my official appointment to the Prefecture of Mont Blanc, and I'm due to leave tomorrow; as soon as my installation is complete and my administration revised, I swear to you that I'll come back to celebrate our clandestine marriage; we'll leave Paris right away, and I'll introduce you to my subjects out there as a long-standing wife."

"Oh, my friend, how happy I am! But you won't be absent for long, will you? Alone, here, I'd suffer too much in expectation."

"Little pedant! If you only knew how much I love you!"

"But Bertholin, what are you doing? Don't embrace me like that!"

"My love!"

"You're treating me in a very cavalier fashion this evening, Monsieur!"

"No, my love! I'm treating you as a wife."

"As a wife! Is that what I am, Monsieur?"

"When two people who love one another have sworn an oath, does it need to be certified by the municipal authorities to be sacred? The law merely ratifies. We shall love one another forever, we are sworn to one another, we are spouses; and if we are spouses, where's the harm?"

"Any liaison without the sanctification of God is a sin."

"God, like the law, merely ratifies."

"I can't contest with you; I'm not subtle in controversy. I can't deny my weakness, but be generous!"

"I am!"

"Let me go, Bertholin—you're unworthy of yourself this evening. What do you want of me...? Oh, it's wicked...a poor girl...! Executioner! Can you really torture me in this way...? I'll call for help!"

"Call."

"I'll rap on the floorboards and have your servants come up."

"They won't come up."

"Alas, alas...it's wicked, Bertholin...!

"Now, my friend, you'll disdain me, you'll reject me; you'll no longer want for a wife a girl so unfaithful to her duty, a young woman without honor?"

"Don't talk like that, Apolline, you're wounding me! You must think my very cowardly and very base. Me, abuse you? Oh, no—never! This raises you further in my heart."

"You still love me?"

"Forever!"

"But your voice just changed suddenly. Heavens! Is it really you, Bertholin? Madwoman that I am...fatal presentiment...of, if I've been deceived! Is it really you, Bertholin? Answer me, I beg you. Speak to me—is it you, Bertholin? Is it you? Let me touch your face—Bertholin has no beard. Oh, if I've been deceived...!"

"Beauty," said the enigma then, aloud, "the moral of this is that one should not receive one's lovers without a light."

At that unfamiliar voice, Apolline collapsed on to the floor.

When, having recovered consciousness, she had collected her thoughts and her strength, she dragged herself silently to the window. A ray of moonlight sliding into the room illuminated the head of the man who was sleeping profoundly in an armchair. Trembling, Apolline studied him. He was dressed in black; his pale face, over which red hair pilled, was titled forward; his eyes were cavernous, his nose long and pointed;

his cheeks were dressed with red side-whiskers, trimmed as sharply as gaiters.

Who is that man? the unfortunate child asked herself. *Oh, the infamous Bertholin—it's him who has foisted this abomination upon me. Who would have believed it? Oh, it's frightful to deceive someone thus!*

She felt a portfolio on the unknown man's breast. She would have given the world to be able to take it out, hoping by that means to discover the identity of her suborner, but it was impossible; his jacket was buttoned all the way to the top.

In that fatal anguish, she cursed Bertholin and God.

Finally, exhausted by chagrin and drowsiness, she crouched down again and curled up on the floor, wet with her tears.

When she woke up, it was broad daylight and the armchair was empty; she was alone, face to face with her shame.

MATER DOLOROSA

The porter came up to Apolline's residence during the day to bring her a bag of money; it was the sum that Bertholin intended to send her incognito after his departure, because he feared that the unfortunate girl, without resources, might succumb to need before his return.

"Who is it from?" Apolline asked.

"I don't know, Mademoiselle. An unknown man brought it to me for you, without saying any more."

"Take the money away!"

"I can't; I was clearly told: for Mademoiselle Apolline."

"Take it away, I tell you!"

The worthy man was utterly nonplussed.

Apolline, proud and noble, rejected it all the more harshly because she presumed in her heart that it was the price of her dishonor, calculated by the nocturnal visitor to humiliate her further and debase her more.

But the porter, while excusing himself, threw the bag on to

the table and retired precipitately.

All day long, Apolline was on tenterhooks; she listened to see whether she could hear any sound down below, in Bertholin's apartment—footsteps, moving furniture, doors or windows opening—but in vain. She spied in that fashion for several days in succession, with no more success. Finally, she dared, one evening, to go downstairs and knock. There was no reply; Bertholin had taken his servants with him.

Her confusion was further complicated, and poor Apolline lost her head.

Has he moved out? she asked herself. *But I would have heard him. Could he have left Paris? And before his departure, could he have planned the infamous imposture with one of his friend? Oh no—it's impossible! That would be very false and very wicked! Oh, no, Bertholin is a sensitive and true man. How can all this be explained?*

In her perplexity, she went so far as to doubt herself, and to wonder whether she might have been mistaken in the darkness, and whether it might not have been Bertholin himself, who seemed strange to her overwrought imagination.

They were not his features, though; I wasn't dreaming. It wasn't his voice, though; they weren't his elegant manners. No, it wasn't him!

About a week after this misadventure, Apollline received a letter postmarked Mont-Blanc. It was from Bertholin, and was conceived as follows.

> Forgive me, my future beauty, if I left without having kissed your hands; I wanted to spare us painful adieux. Summoned to the Prefecture of Mont-Blanc, I have come to take possession of my realm. I hope, within a fortnight, to return to you in order to consecrate our union secretly, and immediately leave again for this region, which, I think, will not displease you at all. You have doubtless not been so awkwardly proud as to refuse the small sum that was to be conveyed

to you by an unknown hand; you are my wife, and I would suffer too much if I knew that you were in deprivation.

This letter only increased Apolline's embarrassment. After so many fine demonstrations, she no longer dared accuse Bertholin of black perfidy, and yet, at the hour agreed for the rendezvous, another, well-informed, had come in his name to violate her. An inextricable mystery! The most plausible explanation was that her note had gone astray, into the hands of a stranger.

Some time after that first letter from Bertholin, she received another, in which he announced that, overloaded with unforeseen work, he had been forced to delay his departure.

At that time, Apolline began to feel a general malaise. Disgusted by all food, she was often gripped by nausea and vomiting; her anxiety grew. A physician advised the use of saffron, which had no effect; then he declared point blank that she was pregnant. At that news, Apolline fell into consternation and despair.

Day and night, she wept bitterly. Her situation became very cruel. Bertholin had finally notified her of his return, and she expected to see him again at any moment. What should she do at that fatal conjuncture? To hide it from him and dupe him would be difficult and dishonest; to tell him frankly would be to lose everything, and yet her delicacy left her no other recourse. So, she resolved to confess everything without dissimulation as soon as he arrived, perhaps hoping that his generosity would forgive her a desperate sin, committed for him and because of him.

Finally, Bertholin reappeared; immediately, he noticed a great change in her: a sadness; a strained expression in his regard; a deterioration and depletion of her beautiful features. He heaped her with so many caresses and so much love that, in spite of her firm resolution, Apolline dared not broach her confession; twenty times over the first word expired on her tremulous lips; she dared not throw a man so greatly smitten into such great disenchantment. Bertholin also became anxious, and did not know to what he ought to attribute so many tears.

The moment to strike the blow arrived; the preparations and legal measures were taken; the marriage was arranged for the following Saturday; it was at Saint-Sulpice, at midnight, before two or three witnesses that they would receive the nuptial benediction, with no ceremony, in order to leave the following morning.

On Thursday evening, Bertholin invited Apolline to come down to his apartment and led her joyfully into the drawing room. The sideboard and the sofa were covered with clothes, shawls, adornments and jewels.

"Here, my beauty, are a few presents offered to you by your humble spouse; may they be agreeable to you."

Apolline suddenly broke into sobs, and stood dismally in the doorway.

"What's the matter, my love? Come in-all this is yours! Do you like this blue velvet Marie-Louise dress? This golden cross? There coral bracelets? These cashmere wraps?"

Then Apolline fell to her knees.

"O Bertholin, Bertholin, if you only knew!"

"What's wrong, my child?"

"If you knew how unworthy I am of all this! Is it not necessary, my God, to tell you everything? I can't deceive you, Bertholin! Oh, if only you knew, you would expel with kicks the one you call your wife!"

He was petrified.

"Listen! Are you, perhaps, guilty of my crime? Look!!!" So saying, she tore off the shawl and the pleated dress that hid her pregnancy. "Look, then! Must I declare my shame?"

"Abomination! You, pregnant, Apolline? Oh, it's infamous to have abused a generous old men so! So this is the wife, the virgin, that I've chosen out of pity! An orphan child I wanted to bring up! Prostituted!!!"

"Rather die a thousand times!" cried Apolline, dragging herself to his feet. "Listen to me, in the name of God! You can kill me afterwards. Listen to me, O my father, listen to the truth."

"Will you shut up, you brazen...."

"God knows my innocence and your crime, for I was pure before knowing you...."

"Wretch!"

"For I was pure when you chose me as your wife, and it's you who have ruined me. Listen! Before your departure, you asked me for a rendezvous one evening, in my home; I granted it. At nine o'clock someone knocked at my door; I opened up and let him in the dark; I believed that it was you, my Bertholin! That demon counterfeited your voice and deceived me. After a long struggle, I succumbed, believing that I was abandoning myself to you. He violated me!"

"Apolline, you're lying!"

"When that monster had consummated his crime upon me, he revealed my error himself. By the light of the moon, I distinguished his features; he was pale, with red hair, red side-whiskers and cavernous eyes; he was tall and dressed in black."

"Apolline, you're lying!"

"Oh my father, believe me!"

"You're lying!"

"I swear by the Christ, by my mother, who can hear me above."

"You're lying!"

"It's to you that I believed I was abandoning my caresses, and you treat me thus! It's you who has ruined me!"

"You're lying."

"You showed me letter to someone else; it must have been one of your friends...."

"You're lying!"

"Oh, my father!"

"Get away from me!"

He was smarting, poor Bertholin: *At fifty years of age, to be stripped of your hatred, to go to abase yourself at the knees of a girl! A cruel lesson! It's infamous! When I think of it...!* "Get out, get out, or I'll trample you underfoot like these jewels! Get out, if you want to spare me a murder! Get out, slut, prostitute!"

Apolline was choking on the tiles.

Bertholin seized her by the feet, dragged her away and threw her out, and left immediately.

MOSES SAVED FROM THE WATERS

Nothing is more demoralizing than injustice; nothing throws more bitterness and hatred into the heart. Bertholin seemed unjust to Apolline; Apolline seemed culpable to Bertholin, and would have seemed so in the eyes of everyone else. It only requires a combination of circumstances to make the most innocent person guilty. It is only on the basis of the probable and the apparent that people can judge with their short antennae.

Crimes are like sealed ballots; it is by the envelope that the judge estimates the contents, and when, by his sentence, he has declared it tallied and counted, and has had the ballot thrown in the sea, the falling ballot breaks upon a rock and opens; all that it concealed rises to the surface of the water and appears in broad daylight; the tribunal's blunder becomes patent, the crowd laughs bitterly; then the judge puts on his robe and stands up and cries, in his risible archiepiscopal tone: "I am infallible!"

Eaten away by mortal chagrin, Apolline was mutely undermined and consumed day by day.

Still so beautiful a few months before, she became emaciated and consumptive, like a specter, only going out in the dead of night in order to avoid malicious gazes. The neighborhood would have believed her dead if she had not, from time to time, played a dilapidated piano that served her as a table, a sad relic of her former opulence. People even remarked and remembered the lines that she often sang languorously, of which she seemed to be uniquely fond.

> Executioner, stop my torture!
> Misfortune has sickened my heart.

Hatred to you, God, world, nature,
Hatred to everything I dreamed!
Before my body, on this wheel
To which fate has bound it,
My soul expires, and I commit it
To Satan, for all eternity!

That refrain in itself shows us Apolline's state of mind, and how suffering and misfortune can pervert the most beautiful soul; once gentle, good, fervent, loving and religious, she no longer had anything but bile in her breast and venom in her mouth. She hated everything, including the creator in whom she denied her faith; she avenged herself by abandoning in her turn the God who had abandoned her. When an individual has been maltreated to that extent, there no longer anything but infernal laughter on her disdainful lips; everything that exists is pitiful, and provokes disgust; the more holy and sacred something is, the more revered by all, the more joy there is in profaning it, in trampling it underfoot. For the unfortunate, blasphemy is voluptuous!

The term of her pregnancy drew nearer, and her misery became profound. For the first eight months she had lived on the meager sum that Bertholin had sent her. None of that remained. By night she went out to pick wild herbs along the deserted roads, but that nourishment for donkeys, so contrary to her delicacy, weakened her to such an extent that toward the end of the ninth month, it became impossible to sink any lower. Her emaciation became, so to speak, absolute, giving her dizzy spells and a chronic headache that degenerated at times into madness. Her dementia was somber. She had atrocious stabbing pains in her stomach, and was often seized by epileptic spasms. When she felt the first pangs of childbirth, she had not eaten for two days; lying on her meager bed, devoured by hunger, she chewed the binding of an old book, out of her mind and at the end of her tether....

At the sight of her child, her somber madness revived, and

recovered its strength; standing up, she embraced it and struck it alternately; she offered it her empty tears; she threw it on the ground, weeping, and lay down upon it.

Finally, having wrapped it in a cloth and put it under her arm like a parcel, she took it downstairs.

It was night.

At two o'clock in the morning, Erman Busembaum, a market-gardener from Vaugirard, was going to market along the Rue du Four, perched on his cart and whistling a Christmas carol. As he drew near one of the filthy side-streets that opened into it, he heard the whimpering of a newborn child. Abruptly, he stopped whistling, uttered an exclamation of surprise in a Provençal accent, and listened; the cries continued, seemingly coming from a nearby drain. He jumped down, put his ear to the opening, and recoiled in fright.

He ran to inform the guards at the Prison de l'Abbaye of this strange event. The commissaire happened to be there, taking the particulars of two whores arrested for stabbing a client. Immediately, he placed himself at the head of a patrol; Erman Busembaum guided a corporal carrying a lantern.

They arrived at the drain in haste; there was a profound silence therein, save for the splashing of the water. The soldier, born evil, was already chaffing Busembaum about hearing things, attributing it to fear; the authority in the sash was preparing to curse the incompetent bumpkin who had disturbed him unnecessarily, when the cries resumed, more loudly. The patrol shivered and the capuchins were summoned.

The corporal carrying the lantern went to the opening of the sewer, bent down and perceived a white package at the entrance, from which the moans were emerging. One of the guards unsheathed his bayonet and held it aloft. Then Busenbaum and the commissaire, playing the role of Pharaoh's daughter, unwrapped the cloth and uncovered a new-born baby.

"Good God! there's a conscript who's escaped a severe punishment!" cried the patrol.

"Poor wee mite," repeated old Père Busenbaum, his heart

melting.

"This is one of those cases in which children are truly unfortunate to have parents," murmured the agreeable corporal.

"Messieurs," said the perspicacious commissaire, then, striking the pose of a Caliph, "a crime has been committed. Let's investigate!" He set about examining the brat, who had no serious injury.

To the great contentment of the army, after conscientious research worthy of being validated by the Académie, it was proclaimed by the majority to be of the masculine or neutral gender.

A smile of satisfaction strayed over Père Busenbaum's lips. "What are you going to do with the kid?" he said to the commissaire. "My wife's just given birth for the third time, but, to her great distress, all the brave woman's children were born dead. If you care to entrust him to me, I'll take it to her immediately by way of compensation; she'll take good care of him and we'll adopt him."

Just as he lifted the infant up in order to climb back on to his cart, however, it stiffened and expired.

The commissaire noticed drops of blood. Lowering the lantern and seeing that the trail extended toward the top of the road, he ordered the patrol to follow it. The drops, although spaced at rather long intervals, were nevertheless sufficient to guide them. In the Rue Beurrière they disappeared, but they found them again in a side-street of the Rue du Vieux-Colombier. Still following attentively, they went as far as the Rue Cassette, where the vestiges continued; finally, the trail of blood stopped at a door.

"Here it is, Messieurs!" exclaimed the commissaire. "Let's go in. He rapped several times with the knocker. "Open up in the name of the law!" the corporal repeated, striking it with the butt of his rifle.

The bewildered porter obeyed. "In the name of God, Messieurs, what's the rush? What do you want?"

"Come with us—we're going to make a search. Look, here's

the blood again! Follow me."

They went up the stairs and into a corridor; there, the trail of blood stopped at a door.

"Who lives here, Monsieur le Porteur?"

"A young woman, good and meek."

"Open up, in the name of the law! Corporal—break down that door!"

It opened immediately under the impact of rifle-butts, and avid gazes peered into the room, seeing, by the light of the lantern, a pale and emaciated young woman lying on the floor in a pool of blood.

They picked her up; she was still warm.

When she returned, Apolline had doubtless collapsed, exhausted by such a long journey and such a considerable loss of blood.

She was taken away on a stretcher to the maternity hospital commonly known as "the Mire."

WELL DONE[28]

The following day, throughout Paris, no one was talking about anything except the child thrown into a drain, and the public criers walked in procession through the city, howling and selling for a sou the exact details of the horrible infanticide committed in the Faubourg Saint-Germain by the daughter of a noble family.

That event had sent shock-waves through the bourgeoisie, who were already avid to see it at the court of assizes, in order to know the whole story, and who, being rancorous, were already enjoying in advance the rare spectacle of a daughter of the aristocracy in the dock and on the scaffold.

---

28. Usually, I have not altered Borel's chapter titles when they are rendered in English, even when some improvement seems possible, but this one, rendered "Very wel" in the original (although someone has kindly entered a second l in the gallica copy by hand), is so important to the story that I have taken the liberty of substituting the phrase that is surely intended.

In the hospital, they had at first despaired of Apolline's life, but they lavished so much care upon her, on the recommendation of the men of law—who feared that her death might cut the matter short, trespassing on their rights and those of the executioner—that after a week or so, she began to recover her strength, and consciousness returned.

She was greatly astonished and distressed when she found that she was in a hospital ward. She had no memory of what she had done, nor of what had happened, just as a drunkard, on awakening, retains no memory of the follies of his intoxication. She asked questions, but only received vague replies. When she was fully recovered, she was told that she was to be transferred to the prison of La Force.

"La Force!" she cried. "Why?"

"On a charge of infanticide."

"Me! Oh, no, you're mad!"

"You threw your child into a sewer."

Then Apolline, in distress, put her hands on her belly, and, seeming to emerge from a slumber with a start and suddenly remembering, collapsed on the ground, out cold.

When she came back to her senses, she was in a narrow and dingy cell.

The investigation of her case took a long time, and after four months of detention and contact with all that is most fetid and most stagnant in the social mire, she was summoned to the court of assizes.

The great scandal had attracted a vast crowd of curiosity-seekers, who wanted to see the beautiful bad mother of the Faubourg Saint-Germain. She had acquired a reputation for beauty equal to that of her ferocity. The windows of print-sellers were garnished with pretended portraits of the beautiful Apolline, as authentic as those of Héloïse or Jeanne d'Arc; one resembled Madame de La Vallière,[29] another Charlotte Corday, another Joséphine, but the public, which wants to be duped at

_____

29. Louise de La Vallière was one of Louis XIV's mistresses.

any price, was entirely satisfied with them.

The Palais was as crowded as if the clerks were going to perform a mystery play on the marble table. A general murmur of disappointment went up when the ushers announced that the tribunal would be in closed session for the judgment.

Soon, Apolline was introduced into the hall; her youth, her charm, her sad and candid expression, her soft voice and her bearing impressed the blasé court considerably.

In order not to compromise Bertholin, she had declared that a man who was entirely unknown to her, and whom she had never seen again, had slipped into her room one night and had raped her violently. As for the crime of which she was accused, she admitted that it might have occurred, but that she retained no actual memory of it, and that, not having had anything to eat for several days when the pangs of childbirth afflicted her, she must have been in a state of complete dementia.

Of five physicians called to establish what her mental state might have been during childbirth, only one had affirmed alienation; the other four having denied it.

When the public prosecutor, Monsieur de l'Argentière, stood up to make his speech, Apolline, struck as by a familiar accent, turned to look at him, uttered a piercing scream, and fell backwards, unconscious.

No speech was ever more violent and more inhumane; there was nothing that Monsieur de l'Argentière did not bring into play to overwhelm the accused. He took his extravagant rage so far as to compare her to Saturn, who devoured his children, and concluded by demanding her head.

"Let us not be seduced," he cried, "by the beautiful exterior of this unnatural mother; the laurier-rose contains a subtle poison; beauty is often the veil of perfidy; do not weaken, Messieurs, it is absolutely necessary that an example is set, to stop infanticide in its tracks. Be inexorable, Messieurs, and you will be just!"

Apolline's advocate, with a rare talent, did himself justice in her defense; his plea would have drawn tears from tigers, but left the tribunal cold, and the prosecutor began his savage reply.

When poor Apolline came to her senses, she stood up abruptly, and pointing an accusing finger at Monsieur de l'Argentière, cried: "It's him! It's him! I recognize his voice. It's him! That man who is speaking! He was the one I saw in the moonlight, pale and red-haired, with the cavernous eyes." Then dissolving in tears, she began howling.

"That child is out of her head," said Monsieur de l'Argentière coldly, his bleak physiognomy not showing the slightest trace of emotion.

"Take the accused away," the President ordered, "and let us, Messieurs, pass into the deliberation room."

After a quarter of an hour, the court came back into session; the jury having responded affirmatively to all the questions posed, the President had the sentence read out, which condemned Apolline to capital punishment.

She listened to her sentence with dignity, and only said, turning to the public prosecutor: "Those who send others to the executioner are the ones who ought to be sent there!"

Her distressed defender, weeping and beating his brow, threw himself into her arms and embraced her, greatly scandalizing the court, who asked whether she wanted to appeal.

"Yes," said Apolline, "but to God's tribunal."

* * * * * * *

On the morning of the appointed day, a priest was sent to prepare her; he did not come out again. Apolline having naively told him her story, the poor man, convinced of her innocence, was weeping desperately. The man who had come to console her was weaker and more inconsolable than her.

"Poor martyr!" he called her, kissing her feet as one kisses a holy relic. He dared not mention his good and just God to her; his providence was too compromised by that fatal life.

At four o'clock the jailer came to summon her. Having finished dressing, she came down, supporting her confessor.

The cart set off immediately. It seemed that the entire population of Paris was crammed into the space between the Palais and the Grève. The houses were packed from top to bottom with avid spectators; no execution had ever attracted such a large crowd.

"There she is! There she is!" was repeated from row to row.

How beautiful she was at the height of her tumbrel, that unfortunate Apolline! What dignity! What resignation! Her complexion was paler than the peignoir that enveloped her, and her hair blacker than the priest who was weeping beside her. She paraded her languorous gaze over the crowd; old women shook their fists at her, and compassionate young men blew her kisses.

Finally, the cart emerged into the Grève. As she climbed the steps, Apolline perceived Monsieur de l'Argentière at a window, staring at her coldly. She uttered a long scream of horror and fainted into the arms of one of the guillotine's attendants. There was then a general hubbub and a fluctuation in the crowd.

It was raining.

There were shouts of "Down with the umbrellas—we can't see!" from all sides.

"Down with the umbrellas!" repeated women's voices. "Be gallant, Messieurs, we can't see!"

All the rabble, craning their necks, were on tiptoe.

When the blade fell, there was a dull murmur, and an Englishman, leaning out of a window that he had hired for five hundred francs, full satisfied, clapped his hands and shouted: "Well done!"

JAQUEZ BARRAOU, THE CARPENTER

(HAVANA)

For love is as strong as death
And jealousy as harsh as an inferno.[30]
The Bible

I am black, but comely...as the tents of
Kedar, as the curtains of Solomon.[31]
The Bible

Eh? Why this jealousy?
P. L. Jacob, Bibliophile

I.
Pesadumbre y Conjuración[32]

It was the Lord's Day, as sufficiently indicated by the calm of the countryside, the jovial atmosphere and the white linen of the slaves passing in the distance without a murmur beneath

---

30. The equivalent line in the A.V., from the *Song of Solomon* 8:6 reads: "For love is as strong as death; jealousy is as cruel as the grave," but the next reference is to hot coals, so "inferno" is probably a more accurate translation than "grave."

31. *Song of Solomon* 1:5.

32. Grief and collusion

enormous burdens—unfortunate men, lacking only a mule-bell. The sun was blazing in the hour of the siesta, but the carpenter Jaquez Barraou, black-limbed and gigantic, came to sit in the doorway of his hut, hunched, so to speak, in a creek, where two pinnaces and a balancelle under repair were moored. The ground was strewn with pieces of wood still bearing bark, blocks and planks.

Jaquez Barraou was still wearing his striped shirt and his working clothes, although, as an exceedingly religious man, he had done no work, for that would have been a mortal sin. His feet were bare. Throughout his being a nonchalance reigned, which contrasted with his energetic bearing. Beneath his curly black hair two large white eyes were rolling; often, he paraded them over the sea and the surrounding land; often, he raised them to the heavens, and then brought them back, fixedly, to his Havana, frowning and scornfully expelling the puffs of blue smoke that he inhaled from the long cigar.

It would have been difficult to explain the man's movements and abrupt sighs; his gaze, chagrined and menacing, which he sometimes rested on the vast sea of the Antilles, whose extent he seemed to be measuring, and sometimes darted at the town, might have give the impression that he was sunk in nostalgic dreams—that his heart was bruised by homesickness, the violent love for an absent fatherland that nothing can overcome, and which still draws tears from old Canadians bent beneath the infamous yoke of the English, at the mere mention of the name of their former homeland, and which sometimes causes them to push away in disgust the young children of their race, who wear out their ears with the rude language of the conquerors. He seemed to be measuring the distance between his Africa and that American shore, and cursing the barbaric Europeans who had transplanted him here after having exchanged him for a saw or a sword with his abductors.

One could have plunged deep into the bile of his thoughts, but none of that was agitating Barraou, for he was a son of Cuba and was only African in his features and his soul.

Suddenly, he threw away his unfinished cigar, stood up and sat down again heavily, muttering hoarse monosyllables like coarse oaths between his teeth. He clicked his jaw and bumped the back of his head against the wall. Finally, seemingly calmed down, he repeated in a tearful voice:

"Jealousy! Jealousy! How ill you're making me feel, how you're devouring me, jealousy! A curse upon me, a curse upon Jaquez Barraou! My breast is burning more than if I'd swallowed a cubeb pepper. Jealousy! You're chewing my heart with a tooth more incisive than a serpent's fang! When I want be rid of you, that's when you besiege me? Get rid of you? All right, but how? They haven't even left me in doubt, for the other evening, when I came back from town, I saw him running away from the hut for the third time. He'd definitely come out of it. Yes, I've seen him, the infamous Juan Cazador—what are you trying to do with my Amada? Trying...how good I am! 'Oh, what!' my Amada replied. 'Oh no!' You're pure, my Amada, yes! But should I believe it? Women are so treacherous. Cruel fate! Horrible uncertainty! Soon, I'll be out of my mind. False friend, you whom I call my Juanito; you who have known me since I was smaller than that kid goat; you who, so many times, have fallen sleep dead drunk on my mat well before nightfall— nights of effusions and dreams sweeter than those brought by sleep! What tafia! What cigaritos! Those times are already long gone, poor Barraou! You made the most of your youth, and now that you're bowing down like your father, you must weep!

"How unjust men are! Have I ever coveted their wives? So why cheat with mine? I'm poor; I have nothing—nothing but Amada. A wretch, I shall never be able to possess anything in this world, unless the tithe is lifted. Nothing! Not even the one I've chosen among a thousand. Oh, I'm too ready to think evil! A stratagem, an ambush might clarify everything; if I'm wrong, if I'm mistaken, I'll be at peace again. Holy Virgin! Help me, and everything will be settled tomorrow...."

Suddenly, he interrupted himself, tilted his head and cocked an ear, as if he had heard a noise; he straightened up again and stiffened in order to feign calmness, when a young woman hurtled out of the hut, ran to him and leaned on his shoulder.

Oh, how beautiful she seemed to me,[33] and worthy of all Barraou's violence! I don't know whether I was blinded by that loving prejudice, the sympathetic prejudice that always attracts me to colored women—who always yield an African beauty to me in my dreams, who caused me to seek the embraces of black women while I was still very young, and remain cold to the caresses of our white creoles. Oh, how beautiful she seemed to me!

She was slim, joyful and merry; her complexion was that of a mixed race, which you would call, scornfully, mulatto; her features were fine, with a profile like that of an Arlesienne, and her almond-shaped eyes were keen. Around her head she had gracefully wound a muslin turban; coral pendants swung beneath her ears. A necklace of Venetian pearls made a golden base for the contour of her beautiful neck. Her slender fingers were imprisoned in precious rings; her short white cotton saya left her rounded legs bare, and her Cinderella feet were only shod in rustic Spanish sandals.

"What are you doing here?" she said to him, lifting her long hair with her hand and plastering her lips to Barraou's depressed forehead. You, today, at this hour, still in such disorder? You're tormenting me, my Jacquez, you seem upset—what's wrong? Share your slightest distress with me—speak, be confident!"

"Nothing's wrong, honestly. Perhaps it's the heat getting me down?"

"No, you're hiding something. Even while speaking, you're still dreaming, and you seem *engolfado*. Besides, didn't I hear you just now talking to yourself, quarreling and complaining out loud?"

"You're mistaken, *Corazón mio*—I was humming, thinking you were asleep, softly singing your favorite song:

---

33. This is one of the most obvious examples of episodes in the collection in which the narrative voice and a character's spoken or tacit monologue become confused.

Paxarito que vienes herido
Por las balos del cruel Cazador,
Cesa, Cesa tu triste gemido.
Mientras duerme mi dulce amor!

"Oh how good you are, my Jaquez, to your Amada! Deigning to think of her!"

"You've deigned to love me; but enough of that. Would you please prepare, for this evening, a copious supper? Good food! I have the intention of inviting Cazador."

"That man...why?"

"Why? Silly question! What's extraordinary about it? Is it the first time that friend has shared my table?"

"Not at all! But you're so sulky, I might even say so sad, that you'll surely give him a frosty reception."

"What does it matter? He'll have the good graces of the hostess! Tell Pablo to come; he ought to be near the worksite—I saw him a little while ago playing with your old dog Spalestro. Go and do it."

My dire presentiments will soon be corroborated. How she blushed at the mere mention of his name. What embarrassment, what surprise! And that female cunning, to receive coldly news that brought joy to her heart!

"You sent for me, Boss—I'm here, what can I do for you?"

"Listen carefully, Pablo; take a packet of tobacco from the dresser, and then go find Juan Cazador at the home of his master, Gideon Robertson. Offer it to him on my behalf, and invite him to come to supper tonight, at the home of his friend Jaquez Barraou. Be quick, and don't come back without him. Go, and may God go with you."

II.
El Corazón no es Traydor[34]

When the *pequeño* Pablo had gone, Barraou went back into the hut. Amada was making the supper. He washed himself and put on his Sunday best. Then he took down the blunderbuss hanging on the wall above a few figurines and images of St. James of Galice and hooded Madonnas, and started cleaning it with a kind of somber joy. Amada noticed it.

"Why are you cleaning that blunderbuss?" she asked him.

"No reason, my love, merely to loosen the wheel, which is getting rusty."

"Oh! Only to loosen the wheel. What's the reason for that new flint, then? Alas! Holy Virgin! What are you doing now? Powder? Bullets? Are you going to load it? That's imprudent—no, I beg you, something bad will happen—that weapon's within reach of all comers."

"Something bad will happen...perhaps...."

"But what's the point? Answer me."

"What's the point? You want to know? Well, tomorrow, I have to go inland, to buy wood; the roads are infested with robber bands; I don't think it's a good idea to go unarmed. Where's my *cuchillo*, Amada? It was there, but I can't find it."

"Here it is, my love, but why do you need to have a dagger on you? Is it for tomorrow's robbers?"

"Please God!"

After Barraou's outburst, without saying a word, Amada finished her coking and laid the table for super. As for him, pacing back and forth in front of the hut, he looked into the distance from time to time, impatiently. While taking care of the housework, Amada, internally agitated and upset, was bruised in her soul by a hundred diverse thoughts. She formulated a hundred conjectures, most of them strange and absurd. She would have give her most beautiful night of pleasure, or her

---

34. The heart is no traitor, although "*traydor*" would normally be spelled *traidor*.

blessed golden necklace, for it to be tomorrow, or to see into the most secret recess of Barraou's heart. Many times, she uttered deep sighs.

Alma de Dios, protect your servant! My good angel, hold back Barraou's arm, as you held back the arm of our father Abraham!

* * * * * * *

Pablo found Juan Cazador ready to go out dancing, excitedly drawing a few twanging sounds from a broken mandolin.

"My Master has sent me, please," he said, "to offer you this tobacco from the royal plantation and to invite you to supper; he told me not to come back without you."

Cazador, surprised and delighted, thanked Pablo for his kind visit, and set out.

On the way, he could not contain his hilarity, and questioned himself.

What, he said to himself, *could have led Jaquez to do me such a favor? Umbrageously, he's done everything for such a long time to keep me at a distance—that can only be because of Amada. What if it were her influence? No, it can't be! Does she, then, have some love for me? Love...love...no, I'm too unfortunate!*

III.
Traycíon y Trayciou[35]

When Juan approached the hut, Jaquez, who was still striding back and forth, saw him coming some distance away, came to met him and greeted him amicably, heaping courtesies upon him, to which Cazador replied effusively. When they went in, Amada started, and without being seen, raised her eyes as if to beg for the mercy of the Good Lord, crossed herself hurriedly, and then turned round calmly.

---

35. Betrayal and stabbing, although the orthography is eccentric.

"*Doy a usted la bienvenida*," she said to Juan Cazador. "Please take a seat; everything's ready."

"*Bien está, querida*," Barraou added, seating Juan to his right. "*Compagnero!* It's a long time since I've had the pleasure of dining with you; it's necessary to signal and celebrate the meal appropriately—let's empty a few old bottles; let's try, my old friend, to reproduce the atmosphere of those old bachelor feasts, which were not embellished by our good Amada. Let he who refuses be reckoned a coward and a babe in arms!"

"Bravo, bravo!" said Cazador. "So be it. I consent, and will pay a forfeit if I lose. Watch out, Barraou!"

"Keep your solicitude for yourself, *Compadre*. How many times have I drunk you under the table, Juanito? Watch out yourself, *Cobarde!*"

As he spoke these last words, Barraou slipped his *cuchillo*, which was on the window-sill, into his sleeve. At that movement, Amada, who was following him with her eyes, uttered a cry of horror; they both immediately caught her in their arms, asked whether she was feeling ill, and lavished a thousand cares on her. Soon collecting herself, she thanked them.

"It's nothing," she said. "Only a sudden palpitation of the heart made me cry out."

"You scared me," said Jaquez.

"You turned my head and my heart," murmured Cazador.

"Aha! That's delicate, Juanito—an adroit admission."

"I said it without malice, and claim no merit for it."

"What do you think, our Amada?"

"Good Lord! You're very tiring, Barraou."

"A joke, my friends, let there be no more doubt about it— *dexada la burlas*. Let's drink to that! Amada, you should go and fetch that bottle of Xerès wine from the back of the cellar. No, don't disturb yourself—I'll go myself, you'll never find it. Excuse me, Juanito—and you can tell me your news."

* * * * * * *

"Without losing any time, Amada of my heart; we're alone—tell me, quickly, is it to you that I owe this happiness?"

"What happiness?"

"Sharing your...."

"No, no, you owe nothing to me; it wasn't me—far from it!"

"You're still as harsh toward me, then? Oh, let me steal the kiss that you refused me the other evening."

"No! I abhor you; I execrate you—and yet I pity you."

"O joy!"

"Listen—danger surrounds you here; watch out, and pray that God is watching over you."

"What do you mean?"

"I'm not saying any more; shut up or you'll doom us, Juan. Shut up—I mean it."

* * * * * * *

"Here's the famous Xerès! Your glass, Juan—taste this."

"*Via usted! Es un amber*—it's delicious."

"Come on, *compadre*! On the double. Do you have a small mouth? Are you afraid of getting drunk?"

"Juan Cazador is no novice; I think, Barraou, that you'd better get ready for your forfeit, for your eye's beginning to glisten. Hey, what are you doing? Be careful—one would think that you were sitting on a blunderbuss."

In fact, Barraou was beginning to pass from enthusiasm to drunkenness. He sang and swayed, getting carried away and thumping the table, bursting into laughter, reciting prayers and lewd jokes, similar to the improvisations of Biscayan arrieros, who set off when their head is reeling, perched on their mules, singing and amalgamating the Old and New Testaments in a manner that is not at all attractive.

After battling for a long time, and uttering a thousand obscene remarks that disgusted Amanda, he slumped over the table and went to sleep.

* * * * * * *

"We can't leave him in that state. Help me, Cazador, to lay him down on that mat; he'll be better there to get over his wine. Oh, the vile drunkard!"

Barraou allowed himself to be transported.

"Take away his *cuchillo*, Cazador—there, by his side—he might injure himself. Throw this cape over him. What are you doing Cazador? Don't cover his face, you'll stifle him! No, no, don't cover him, I tell you.

"How silly you are! Oh, forgive me for that word—I got carried away, Amada, because chance has served me so well! Thanks to his drunkenness, we're liberated from his inquisitive gaze, and he's facilitated this *tête-à-tête* for me himself. Let me cover with kisses the hand that is pushing me away, Amada— don't be so surly."

"Shut up!"

"Be less surly for the man who loves you more than his freedom!"

"Stop, Cazador—I'm the wife of Jacquez Barraou, your friend!"

"Are you still a rock? In our last conversation you let me fall at your feet rather than grant the smallest favor to this unfortunate lover. You're annoying me, Amada—fear my violence!"

"*Alma de Dios*, save me! Stop, Juan! I'll call Barraou!"

"Wake him up, if you dare. What does it matter to me? Call him, then, your husband—he's drunk!"

At these words, Jaquez Barraou, throwing off the cape, suddenly stood up.

"*Carajo, cobarde!* Do you think, ruffian, that Barraou gets drunk as Cazador gets drunk? Wretch—you've been caught in a trap. Die!"

He seized his blunderbuss then, and took aim at Cazador, who fled toward the door. Amada, hanging on to the weapon, cried for mercy, and stopped him.

He freed himself, grabbed a knife from the table and raised

his arm to strike Juan, who leapt outside, slamming the door. The blade dug deeply into the wood. Barraou, foaming at the mouth, pursued him, roaring infernal oaths.

"Stop! Stop! Jaquez, stop! It's Amada who's begging you; be generous, let the man go!"

Without hearing her, though, as rapid as a gust of wind, he followed his agile enemy, who plunged into the clumps of the neighboring plantations.

Fainting, Amada dragged herself into the hut, accusing herself of Juan's death and weeping profusely.

Amada, however, was irreproachable; she had not given Juan any hope, she had rejected his declarations of love out of hand; in sum, she did not love him. But when a person for whom a woman has the least sympathy suffers unhappiness because of her, nothing can prevent her from feeling a tender sentiment that expands in her soul; she does not love him, it is true, but she feels a great deal of pity.

Scarcely had she conceived the hope that he would escape her husband's fury that the explosion of a firearm burst forth nearby.

"There no more doubt as to his fate!" she exclaimed, falling to her knees. "*Virgen María*, have pity on us! *Jesu Cristo*, who redeemed humankind, have pity on him! *Buon Dios, Dios de mi Corazón*, grant him mercy at your tribunal!"

And, her voice gradually fading away, she remained plunged in her grief.

* * * * * * *

Suddenly, she heard precipitate footsteps outside. Barraou came back in, completely out of breath, his eyes haggard, dragging his blunderbuss lazily by the strap.

"Get up, Amada, you can pray later; give me water."

Trembling, she went to him, presenting him a water-jug. Barraou rolled up the sleeves of his shirt. Amada, seeing his hands wet with blood, dropped the jug, which broke.

"Oh Jaquez, you've killed him!"

"It's nothing. No, unfortunately, God did not grant me that mercy. I thought so when he fell; I was running to finish him off when he got up and escaped my claws; his wound was slight. I swear by all the saints that I'll have his life! Nothing can save him from my rage!

"I'm tired, Amada—aren't you weary? Let's go to bed; perhaps I'll find calm and rest in your arms.

"Jaquez, at least change that stained shirt; you reek of blood!"

IV.
A las Oraciones[36]

The next day, Monday, at daybreak, while Amada was still awake, Barraou went to Havana.

He was seen all day long in the neighborhood in which Gideon Robertson lived.

For four days and four nights he prowled around the city with no success; Juan's wound was doubtless keeping him in bed.

Finally, on the fatal Friday, Barraou saw him on the harbor, and followed him closely. When he went into a deserted sidestreet behind the big fort he cried "Stop, bandit! I've been looking for you!"

"You've been looking for me? Here I am."

"That's good. Defend yourself if you can!"

As he spoke these words he threw himself upon him like a hyena, in order to strike him with his dagger. Juan dodged the blow and, quickly taking out his knife, he slashed Barraou's forearm. The latter seized him around the waist and stabbed him in the side. Juan, desperate, let himself fall upon him, and bit his cheek, tearing away a strip of flesh that uncovered his jawbone. Barraou spat blood and foam into his eyes.

At that moment, eight o'clock and the *Oraciones* sounded at the nearby convent. The two furious men separated and fell to

36. *Oraciones* means "prayers," but the reference here is more specific, to one of the daily offices observed by monks and nuns.

their knees.

BARRAOU

The angel of the lord has appeared to Mary and she has conceived, by the action of the Holy Spirit.

JUAN

Hail Mary, full of grace, the Lord is with thee; blessed art thou amongst women, and blessed is the fruit thy womb, Jesus. Holy Mary, Mother of God, pray for us poor sinners, now and at the hour of our death. Amen.

BARRAOU

Behold the servant of the Lord, that he might act according to thy word.

JUAN

Hail Mary, full of grace, the Lord is with thee; blessed art thou amongst women, and blessed is the fruit thy womb, Jesus. Holy Mary, Mother of God, pray for us poor sinners, now and at the hour of our death. Amen.

BARRAOU

And the word is made flesh, and it has lived among us.

JUAN

Hail Mary, full of grace, the Lord is with thee; blessed art thou amongst women, and blessed is the fruit thy womb, Jesus. Holy Mary, Mother of God, pray for us poor sinners, now and at the hour of our death. Amen.

"Come on! Get up, Cazador; what are you doing still on your knees?"

"I was praying for your soul."

"There's no need; I was praying for yours. On guard!"

Immediately, he stabbed him in the breast. Blood spurted a long way. Juan uttered a cry and fell on to one knee, seizing Barraou's thigh. Barraou pulled his hair and struck him, with redoubled violence, in the back; a counter-thrust slit his belly. Both falling to the ground, they rolled in the dust. Sometimes Jaquez was on top, sometimes Juan. They roared and writhed.

One raised his arm and broke his blade against a stone wall; the other stuck his into the throat. Bloody and lacerated, they uttered frightful groans, and no longer seemed anything but a mass of flowing and clotting blood.

Already, thousands of flies and filthy beetles were going into and coming out of their nostrils and mouths, wallowing in the suppuration of their wounds.

* * * * * * *

At dusk, a merchant tripped over their cadavers, said "they're only negroes," and passed on.

DON ANDREA VESALIUS, THE ANATOMIST
(MADRID)

When this story of Andrea Vesalius was finished, it was taken to the *Revue de Paris* and offered to Monsieur Amedée Pichot as a translation from the Danish of a supposed Isaiah Wagner; its form being unsuited to that literary magazine, Monsieur Amedée Pichot would not insert it, but, having paid for the pretended translation, he made use of the same hero to embroider the charming anatomical tale that you have doubtless read in the periodical.[37] That story having no detailed resemblance to this one, however, we are therefore reclaiming for Champavert the priority and discovery.

I.
Chalybarium[38]

At the hour of darkness and peace when cities resemble necropolises, only one tortuous back-street in Madrid, an

---

37. The issue of the *Revue de Paris* in which Pichot's own version of this story is contained appears to be missing from the Bibliothèque Nationale's run of the periodical, but Pierre Lacroix refers to it in his review of *Champavert*. The anatomist's forename is usually rendered Andreas, but he was originally Andries van Wesel, and his name acquired so many variants during his career that I have retained Borel's.

38, A variant of "charivari" (making a racket by banging saucepans and other metal vessels).

obscure artery, was still beating with a violent and febrile pulse. That somnambulistic back-street in the sleeping city was the Callejuela casa del Campo. At one of its extremities stood a rich dwelling inhabited by a stranger, a native of Flanders. The window-panes were resplendent with interior fires, projected upon them obliquely and cutting out ardent lattices and golden threads on the black face of the house opposite, seeming in the shadows to be speckled with the mouths of furnaces.

The door of that large house was wide open, allowing the sight of a vast porch with a ridged vault and a pendant keystone, at the foot of a great stone staircase with balustrades carved in light, like the ivory of a fan, and strewn with odorant flowers.

There was, one might say in jest, a carnival of walls, all their partitions being disguised and masked by tapestries, velvet and sparkling candelabras.

A few halberdiers were marching up and down at the entrance.

When the shouts of the crowd gathered outside eased from time to time, a sweet and melodious symphony could be distinguished, descending along the stairway and making the sonorous vault speak.

The entire palace was celebrating, but a rabble of poor people was howling and milling at the door; there were the organs of the temple and, at the very bottom, beggars on the flagstones of the parvis.

Sometimes, frightful hurrahs, sniggers and the sounds of brass instruments spread from group to group in the darkness, dying away among satanic laughter strayed from the clouds.

* * * * * * *

"The doctor has chosen his wedding day well—a Saturday, the festival of the sabbat; a sorcerer could do no better," said a toothless old woman, huddled in the embrasure of a gate.[39]

"True. My dear, and in the name of the God I adore, if all his defunct clients were to come back for it, the round-dance would make a tour of Madrid."

"But what would happen," the first old woman went on, "if all the poor Castilians that executioner of death has peeled—may God compensate them!—came to reclaim their skin?"

"I'm assured," said a small bearded man, buried in the crowd and raising himself up on tiptoe, "that he often dines on cutlets of meat that don't come from the butcher's."

"It's true! It's true!"

"No, no, it's false!" shouted a tall young man, jammed against the trellis of a window. "It's false—ask Rivadeneyra, the butcher."

"Silence! Will you shut up?" shouted, even louder, a man embossed in a brown cape, with a sombrero over his eyes. "Don't you recognize him? That's Henrique Zapata, the apprentice flayer! It's true, Verdugo and Ahorcador support it.[40] I'll wager that if one searched beneath his doublet, one would find a hand or a leg."

"What an idea—that old corpse-eater taking a young woman!" the old woman replied. "If I were King Philippe, I'd certainly put a stop to that ogre...."

"Oh yes," said the unknown man in the brown cape. "Philippe II protects him, that Flanders dog. Just yesterday, Torrijo, the baker of the Cebada, disappeared, surely for the pâté at the

---

39. Vesalius (1514-1564) married Anne von Hamme in 1846, long before he became imperial physician to Charles V; there is no evidence of a second marriage in the 1550s, but if there had been such a marriage, he would only have been in his forties, so the decrepit figure represented here is an invention.

40. Both these apparent surnames carry the approximate meaning "executioner," the latter being more narrowly construable as "hanging judge."

feast. It's a horror! It must be stopped!"

"The king might well protect him," murmured the people. "He ought to be burned alive."

"Christians! The man is a heretic! A necromancer! A Fleming! He deserves to die!" said, benignly, some monks from the convent of Nuestra Señora de Atocha, newly founded by the Fathers García de Loaysa, inquisitor general, archbishop of Seville, and Juan Hurtado de Mendoza, the confessor of the Emperor Carlos V, with whom the monks of the royal convent of San Geronymo joined in chorus.[41]

"To death!" cried the crowd, driving back the halberdiers, swearing in front of them.

"To death!" repeated the cloaked cavalier.

"To death!" howled the monks, who were inflaming the populace, crucifixes in hand. "To death! Put him on the fire!"

Suddenly, the imminent storm burst. Cries of rage and death rained down; the mob rushed into the porch, one monk brandishing a torch over his head—but the halberdiers, assisted by Henrique Zapata and several other students, put up a vigorous resistance, and gave battle as they retreated to that unleashed rabble, roaring as they did so. In return, the racket was redoubled; the mob struck bells, blades, saucepans; it was a scathing, deafening thunder, an almost homicidal symphony.

II.
Saltatio, Turba, Mors[42]

In the reception-rooms, a cordial or mocking hilarity reigned; no one paid any heed to the noise outside, the custom being to make such a fuss when an old man married a young woman.

A brown cape was suspended at the entrance to the gallery

41. Juan García de Loaysa y Mendoza died in 1546, eight years before Philip II became King of Castile. The most famous bearer of the name, Juan Hurtado de Mendoza, was long dead by then, but was a member of an extensive family.

42. Dancing, Crowd (or Chorus), Death.

that served as a vestiary. The bride was dancing with a handsome cavalier, who had not previously been seen at the celebration. They seemed more interested in their whispering than the dance. The groom, in the opposite corner of the room, was flirting with the daughter of a relative.

The great hall terminated in an anteroom opening into a courtyard; it was full of guests—ladies, cavaliers, old men, duennas—who, under the pretext of breathing the fresh night air, were giving free rein to their satire and malice. It was a battle of influences and interlocutions; an orchestra of shrill, deep, hoarse and tremulous voices; a collection of pretty faces and expressions wrinkled by coarse laugher or enlivened by sardonic smiles, revealing ivory keyboards or mouths crenellated like a tower, or denticulated like the cornice of a vault.

"So who's the cavalier at whom the bride is simpering?"

"You're wicked, Señorina!"

"Ha ha ha! Look over there, then, at Don Vesalius, encased in his *calzas bermijas* and black doublet. By Mahomet, don't his legs look to you like quills in an inkwell? Watch him dancing with Amalia de Cardenas, plump, fresh and rosy. Does he not remind you of Monsieur Saturnus?"

"Or Death making the living dance."

"Holbein's dance."

"Tell us, Olivares, what will he do *con su Machacha*?"

"An anatomy lesson."

"Conversation."

"Thank God for the *Novia*!"

"That's the saraband concluded—look at him kissing the hand of our cousin Amalia."

"This isn't a bourgeois wedding, a *saraguete*, but a brilliant *sarao*."

"Where's the bride, then?"

"Where's the handsome cavalier?"

"Don Vesalius is looking for them, alarmed—*busca, busca, perro Viejo!*"

"Go ask him, Olivares—he, who passes for a sorcerer—what

Maria is doing at this moment."

"Friend! Don't put a finger between the hammer and the anvil."

The dance resumed. Vesalius offered another invitation to Amalia, who pulled a face, and laughed at him behind his back.

The bride was no longer in the room, nor the brown cape in the vestiary, and in a dark corridor, footsteps could be heard, and this:

"Cover yourself with this cape, Maria, quickly—let's go."

"Alderan, I can't."

"Me, leave you prey to that Vesalius? No—you belong to me. I learn that you've betrayed me in my absence; I arrive in haste, this very morning, I mingle with the celebration; I take you to one side, alone, and I say 'let's go'—and you refuse? Oh, no, Maria, you're mistaken. Come—there's still time; break this ignominious bond; we'll be happy; I'll be entirely yours, yours alone, and forever. Come, Maria!"

"Alderan, my family has imposed this yoke upon me; I shall submit to it—but you'll always be my lover, and I'll always be yours! What does that man matter? What is he? One more valet, a screen that will veil our mysterious love. Leave me, leave me—adieu!"

"So you don't want to, Maria—that's all right! Go dirty yourself with that man! Do as you wish, and I'll do likewise—go!"

Pulling away from his arms, she fled abruptly from the gallery into the drawing room.

Alderan stood there for a few moments, as if devastated; he blasphemed, he stamped his foot—and then, suddenly, he disappeared into the depths.

In the meantime, the crowd had swollen, like a pond in a storm. The tumult became more and more intense, and the bacchanal terrifying. The people had recovered their initial audacity, and, having gradually drawn closer, were laughing in the faces of the halberdiers. Imprecations and mortal threats were rumbling again; stones were being thrown at the windows and the walls spattered with ox-blood and faeces, when, suddenly, the groups opened up to make way for a disheveled woman who was howling like a dog at the moon; it was the wife of the baker Torrija, who had come to reclaim her husband, and demand vengeance.

"It's Torrija the baker's wife," people said, on all sides. Then, the compassionate mob fell silent, and La Torrija sobbed and uttered roars.

Then the man in the brown cape, climbing the steps, shouted in a loud voice; "Friends! Let's have justice! Cowards, those who won't follow! Vengeance! Death to Vesalius! Death to the necromancer!"

The reply was a hail of stones on the windows and on the halberdiers, who retreated all the way to the staircase. The mob vomited into the porch, its members throwing themselves at the raised pikes, seizing them and breaking them. They climbed the flight, and were breaking down the door to the reception room when the sound of galloping horses was heard in the distance.

"It's the *alguazils*! Every man for himself!"

Gripped by panic terror, the mob flowed back down the staircase, rushing into the corridors or jumping out of windows; only a few brave men stood firm.

"In the name of the king, disperse!"

"The king punishes murderers, heretics and sorcerers with death! Death to the Fleming!"

"In the name of the king, disperse!"

Then the *alguazils* rode into the porch; a rain of furniture greeted them; they replied with musket-fire, which felled the most audacious. The man in the brown cape, uttering a cry, put his hand to his side. The sound and the wounded took flight, leaving five cadavers lying on the tiles.

Suddenly, the palace and the street became bleak. The watch took away the bodies of the vanquished; the guests, trembling, escaped via the rear entrance. The doors were bolted, the lamps extinguished; the scene of life was followed by a scene of death—except that, in one wing, in Vesalius' apartment, two windows were alight in the darkness.

III.
Quod Legi Non Potest[43]

Through the broken-down battens of the door of the reception room, Maria had seen the man in the brown cape hit by a gunshot; at his heart-rending cry, she had fainted. She had been carried to her bedroom and laid on a sofa, where she remained negligently extended for some time. Vesalius, on his knees beside her, tearful and trembling, kissed her hands and forehead.

"How do you feel, Maria, my love?"

"Better—but is everything calm now?"

"Yes—that ugly mob has had its reckoning. Can you imagine what those good folk have against me? Me, placid and retiring, spending my days obscurely in the somber study of anatomy, for the good of humankind, for the progress of science, or the glory of God! Those good folk are demanding my head; they believe me to be a sorcerer; if anyone in the city disappears, it's me, Vesalius, who has stolen them for my experiments. The masses will always be ugly and stupid! Stupid and ingrate! That's the fate reserved for all those who exert themselves on their behalf—all those who want to show them a new path, say something new. They crucified Jesus of Nazareth, laughed in the face of Christopher Columbus. The masses will always be ugly and stupid, stupid and ingrate!"

"Dispel those dark thoughts, Vesalius—but frankly, that skirmish is unlikely to win their love."

"Of, what do I care, after all, about the love of that rabble, so long as I have yours, Maria. Oh, you love me, don't you? You love me a little."

"Can you still ask me such a question?"

"I know, Maria, that I'm old, and when one is old, one doubts; I know that I'm devoid of gallantry, broken by sleepless nights, that I've grown thin, not unlike the skeletons in my workroom—

---

43. This phrase is usually used to mean "illegible," although it can be construed more literally as "what is written (or legislated) cannot be accomplished."

but my heart is young and warm! You see, the passion I feel for you is not a stale passion; in this old envelope, it's a new soul I bring you; I've encounter many women in my life, but none, I swear, has lit such a fire in me. Fatality! Is it necessary to arrive at decrepitude in order to know love and its violence? Maria, accustom your gaze to the coarse coffer imprisoning my young soul; sap remains beneath the bark of a centenarian oak."

Maria threw an arm around his neck, passing her mouth over his bald head and his whitened beard. Vesalius wept with joy.

Bedtime! An hour so delirious, so palpitating with modesty and sensuality! An hour that confuses people, who revive and drown in desire! Bedtime, betraying lies or beauties! An hour, too often, of painful contrasts! An hour that is sometimes fatal!

Gracefully, the bride took off her nuptial dress and her jewels; the rose seemed stripped of its sepals; she was a Castilian beauty such as one sees in dreams!

Awkwardly, Vesalius took off his party clothes and laid bare his ugly frame; he was a mummy taking off his bandages!

* * * * * * *

The lamp was suddenly snuffed out; the rings of the bed-curtains creaked on their rods; there was a profound calm, tumultuously interrupted at intervals; but Maria uttered no cry....

Far into the night, however, there were caresses and kisses without response, and then murmurs and curses—and the savant professor of anatomy repeating, tremulously: "Oh, don't think that it's weakness, Maria! It's the violence of my love that is breaking me; your beauty fills me with shame; it seems to me that I'm touching something sacred; I love you so much, Maria, I love you so much! But don't think that it's weakness! Tomorrow, by daylight, I'll show you in twenty authors, you'll see in Mundinus, in Galianus, in Gontherius Anderaci, my master and the chief physician of François I of France, you'll see that, on the contrary, it's potency, a excess of love—I love you so much, Maria!"

It is necessary to believe that this excess of love did not abate, for only a few days had gone by when Maria moved into an isolated apartment in another wing, with one of the professor's former housekeepers, who was utterly devoted to him, and whom he had metamorphosed into a duenna for his wife. The owl only saw his turtle-dove at meal-times; he treated her with all the coldness and strict politeness of one stranger to another.

Vesalius was married to his studies again; buried in his research, he went from the laboratory to the amphitheater and from the amphitheater to the laboratory.

Puberal and nubile young women, this is the lesson you can learn from this: that it is necessary, if you have ardent passions, no matter how much you want to, not to marry a doctor of the Faculté, a member of the Académie des Inscriptions et Belles-Lettres or, above all, an immortal of the Académie des Quarante Fauteuils and the inexhaustible dictionary.

IV.
Nidus Adulteratus[44]

About an Olympiad after these events. Doña Maria—who, contrary to custom, had not appeared at table for several days, sent for her husband, Vesalius. He went to her immediately; pale and exhausted, with dark circles around her eyes and her voice faint, she was lying on her bed. Vesalius, bringing up a chair, sat down and leaned over in order to listen. Maria, feeling warm breath on her forehead, raised her eyelid, recognized Andrea Vesalius and, sighing, began speaking in an agonized tone.

"You are my lord and master, Andrea! I feel myself weakening by the moment. Soon, I shall be at the feet of God, the austere judge, and I am impure. I have sinned against you so much! But the sinner begs your forgiveness. Don't get carried away; you're a wise man, you are my good husband and my

---

44. Adulterous Nest

master! Allow me to lay my soul bare."

"Señora, you are not as base as you seem to think; your mind is afflicted."

"No one knows an illness better than the patient. Something is crying out in me, that my end is nigh. You are my husband and my good lord; listen, and forgive; perhaps I shall even be excusable in some respects.

"We both swore an oath at the altar; we have both been unfaithful to it—me because I was young and superabundant with life, you because your hair was whitened by study and your body broken by work. Woe, woe, to have to curse one's youth! O Vesalius, if you knew what it is to be a young woman, if you knew all that passes within her...forgive me, O Vesalius!

"Listen coldly.

"Now, I say that I am an adulteress, that I have deceived you vilely. I am direly criminal, Andrea; I have introduced my lovers into your home; I have intoxicated them with your wine, I have gorged them at your table; and, while you were plunged in study or sleep, I have laughed with them at you; our filthy iniquity rejoiced in your complacency; you were the aliment of our laughter. Is that not infamous? This very bed, here, in which I am dying, is still quivering with out lasciviousness—and God is summoning me! I'm dying! Oh, if you reject me...."

Her voice was stifled by sobs; then, after a momentary pause, she continued, distinctly.

"Already, I have been harshly, atrociously punished. An adulterous woman must be very repulsive. She must trail disgust wherever she goes. Since our marriage, I have had three lovers, but in truth, I possessed each of them only once. When, after long courtship, I ceded to their obsession, when I surrendered my body to them, a share of this bed...yes, a guilty woman must be very repulsive; the next day, when I awoke, I was alone! And I never saw them again—never! Can one be more severely punished? Crime is linked to punishment; crime summons torture; and if it is necessary to tell all to obtain remission—you are merciful, Andrea!—the last one, I loved recklessly, with a boundless love, you see! His loss has killed me; abandoned by him, I'm dying of it!

"Now, I've said everything; in the same of Nuestra Señora de Atocha; in the name of San Isidro Labrador; in the name of San Andres, your patron; in the name of my father, your *tocayo*, your *colombroño*;[45] forgive the weak woman who has offended you so much, whom your blessing will purify. Oh, forgive her—she is dying!"

And, taking his hand, she covered it with tears and kisses. Vesalius withdrew it rudely, pushed back his chair, and said to her, in an intense voice: "Get up, Maria. Come with me."

"I'm too weak; I can't."

"Come with me, I tell you."

Maria, getting up with difficulty, wrapped herself in a peignoir, and followed Vesalius unsteadily.

He went down the great staircase and across the courtyard, opened a sunken door pierced with loopholes that gave access to a small building illuminated by great stone bay-windows. That gate closed behind them, and the interior bolts grated in their varvels.

V.

Opificina[46]

We are now at the entrance to Vesalius' laboratory: a large square room in the arch of a cloister, with stone walls and flagstones. A few tables of dirty and greasy wood, a few work-benches, two or three vats, a dresser and cupboards comprised its only furniture. A few cauldrons were scattered around a fire-place, whose projecting mantle descended from the vault; on its pot-hook hung a kettle, boiling over an ardent fire.

The workbenches were laden with partly-dissected cadavers; there were shreds of flesh and amputated limbs underfoot, and

---

45. Both these words mean "namesake."

46, Workshop.

muscles and cartilage were crushed by the professor's sandals. A skeleton was hanging on the door, which, when it was agitated, rattled like those wooden candles that candle-makers hang up as their sign, when they are stirred by the wind.

The ceiling and the walls were covered in bones, spines, skeletons and carcasses, some of them human but the greater number monkeys and pigs—the animals most closely resembling human osteology in their framework—that had served the studies of Andrea Vesalius, the first man who had, so to speak, made anatomy a real science, who had dared to dissect cadavers, even those of orthodox Christians, and work on them in public.

Only Mundinus, a professor in Bologna, long before, in 1315 or thereabouts, had previously offered the spectacle of three dissected human skeletons. That audacious scandal had not been repeated; the Church had formally prohibited it as a sacrilege.[47] Frightened himself by the edict of Boniface VIII, still warm, Mundinus had not obtained any great advantage from his research.

Contact with, or the mere appearance of a cadaver, among the ancients, imprinted a pollution that obligatory lustral ablutions and other expiations could scarcely efface. In the Middle Ages, the dissection of a creature "made in God's image" was reckoned an impiety worthy of the scaffold.

VI.
Enodatio[48]

"Now, here, in this laboratory, what do you want from me, Vesalius?" Maria repeated, weeping. "What do you want from

47. In fact, the Vatican had sanctioned the public dissection carried out by Mundinus (Mondino de Luzzi) in January 1315. Boniface VIII, famous for his disputes with Dante, who died in 1303, was widely believed to have issued a decree banning dissection, but that interpretation was probably mistaken.

48. Untying—i.e., explanation or denouement.

me? I can't stay here; the putrid odor of these corpses is suffocating me—open the door so that I can go out. I'm suffering horribly!"

"No, what does that matter to me? Listen in your turn. You've had three lovers, have you not?"

"Yes, my lord."

"You intoxicated them with my wine, did you not?"

"Yes, my lord."

"Well, that wine was not pure; your duenna poured a narcotic into it—opium—and you slept for a long time, didn't you?"

"Yes, my lord—and when I awoke, I was alone."

"Alone, were you not?"

"Yes, my lord—and I never saw them again."

"Never! That's good! But come here!"

And, pulling her by the arm, he drew her to the back of the room; there, he opened a cupboard in which a complete skeleton was hanging, with its natural articulations, and an ivory whiteness.

"Do you recognize this man?"

"What? These bones?"

"Do you recognize this doublet, this brown cape?"

"Yes, my lord—it's the cavalier Alderan's cape."

"Look hard, then, señora; do you also recognize the handsome cavalier who wore that cape, with whom you danced so gallantly at our wedding?"

"Alderan!" Maria uttered a scream that might have woken the dead.

"At least, Doña, you can see that everything is to the advantage of science," he said, turning toward her with a chilly expression. "You can see that science is greatly obliged to you."

Then, laughing sardonically, he led her to a kind of reliquary, or cage garnished with glass, which displayed a carefully-preserved human skeleton; the arteries were infused with a red liquid and the veins with a blue liquid; the bony frame seemed to be enveloped by a silken network; its study was easy. A few tufts of beard and hair were still adhering to it.

"Does this one, Doña, remind you of anyone? Look at his beautiful beard and his blond hair."

"Fernando!!! Did you kill him?"

"Until now, not having yet dissected living bodies, we have only had vague and imperfect notions of the circulation of the blood, of its locomotion—but thanks to you, señora, Vesalius has lifted the veil, and has acquired an eternal glory!"

Then, seizing her by the hair, he dragged Maria toward an enormous chest, whose lid he raised, with difficulty. Clutching her hair, he forced her to lean over the opening.

"Finally, look at this one! It's your most recent, is it not?"

The chest contained bottles full of liquids, in which body-parts were steeped.

"Pedro! Pedro! You've killed him too!"

"Yes, him too!"

Then, with a frightful croak, Maria fell heavily on to the flagstones.

* * * * * * *

The next day, a procession emerged from the house.

The gravediggers who took the bier down into the cellars of Santa Maria la Mayor, remarked on the fact that it was heavy and sonorous, and that there was a sound as it fell that was not the sound of a body.

And the following night, through the loopholes of the door, one might have seen Andrea Vesalius in his laboratory, at his workbench, dissecting a beautiful female cadaver, whose blonde hair hung down to the ground.

VII.
Affabulatio[49]

In the opulent court of Madrid, gorged with all the treasures of the world of Christopher Columbus, which dominated all of Europe powerfully, Andrea Vesalius reclined in his glory, rich and highly esteemed. Between the Inquisition and Philippe II, he was pleading the cause of the study of anatomy as much as possible, when an accusation brought horrible misfortune down upon him.

While performing the autopsy of the cadaver of a gentleman in public, the heart appeared to beat under the blade of the scalpel. The rancorous Inquisition, accusing him of homicide, demanded the scientist's death, and Philippe II had great difficulty obtaining a commutation of the sentence to a pilgrimage to the Holy Land.[50] Vesalius set off for Palestine with Malatesta, the leader of the Venetian fleet.

Having braved many dangers in the scabrous voyage, during his return journey he was thrown by a storm on to the coast of Zante, where he died of hunger on the fifteenth of October 1564.

The Republic of Venice then appealed to the University of Padua, to its pupil Gabriel Falloppe, whim it had lost prematurely that same year.[51]

If one can believe Boerhave and Albinus, Andrea Vesalius perished a victim of his eternal mockery of the ignorance, costume and mores of Spanish monks, and of the Inquisition,

---

49. This term is usually used to refer to the moral of a story, as in a fable, but it can be construed as "fabulous distortion."

50. Vesalius did indeed go on a pilgrimage to the Holy Land, and died on the return journey having been landed on Zakynthos after a shipwreck, but the story that he went because of a penance demanded by the Inquisition, although widely believed for centuries—like many anecdotes posthumously blackening the names of great scientists—is apocryphal. The Malatesta with whom Vesalius sailed was a descendant of the more famous military leader and poet of the same surname.

51. Gabriele Falloppio actually died in 1562

which seized the opportunity to get rid of that extremely inconvenient scientist.

The great anatomy of Andrea Vesalius, *De Humani Corporis Fabrica*,[52] was published in Basle in 1562, ornamented with drawings attributed to his friend Tiziano.

---

52. This book actually first appeared in 1543 and a revised edition appeared in 1555. The illustrations were not by Titian himself but various pupils in his studio, probably including Jan Stephen van Calcar.

THREE-FINGERED JACK, THE OBI
(JAMAICA)

....Everyone born on this earth,
Bears like dogs the hereditary chain,
Still howling......
As for Jacob, he is free, returned to the desert.

Alexandre Dumas.[53]

When fortune means to men most good,
She louks upon them with a threat'ning eye.

Shakespeare.[54]

Jealousy ambitious, corsair to corsair
and a half.

André Borel.

I.
Next night, at the three palm-trees

"Abigail, Abigail. Tell us a story! A story!" cried a troop of children with skins of ebony, ivory, boxwood or copper, who, sucking long sugar-canes, were playing on the gravel, at the feet of a young black woman, naively beautiful, dressed in simple

---

53. From the play, *Charles VII chez ses grands vassaux* (1831).

54. *King John* Act III scene 4.

fabric. Abigail—that was the name her puritan master had imposed on her—sitting on the ground before a rich dwelling, had a white bird[55] perched on her pretty finger, which she was caressing. Sometimes, she sang to it, a little creole ditty from the French Antilles, whose meaning she surely did not understand.

> *Mounché Béqué li un boun blan,*
> *Quand li conqué li payé compant,*
> *Résonnablément!*

Sometimes, calm and melancholy, her head tilted over her shoulder, she seemed lost in intuitive dreams of a happiness to come, which all your women nurse.

"Abigail! Tell us a story, then!" the children were still shouting. "We'll be good, we won't beat little John Blackheart any more!"

The young woman was wrenched out of her sweet meditation.

"What do you want from me, children?"

"A story, Abigail!"

"A story—I don't know about that, my little friends."

"Yes, yes, yes...the one about the picaroons—you know? Who carried you away, and where the obi...you know?"

Then Abigail, while passing her fingers through the bird's feathers, began to speak in a slow voice, and all the children opened their black-irised eyes and white-toothed mouths wide.

* * * * * * *

---

55. The original text has *"haras*," which must, in this context, be a corruption of *"ara*," then used as a general term for what are nowadays known as macaws. There were two species of macaw native to Jamaica at the time (both are now extinct), but both were brightly-colored, so I have substituted a vaguer term; it is possible that Borel had an image of a cockatoo in mind, but cockatoos are Australasian, unlikely pets in Jamaica.

In those days, there was a war, and the picaroons of Hispaniola—San Domingo—often made night raids on the island; they captured black men sleeping in their huts in order to sell them in the markets of their homeland.

This time, in spite of the vigilance of the sixteen coastguard boats, they slipped into a creek and ventured as far as the outskirts of Saint-Anne. When they got there, all armed to the teeth, they crept into the plantation. They'd already carried off a hundred backs to their sloops when they got to the hut where Abigail, your maid, who loves you when you're good, was asleep. Several men who resembled monsters in the shadows fell upon her, and grabbed me while I was asleep, tied my arms and dragged me to the river bank.

Take note, little friends, that these wicked men were white, but that, although they were white, they didn't talk like the white men here; the words that they growled like dogs all ended in *o* or *a*.

The sloops, loaded with poor blacks who were weeping and moaning in spite of their gags, set out to sea. I was in a canoe with the last picaroons, who had stayed behind as lookouts. Scarcely was it unmoored and launched a short way from the shore, than we heard something like the sound of a body falling in the water, and soon made out a black man who was swimming hastily toward us,

"*Que biba?*" shouted the picaroons—which, in their lingo, doubtless means: "Look out."

The man swam beneath the surface impetuously, and when he reached the canoe, whose side he grabbed with one hand, one of the savages raised a hatchet to strike him—when, lifting himself out of the water and putting all his weight into shaking the boat, he overturned it and submerged all those who were manning it.

I soon bobbed up to the surface, and suddenly felt myself gripped around the waist. Carried to the shore, so to speak, by the tall black man who had overturned the canoe, I was laid down there, choking. The brave young man lavished cares upon me, wiping my face and my wet hair.

"You've saved me—oh, I owe you my life," I said to him when I came round.

"Few people owe me that," he replied, dully.

"But let me kiss your hands—at least tell me your name so that I can bless it."

"My name...you'd shiver!"

Suddenly, he stood up, at the sound of musket-fire, footsteps and shouts, coming closer; it as the neighboring colonists and the people of the house, who, awakened by the racket made by the picaroons and the shouts of the captured blacks, were running belatedly to the rescue.

"Adieu, adieu," whispered unknown man, squeezing my fingers, which clicked in his rough grip. "Adieu!"

"But your name, please? I'm Abigail, John Fox's girl."

"For men, I'm less than a lynx that they hunt. I'm Three-Fingered Jack from Libanus."

"Three-Fingered Jack the obi-man?"

"Yes, the obi-man!"

I uttered a scream of terror; he disappeared into the darkness, and I lay there, stunned, as if I had fallen from the sun. Soon, all the colonists arrived on the shore. No boat was moored there that could be used for a chase at sea. Furious, they fired a few volleys, which only carried half way. The picaroons saluted them with distant laughter and ferocious songs, which drowned out the howls of the poor captured blacks....

* * * * * * *

The children opened their black-irised eyes and white-toothed mouths wide—and at that moment, a half-breed came from behind the hut and said: "Abigail, tonight at the three palms by the spring."

II.
Voices in the Desert

It was late at night; everything was plunged in the oblivion of sleep; the air, sky and land were silent; and nothing could be heard on the island, on the mountains, but the spare melodious chirping of little birds, which only sing when the earth is asleep and only the heavens are listening, and a male voice under the three palms by the spring, saying:

"Abigail, stop for a moment! Amour! Amour! That's all very well, but I'm ambitious. I invited you here tonight, you see, to bid you farewell for a while, and to tell you about a plan I've made.

"I'm ambitious, as I said, for beneath a frivolous exterior I hide a heart that is being eaten away. A blood flows in my veins that is wearing me down, and this thinking forehead and this powerful back are bent down beneath the whips of stupid and ferocious beings with white skin, who savor our sweat and laugh at the groans that fatigue bring out of me.

"I've suffered enough! This cowardly life is killing me; I need another! The slave wants to stand up and break his chains. I'm proud, you see, I'm ambitious; something within me is driving me—me, a slave—to domination; as a child, I dreamed of royalty, I dreamed of golden vestments, a long sword, a horse...."

"Poor Quasher! Your royalty is misfortune!

"Now an opportunity, a chance has presented itself; I can become rich, great; I can be gorged with gold! Those who reject me today will soon offer their hands to me, and I shall spit in their faces in my turn."

"Oh, Quasher, remain poor: wealth makes men wicked."

"A price has been put on the head of the obi-man Three-Fingered Jack—an enormous sum. I shall have it!"

"You're mad, Quasher! You're going to attack Three-Fingered Jack, an obi? You're mad!"

"I know that Jack and his obi are strong, but Quasher and his heart are strong too; besides, am I not resigned to death, to living free or not at all?"

"No, no, Quasher, I beg you, protect your life; if you love me, remain poor; only the poor are happy, happier than their masters; remain where fatality has thrown us!"

"Eh! Why remain poor?"

"Oh, why, why? Quasher, you understand only too well."

"What do you have to fear, Abigail? I'll buy you back; I'll buy myself back; we'll be free; we'll have our own house; we'll have our own slaves; we'll be able to make love all day; to be alone together, at any hour, to go anywhere we please. Can you imagine it? To be free!"

"My Quasher, you're ambitious, you tell me, you were boasting about it just now. When you're rich, you'll push away this poor negress, who loves you so much, with your foot, you'll want a white European woman—I know full well that I'll lose you."

"Listen, Abigail: a woman who softens a strong man is a base woman! Do you think that your charms are powerful enough to nail me to you? Do you think that your tears will change my mind? No, your embraces are in vain. 'I want,' Quasher has said. 'I want!' Have confidence in him; he has given you his love; he has remained faithful to you, as God as his witness, he is yours for life. Don't be suspicious or jealous, and it's at your feet that he will lay down that gold. Weep, weep, but don't hope to soften me. Adieu!"

III.
Hatsarmaveth Abraham Westmacot

Left alone, Abigail got to her feet abruptly, moved by a profound jealousy and an intimate sentiment of the loss of her lover. She feared, no doubt rightly, knowing his proud ambition and his audacity, that he would either lose his life in such a combat, or that, on receipt of the large sum promised, he would yield to all his unbridled appetites and glorious penchants, and that, swollen with pride and opulence, he would not turn his head to her appeal; that he would turn her away from his new hut, a poor and virtuous black slave, in favor of those great ladies with beautiful exteriors, who hawk childish hearts and base and venal souls to all the young men whose wealth they covet, as the scorpion covets its prey; or that, if he were wiser, he would choose among fortunate maidens in order further to increase a large patrimony with a large dowry. The poor child foresaw her inevitable abandonment, and that heart-rending thought overwhelmed her.

Instead of taking the route that led back to the habitation, as if she had made a sudden resolution, she headed into the savannah, walking incessantly, heading toward the mountains, hiding whenever islanders approached, especially avoiding meeting maroons and cudjos.[56]

That difficult pilgrimage through the hills, bogs, ravines and virgin woods wore her out. Her feet, bruised by walking, refused to touch the ground. She had not had anything to eat except a few of the cashew-nuts that grew in the mountains, or anything to drink but the water of streams, in which she bathed her lovely legs, swollen by walking on the burning earth.

On the third day, at the approach of that afternoon hour solemnly called dusk by writers of pianoforte romances, and "between dog and wolf" by Madame de Sévigné—the hour when nature becomes drowsy, and veils herself mysteriously, like a beautiful woman lowering the gauze of her hat and rendering her beauty dubious to avid gazes; the hour when colors fade and contours stand out sharply like phantasmagorical shadows against an azure background—by way of a sheer and stony path bordered, or rather cluttered, by larches, Abigail, head bowed, leaning on a flexible branch, was dragging herself along like those poor travelers that one sees arriving in the evening in the outskirts of towns, searching with weary eyes for the consola-

---

56. The maroons of Jamaica were runaway slaves who established communities in the mountains, sometimes called Cudjoes or Cudjos after the most famous of their leaders, who died in 1744 and whose name was presumably originally Kojo or Kwajo.

tory sign of an inn. Sweat was streaming down her forehead; she sighed violently, and sometimes uttered plaints when her foot bumped into a pebble.

The path went all the way to the top of a steep rock, around which it wound; at the summit of the rock, someone less weary and less pensive would have observed a motionless black body lying down, reminiscent of the broken mast of a sunken ship, or a druidic menhir in the Armorican dunes of ancient Gaul.

Abigail was scarcely three hundred paces from that mysterious being when it was suddenly illuminated by a flare, accompanied by a detonation similar to that of a firearm, which rumbled for a long time in the plain. She uttered a terrible scream and fell face-down. Immediately, with the speed of a greyhound precipitating itself upon the prey hit by a hunter, the black gnome came down the rock and the path, hurtling straight toward Abigail. At the sight of her he recoiled, in consternation, letting slip the brief remark: "A woman!"

Beating his breast and kneeling down, he lifted her up and laid her in the grass. The phantom was simply a black man of tall stature, carrying a carbine like the Bedouins, a long saber and a cutlass in his belt.

"Woman, woman, you're hurt!" he repeated, trying to soften the hoarseness of his voice.

Abigail remained mute in her pain, however; the bullet had struck her in the flesh of her leg.

The black man, parting her dress and applying his lips to the wound, sucked up the flowing blood. A traveler witnessing the scene, so frightful in appearance, would doubtless have thought he was seeing a vampire feeding on a woman. Then he poured eau-de-vie from his flask on to leaves, bound that compress to the wound, and rubbed her temples with the remainder of the liquor.

Soon, Abigail opened her eyes and looked around wildly.

"Have no fear, Woman—the man beside you is your friend."

"It's you who have shot me, though," she relied, lifting herself up and setting her back against a tree.

"Don't hold it against me, Woman. Jack has many enemies, whom he cannot allow to approach his lair. The feeble light of the setting sun deceived me; I thought I was shooting at a man. Forgive me; it's men that I hate, because they're cowardly and ferocious, all the more ferocious if they are more cowardly. Don't worry—the wound isn't serious."

"Are you not Three-Fingered Jack? Oh, thank God! I've finally found you—I've been looking for you."

"Eh! Why?"

"I'm Abigail—do you remember her?"

"No."

"Do you remember the woman you saved, two years ago, from picaroons who were carrying her away?"

"What—that's you!"

"Jack, there's a price on your head."

"I know."

"I owe you my life, and if I've come to the mountains to look for you, it's to pay back that debt. Be on your guard. In order to claim the price of your blood, Quasher is coming any day now to pursue you and kill you."

"Kill me..." Jack repeated, coldly.

"Avoid him, but don't kill him, I beg you."

"Woman, I thank you; forget the harm I have done you involuntarily."

"Oh, I forgive you! Do I not owe you my life? You have disposed of your property."

"Woman, now, what can I do for you? Would you like to come and rest in my lair?"

"It's three days since I left my master's habitation; he must be very worried. If I weren't wounded...."

"Oh, if that's all," Jack continued, "here, take this in memory of me; always carry it on your person; with that, you'll be strong. It's an obian sachet."

And, lifting Abigail up gently, he placed her on his strong shoulders, went down the path, and disappeared into the cashew-trees.

* * * * * *

Dawn was breaking, although everything in the vicinity of Saint-Anne was still asleep, when Three-Fingered Jack appeared in front of the habitation, carrying Abigail. He was carrying her as lightly as a young woman carries her pitcher to the spring. Having reached the house, he laid her down at the entrance.

"Adieu, Abigail!"

"Adieu, Jack—look out for yourself!"

The obi knocked loudly on the door with his cutlass and fled, as swift as a deer.

Hatsarmaveth[57] Abraham Westmacot emerged, accompanied. When his foot encountered the woman, recumbent and bloody, he uttered a cry of fright.

"Calm down, Master, don't be afraid. It's your servant Abigail."

"Abigail!"

"Yes. Maroons, after having wounded me, brought me back from the mountains and dropped me at your door."

IV.
Tiresome Chapter

Before going any further, as I have already mentioned obi, an obi-man and an obian sachet, it would be as well if I told you Europeans what an obi is.

As for the erudite who think that they know, or have read what follows in Dr. Moseley, they have only to skip this pedantic and academically fastidious chapter.

Dr. Moseley, to whom I owe this Jamaican story, gravely claims, in his *Treatise on Sugar*, that the obi and the swindler or gambler are the only examples he has been able to discover among the natives of the African continent in which an effort of

---

57. This unusual forename is Biblical in origin, taken from the list of Noah's descendants included in *Genesis* 10.

combining ideas has ever been demonstrated.[58]

Oh, Master Moseley, you're no negrophile! Poor fellow! He can scarcely have guessed, when writing in Jamaica about his sugar-canes, that he would have a posterity, and that his *Treatise on Sugar* and the story of Jack would still be a matter of interest in 1832. Oh the incomprehensible *encatenation* of events! To produce that it required an Alpine montagnard to be born, to descend therefrom, and, seeking to use his vigor along the men of the plain, to start riffling through a second-hand English book.

Generally, the word obi designates both the magic and the magician; in the English colonies, however one speaks of an "obi-man." I shall offer no other etymological probabilities regarding the origin and significance of the word, imported from Africa by the blacks into the world of Christopher Columbus than this one: *nobi*, in Arabic, means "prophet," and there is certainly a great similarity between the two words; contract by the corruption of the nasal initial in the singular, as the Arabs do for the plural, and you have the identical word. I do not offer that as an article of faith; modesty aside, however, I believe myself to be a rather competent etymologist, having done considerable paleographic and paleological research—producing, among others, at the tender age of sixteen, a large folio volume, worthy of the Benedictines of Saint-Maure, on the origins on the origins of proper names, of people and places, a little artesian well of science and erudition; I only required fifteen years of hard work to complete it—and a publisher, because the royal printing press would not issue it—when I abandoned it for more digestible works more in harmony with our glossy era: studies of Pasquier, Fauchet, Ménage and P. Borel, etc. etc.

All in all, I sincerely believe that etymology to be as good as any other, even those of Monsieur Arouet de Voltaire, who

58. Benjamin Moseley, *A Treatise on Sugar*, London: G. G. & J. Robinson, 1799. The famous account of Three-Fingered Jack is on pp. 173-180; thanks to that oft-cited inclusion the book is still in print. The original text of *Champavert* misrenders the author's name as Mosely.

claims that "boulevard" comes from the fact that people played *boule* there, and that it was green. See the philosophical word "boulevard" in his Philosophical Dictionary.

The science of the obi is very extensive—more extensive than that of pharmacology or pharmacochemistry, and, if there were an examination to pass in order to be qualified as an obi, more than one of our brilliant pharmacopoles would have his nose broken and by kicked out; I only know, as profoundly worthy, Monsieur Roux with his paraguay,[59] Maître Guérin with his mixture,[60] and the parabolain Labaraque, with his chlorine[61]—all three past masters in obi, but whom, nevertheless, the envious ignorant would like to see fall, with stones around their necks, into sequanic hydrogen protoxide.

The obi, whose objective is the bewitchment of the poor, or their consumption by maladies of languor and spleen, makes use of grave-dirt, hair, the teeth of sharks and other creatures, blood, feathers, eggshells, wax figures, birds' hearts, powerful roots, herbs and brambles still unknown to Europeans, which the ancients used for the same purposes. Certain mixtures of these ingredients are burned, or buried very deeply in the earth, or hung from a fireplace, or placed on the threshold of a door of the person who is subjected to the spell, with the accompaniment of incantations and imprecations, proffered at midnight, with due regard to the phases and aspects of the moon.

A negro who believes himself to have been bewitched by obi goes to an obi-man or obi-woman in the same way that a sick person, made ill be his doctor, goes to a apothecary.

Sugary laws have been set up in the West Indies to punish obian practices by death; they have had no effect. Stupid legislators! The bloody laws passed in your Indies cannot annihilate

---

59. The French surgeon Philibert-Joseph Roux (1780-1854).

60. The Belgian physician Jules Guérin (1801-1886), the editor of *La Gazette de la Santé* when *Champavert* was written.

61. The French chemist Antoine-Germain Labarraque (1777-1850) was responsible for the chlorinated disinfectant known as "eau de Labarraque."

the effect of ideas whose origin is in the heart of Africa, where you go to harvest your slaves!

Our old Dr. Moseley, again in his *Treastise on Sugar*, speaks of having seen the obi of the famous negro Three-Fignered Jack—a thief, as he calls him, the terror of Jamaica in 1780 and 1781, and which the runaways who killed him brought to him. That obi "consisted of the end of a goat's horn filled with a compound of grave-dirt, the blood of a black cat and human fat, all mixed into a kind of paste"—it was only after a long and savant analysis that he was able to ascertain that formula. A dried toad, a cat's foot, similarly black, a pig's tail and a strip of parchment from the skin of a goat-kid, on which characters were traced in blood, were also found in his obian bag.

"These, with a keen saber and two guns, like Robinson Crusoe, were all his obi, with which and his courage, [as a true highlander],[62] in descending into the lowlands to devastate and pillage in order to supply his wants, and his skill in retreating into difficult fastnesses, among the mountains commanding the only access to them, where none dared follow him, he terrified the inhabitants, and set the civil power, and the neighboring militia of the island at defiance for nearly two years.

"He had neither accomplice, nor associate. There were a few runaway Negroes in the woods, in the woods near Mount Libanus, the place of his retreat; but he had crossed their foreheads with some of the magic of his horn, and they could not betray him, but he trusted no one. He scorned all assistance. He ascended above Spartacus. He robbed alone; fought his battles alone; and always killed his pursuers.

"By his magic, he was not only the dread of the Negroes, but there were many white people, who believed he was possessed of some supernatural power."

---

62. This is Borel's insertion into a passage which is otherwise a direct translation of Moseley; I have restored the original text for my translation where appropriate. I have, however, retained Borel's spelling of Quasher, where Moseley has "Quashee." The bounty-hunter's name was presumably an adaptation of Kwashi or something simlar.

In hot climates, women marry very young and often with a great disparity of age; Jack was reputed to be the author of discords and disturbances, for at that time—as at all times, as today—unhappy unions, adultery and God knows what else were abundant.

Give a dog a bad name and hang him, says the English proverb. Clamor after clamor, and more clamors, rose up against the cruel sorcerer, and almost all conjugal misadventures were attributed to spells cast by Three-Fingered Jack on the day of the wedding.

God knows that poor Jack had enough sins of his own without being charged with those of others. "He would rather have made a Medean cauldron for the entire island," says Dr. Moseley, again in his *Treatise on Sugar*, "than trouble the happiness of a single woman."

I will confess frankly, for my own count, that I am not too sure what a "Medean cauldron" is, being a dunce in mythology and a puritan, never having touched, even with my foot, the dictionary of the pagan Chompré.[63] At any rate, it was definitely not the opportunity he lacked, and yet, in spite of his hatred for the whites, no one ever heard it said that he did the slightest harm to a child, or hurt a woman.

V.
Hound's Fee[64]

"But even Jack himself was born to die. Allured by the reward promised by Governor Dalling, in proclamations, dated December 12, 1780 and January 13, 1781; and, by a resolution

---

63. Pierre Chompré (1698-1760) published a *Dictionnaire abrégé de la fable* (1727) and a *Dictionnaire abrégé de la Bible* (1755) as well as other works adapted for pedagogical purposes.

64. This chapter is, in essence, a straightforward translation of Moseley; I have restored the original text, except for the name Quasher, in the passages in quotation marks; the unmarked paragraph and phrases in square brackets are Borel's comments.

of the House of Assembly, whih followed the first proclamation; two Negroes, named Quasher [whom you already know] and Sam (Sam was Captain Davy's son, he who shot a Mr. Thompson, the master of a London ship, at Old Harbor) both of Scot's Hall Maroon Town, with a party of their townsmen, went in search of him. Quasher, before he set out on the expedition, got himself christianized, and changed his name to James Reeder.

"The expedition commenced, and the whole party had been creeping about in the woods, for three weeks, and blockading, as it were, the deepest retreats of the most inaccessible part of the island, where Jack, far remote from all human society, resided—but in vain."

Jack was one of those strong constitutions, one of those powerful brains, born to dominate, who lack air in the narrow cage into which fate has thrown them, in that society, which wishes to bend and shrink everything to vulgar dimensions, breaking forever with they execrate if they cannot break them with life. Three-Fingered Jack was a lycanthrope!

* * * * * * *

"Reeder and Sam, tired with this mode of war, resolved on proceeding in search of his retreat; and taking him by storming it, or to perishing in the attempt. They took with them a little boy, a proper spirit, and a good shot, and left the rest of the party.

"These three, [whom old Dr. Moseley flattered himself on having known well], had not long been separated from their companions, before their cunning eyes discovered, by impressions among the weeds and bushes, that some person must have lately been that way. They softly followed these impressions, making not the least noise. Presently they discovered smoke. They prepared for war. They came upon Jack before he perceived them. He was roasting plantains, by a little fire on the ground, at the mouth of a cave.

"This was a scene not where ordinary actors had a common role to play. Jack's looks were fierce and terrible. He told them he would kill them.

"Reeder, instead of shooting Jack, replied that his obi had no power to hurt him; for he was Christianized; and that his name was no longer Quasher. Jack knew Reeder; and, as if paralyzed, he let his two guns remain on the ground, and took up only his cutlass.

"These two, had a severe engagement several years before, in the woods; in which conflict Jack lost two fingers, which was the origin of his present name; but Jack then beat Reeder, and almost killed him, with several others who assisted him, and they fled from Jack.

"To do Three-Fingered Jack justice, he would now have killed both Reeder and Sam; for, at first, they were frightened at the sight of him, and the dreadful tone of his voice; and well they might: they had besides no retreat, and were to grapple with the bravest, and strongest man in the world. But Jack was cowed; for, he had prophesied, that white obi would get the better of him; and, from experience, he knew the charm would lose none of its strength in the hands of Reeder.

"Without further parley, Jack, with his cutlass in his hand, threw himself down a precipice at the back of the cave. Reeder's gun missed fire. Sam shot him in the shoulder. Reeder, like an English bull-dog, Reeder, never looked but, with his cutlass in his hand, plunged headlong down after Jack. The descent was almost perpendicular. Both of them had preserved their cutlasses in the fall.

"Here was the stage on which the two of the stoutest hearts, that were ever hooped with ribs, began their bloody struggle. The little boy, who was ordered to keep back, out of harm's way, now reached the top of the precipice, and during the fight, shot Jack in the belly. Sam was crafty, and coolly took a round-about way to get to the field of action. When he arrived at the foot where it began, Jack and Reeder had closed, and tumbled together down another precipice, on the side of the mountain, in which they both lost their weapons. Sam descended after them, though without weapons, they were not idle; and, luckily for Reeder, Jack's wounds were deep and desperate, and he was in great agony. Sam came up just time enough to save Reeder; for, Jack had caught him by the throat, with his giant's grasp; Reeder then was with his right hand almost cut off, and Jack streaming with blood from his shoulder and his belly; both covered with gore and gashes. In this state Sam was umpire; and decided the fate of the battle. He knocked Jack down with a piece of a rock.

"When the lion fell, the two tigers got upon him, and beat his brains out with stones. The little boy soon found his way to them. He had his cutlass, with which they cut off Jack's head, and three-fingered hand, and took them in triumph to Morant Bay. There they put their trophies into a pail of rum; and followed by a vast concourse of Negroes, now no longer in fear of Jack's obi, blowing their shells and horns, and firing guns in their rude method, they carried them to Kingston, and Spanish Town; and claimed the rewards offered by the King's Proclamation, and the House of Assembly."

VI.
Blood's Reward

When Reeder and Sam passed through, I was in Spanish Town at the home of two exceedingly old women, two sisters almost a hundred years old, the daughters of Spanish colonists, born a long time after the island was taken from the Spaniards by Admiral Penn, aided by a large number of English and French filibusters, in 1655. A sole and double monument to Spanish dominion over the territory, a sort of living cippus,[65] still attested to their passage, as druidic dolmens are there to remind us of our ancestors the Gauls, who now form the vegetative layer that covers the soil of France like fertilizer. Those saintly

---

65. Cippus is an architectural term, whose original Latin reference was to a stake or pole, but it had been borrowed for application to a pair of wooden stakes used in punishment, and hence to the stocks.

dowagers, although receiving a government pension, mortally hateful, never wanting to speak the language of the conquerors, spent several generations without any contact, still spoke the divine Castilian language.

A religious pilgrim of all ruins, I had come to salute them; my visit had filled them with joy, had rejuvenated them by almost a century, and had awakened a thousand tender and dolorous memories in their souls; they had retained me for a few days. I was like a son to them; they told me all the old things that no one but them knew about the world, displaying in broad daylight, and doubtless for the last time, the gilded shreds of their memory, shaking the dust pages of that book of *gai-savoir*,[66] which time gnaws away like a stupid rat, and would soon be enclosed with their lives in the grave.

We were sitting by a window and chatting when we heard a distant tumult and musket fire. We got up and leaned out of the window; we saw Reeder sand Sam, our heroes, marching triumphantly, carrying, at the end of a pike, the head and hand of the unfortunate Jack. They were followed by a large procession, mainly composed of *cudjos* from Maroon Town, clad in the loincloths and coarse waistcoats that the government gave them every year, as well as a rifle every five years, in payment for the services they rendered the colony.

Those worthy men serve almost as the island's police force, like a constabulary, arresting and bringing back fugitive negroes, vagabonds who withdraw to the mountains and prisoners of war escaped from Port Royal. It was a mass of men of every origin, true klephts,[67] with whom the English had been forced to make

---

66. This phrase, whose implications are not communicated by a crudely literal translation such as "cheerful knowledge," is a French translation of the Occitan "*gai saber*," which referred portentously to the art and world-view of the Medieval troubadours, in which formalized eroticism and a defiant rebellious spirit were deftly alloyed.

67. The klephts were Greeks who took to the hills after the Ottoman conquest to form a kind of resistance movement fighting a guerrilla war, or gangs of bandits and terrorists, depending on one's point of view.

a capitulation entirely to their advantage, never having been able to tame them. The nickname of *cudjos* came to them from the name of one of their valiant captains. No longer being able to make war, they had devoted themselves to the education of animals, which they came to sell at the island's markets. Most of those mountain folk were remarkable for their handsome faces, tall stature, strength and skill.

Not far from the house of my old ladies, a young black woman, who seemed to be wounded in the leg, was sitting on a stone pensively, her head bowed over her bosom. Abruptly awakened by the gunshots, which the blacks were letting off as a sign of joy, she turned to face the direction from which the tumult was coming, and remained motionless, like a she-wolf scenting her prey. When Reeder passed by she shouted several times: "Quasher! Quasher!"

Reeder, who had seen her from a distance, turned his head away.

"Quasher! Quasher! Have you forgotten Abigail already?"

He did not reply, and seemed to increase his pace.

The young negress sat down on the stone again, turning her back to the road, and remained thus all evening.

Before going to bed, strolling in the moonlight in the vicinity of the house in order to get some air, I distinguished a body lying on the ground against the stone. I went closer. She was asleep.

The next day, at dawn, I was woken up by a racket similar to that of the previous day. Moved by curiosity, I went out. It was Reeder and Sam, who, having received the reward promised by the royal proclamation and the colonial assembly, were going back with their compatriots.

The mob were shouting hurrahs, the cries of wild beasts, singing unknown words in chorus, dancing to the sound of balaphons and that kind of instrument whose name escapes me, widely used among the blacks, comprised of a horse's jawbone made to vibrate by passing a stick over the teeth. Most of them were drunk and in a complete and repulsive state of disorder.

They had spent the night partying, dragging with them a few loose women from the town, attracted by the scent of money.

In the van, four negroes were carrying, in baskets hanging from a pole, the price of blood, already eroded by the night's bacchanal. Reeder preceded them, so drunk that he was almost falling over, giving his arm to a drunk and emaciated young woman.

When they arrived at our house, the young negress lying by the stone suddenly stood up on seeing Reeder, and then suddenly hurled herself upon him like a tigress.

"Quasher!" she cried, plunging a dagger into his breast. "You're a coward and a traitor!"

At a shout from Reeder, the negroes ran to surround Abigail, but, brandishing above her head the bloodstained knife and the obi that Jack had given her, she terrified them, and caused them to fall to the ground face down, thus opening a passage over their bodies, and she fled into the mountains.

* * * * * * *

When I said that I was in Spanish Town when Sam and Reeder passed through, it wasn't true; I was lying in my teeth! But let no one accuse me of taking delight in the horrible—this is history! I have the testimony of Dr. Moseley and his *Treatise on Sugar* that it's history—which I would not dare to prune as Père Jouvenci[68] pruned the Latin classics *ad usum scholarum*.

At the moment when I was writing this, 6 January 1832, the black population of Jamaica having imagined that the king had signed a decree freeing the slaves, a revolt broke out in the parishes of St. James and Trelawney; in the former, fifteen properties were destroyed. At Montego Bay in Westmoreland, martial law was declared by Sir Willoughby Cotton. The anabaptist missionaries were put in irons, as fomenters and instiga-

---

68. The Jesuit scholar Joseph de Jouvancey (1643-1719).

tors of the insurrection.[69] A military tribunal was established at Montego Bay, and compensation promised for the arrest of several chiefs.

At present, no doubt, some of those brave Africans are laying their heads on the block, and, in the name of Christian equality, the English ax is steeping itself once again in the blood of slaves.

---

69. The rebellion put down by Willoughby Cotton's troops was inspired by the peaceful protests of the native Baptist preacher Samuel Sharpe (1801-1832), who was not only clapped in irons but hanged (in May 1832), setting an example of courage and injustice that assisted the abolitionist cause in England; he was later declared a National Hero and now embellishes the Jamaican fifty-dollar bill.

DINAH, THE
BEAUTIFUL JEWESS
(LYON)

Reader, without hyperbole, she was truly beautiful;
Truly beautiful! Which is to say that she seemed so,
And that is the same thing. It is sufficient for the eyes
To be deceived, and they always are when one is in
    love:
The joy that come to us from a lie is the same
As if it were proved by algebra. To be happy,
What is that?—if not to believe....

                Théophile Gautier[70]

Rosa mystica.
Turris Davidica.
Turris eburnea.
Domus aurea.
Foederis arca.
Janua coeli.
Stella matutina.
Regina virginum.[71]

                Litanies of the Holy Virgin.

---

70. From *Albertus* (1832).

71. Mystic Rose/Tower of David/Tower of Ivory/House of Gold/Ark of the
Covenant/Gate of Heaven/Morning Star/Queen of Virgins

Hurry up and give in; you will have done well, darling, it's to retreat in order to bounce back! Oh the bitch, is she biting? Come on, calm down Mademoiselle. Dammmn!

P. L. Jacob,
Virtue and Temperament

I.

Amour é râsco, rëgardo pa ountë s'atâco[72]

Where there is no hedge, the possession
shall be spoiled, and where there is no
wife, he mourneth that is in want.
Who will trust him that hath no rest?
The Bible.[73]

The curfew was sounding, the drawbridges being hoisted and a few belated townspeople were hurrying home; Lyon the Rich, seated between its two rivers, was asleep, girt within its walls like a warrior in his suit of armor.

Moving along a narrow and deserted quay, two men, one young and one old, were preceded by a lackey bearing a lantern.

When I say a quay, I am not being exact, for in those old times, enclosed by a double row of houses, the majority of

---

72. Borel probably found this Occitan proverb in the 1785 edition of Abbé Pierre-Augustin Boissier de Sauvages' *Dictionnaire Langudeocian-François*; other versions of the saying seem to differ in their orthography; its approximate meaning seems to be: "Love is a trap; beware of being caught in it."

73. Borel's version of this quotation is taken from the version of *Le Livre de l'Écclestiastique ou le sagesse de Jésus, fils de Sirach* XXXVI: 26 in the so-called Louvain Bible of 1550. The text is usually known in English as the *Book of Ecclesiasticus*, but sometimes as the *Book of Sirach*; although accepted as canonical by the Catholic Church, it was not included in the Authorized Version of the English Bible; I have substituted another English translation taken from the Latin of the Vulgate, where it is represented as 36:27-28.

quays were like streets; the basements of houses hemming the river were sunk in the water; suspended on piles or founded in the mud, those amphibious dwellings had gables overlooking the streets and gables mirrored in the water, and stone stairways down below, steep and profound, which descended into the water like a Spanish cistern, sometimes separated from the current by a narrow strip of land, sometimes inundated to the mid-point of the steps.

How many crimes those stones must have witnessed! How many murders must have made those walls quiver! Damnation! How easily one could get rid of an enemy, a rival, an abused woman, a stubborn father—one pushed them from above, through an open window, and it was done. At the most the sound of a body was heard falling into the waves, whose lapping stifled the death-rattle. Oh, if those confidential ruins could talk!

The young one, enveloped in a bleached mantle, hiding beneath a felt hat pulled down over his face, was tall and thin; by his cavalier and mincing gait, the clink of his spurs and the sword denting the hem of his mantle, it was easy to scent a gentleman.

The old one, wrapped in his black robe, with a black magistrate's cap perched on his graying mop and parchments in his hand, advertised a doctor of law to anyone within arquebus-range. Capitulary or privy councilor, prosecutor, judge or scrivener, that bird of prey abruptly broke the silence:

"Seigneur Aymar," he croaked, "the minor with regard to whom I'm going to adjudicate, to judge by your exquisite taste, is beautiful, is she not?"

"Oh, is she beautiful! Maître, I confess, that question offends me; it seems to me that everyone ought to have prescience of her beauty. O Dinah, someone is asking me whether you are beautiful! Maître, she is more beautiful than the most beautiful Saracen in the Sudan! She's an ivory turret! She's a silver ewer!"

"At least, Seigneur Aymar, you're not, I hope, demanding prescience of her wealth. Does she have gold?"

"You're asking whether gold has gold, whether the sun is

radiant! Yes, Maître, she has gold enough to crush the strongest hack beneath the weight of her dowry."

"You're young, Seigneur Aymar—who, then, can push you so soon into marriage? Take my advice; it's necessary to use up coltish fire in fallow fields; it's necessary to run around and make the most of the world before cloistering one's love in a woman; it's a grave matter to pledge eternal fidelity. Look, personally, I entered into association at forty—it's the best age to do it! One is beginning to descend the slope of life; one needs support, as a weary pilgrim needs a staff, a hostess to care for one; then one chooses a meek and respectable woman with an alluring patrimony. That's what I did; one can't do better. Youth, you see, ought to be spent in storm and tumult; when I think about my life in Paris, at twenty years old, as a clerk of the court...! So, I made history then; I still have it, proverbially; I make use of that era in order to tolerate the present: at the Palais, they still talk about the joyous times of Bonaventure Chastelart."

And raising his cap and bowing, the jocular lawyer laughed and croaked, utterly triumphant, over his old follies, perhaps his turpitudes.

"Without wishing to offend you, Maître Bonaventure Chastelart, permit me to tell you that your advice seems scarcely noble to me, but I can affirm that in my regard, they are not pernicious."

"You're peremptory, young man, but I don't believe myself disbarred for that, and refer myself to the wisdom of Pierre Charron, Parisian doctor-in-law.[74] The Holy Sacrament of marriage has no value in itself; listen, this is exactly what he says in a certain malicious chapter in his three books of wisdom, to which, during life, I direct my prayers:

"Although the state of marriage is like the wellspring of human Society, *prima societas in conjugio est, quod principium urbis, seminarum reipublicae*, it is denigrated and decried

---

74. Pierre Charron (1541-1603) is now best-remembered as a close friend of Michel de Montaigne; his significant work of moral philosophy, *De la sagesse* (1601) is based (a trifle loosely) on Montaigne's principles.

by several great persons, who have judged it unworthy of men of heart and intelligence and have raised objections to it. Its bond is an unjust and harsh captivity; if it happens to have been unfortunately entered into, miscalculated in choice and in price, in terms of gold or flesh, one remains miserable for life. What iniquity can be greater, for a moment of bad bargaining, a sin committed without malice or by mistake, and often in order to obey, to follow another's advice, than being obliged to perpetual punishment? It would be better to put a rope around one's neck and throw oneself into the sea head first in order to end one's days sooner, than to suffer incessantly by one's side a tempest of rage and mania, a stubborn stupidity, and other miserable conditions.

"Whoever invented the marriage knot found a fine and specious expedient to avenge himself on humankind, a pitfall-trap or net to capture the beasts, and then roast them over a slow fire. Marriage is a corruption and bastardization of good and rare minds, since the charms of the party that one loves, the affection of children, the cares of the household and the advancement of the family relax, dilute and soften the vigor of the most generous spirit there ever was; witnesses, Samson, Solomon, Mark Antony. It is only necessary to marry, as a last resort, for those who have more meat than soul, in order to lighten the load of petty and base things, according to their scope. But for those who are feeble in body but great in spirit, is it not a great pity to shackle them and garrote their flesh, as one does with domestic animals?

"Utility might well be on the side of marriage, but honesty is on the other. It prevents traveling in the world, either to learn wisdom oneself or to inform others and publish what one knows; it makes strong minds small and binds them to a woman's apron strings, around small children."

"Enough, enough, Maître Chastelart, enough, if you please!"

"It is, all in all, a great evil..."

"Enough, enough, I tell you, Maître Chastelart, that you're stunning me! End this sermon!"

"Debauched humors, turbulent and unhinged souls, are not appropriate to that bargain...."

"Enough, enough, Maître, I beg you. Accursed loquacity!"

"Don't get carried away, handsome cavalier; at least you can't accuse me, a lawyer and royal notary, of preaching in my own interest."

"That's all well and good, perhaps even orthodox, Maître Bonaventure Chastelart, but not absolutely by the book. You say that it's sometimes necessary to sow one's wild oats—agreed; but the man whose soul is lively, warm and loving, who avoids taverns, hates dice and ribaldry, for that man, a beloved, comely woman, a peaceful home and a flock of children, is happiness! I'm seething, but pure; my ardent heart needs to embrace someone in its chaste and tranquil love. At first, I devoted that love to the liberal arts; I wanted to dispense my activity with them, consecrate my vigor to them—but my father, a typical lord of the manor, who calls artists vagabonds and artisans beggars, broke my easel and burned my studies of Philibert Delorme.[75] Idle and bored, my soul set forth to wander like the dove from the ark, seeking a green branch on which to perch; it has found a flourishing myrtle, and has settled thereon. If there are Delilahs who shear the strength of their lovers and sell them, there are others too, who comfort them, and spread around them an aromatic essence of happiness and who pour balm on their wounds."

"Oh, Seigneur Aymar, what a pretty speech! Love has made us delirious, and we're wandering. Now, we've been walking for some time, aren't we going to get there soon? By Saint Polycarpus, where the devil are you taking me?"

"In your turn, don't get impatient, Chastelart, we're getting close; the Juiverie can't be far away now."

"The Juiverie!"

"Yes—the Juiverie, where we're expected."

"Your future is a heretic, then? A Jewess?"

---

75. The Lyonnais architect Philibert DeLorme (1514-1570) was one of the stars of the French Renaissance.

"An Israelite, Maître."

"Lord Jesus! That's the last straw, I hope! And you wanted to drag me, at this hour, to the abode of those miscreants! Thank you! Would you like me to preside over a Sanhedrin or observe a Sabbath? Thank you! I have no desire to have any dealings with these damned souls; it's a conspiracy to dress me in a sulfurous shirt and have me scorched in the Place des Terreaux by Maître Carnifex,[76] the roaster of vampires! Thank you!"

"What do you have to fear, Bonaventure? You're in the company of a trusty gentleman. It's not a matter of a Sabbath or a Sanhedrin, but simply of drawing up a contract."

"Child! Do you take me for the Devil's Advocate? It seems to me that you can make your own pacts! Good night!"

"You're going with me, I tell you; if not, I'll run you through and pin you to that door like a screech-owl! Churl! Donkey-driver in a doctor's doublet! You'll come with me and do your duty, and afterwards, I'll throw this purse in your face and put my boot up your backside. March!"

"Cavalier, I'll do whatever you want—but put that sword back in its scabbard!" The worthy man was shivering with fear. "Calm down, I beg you; I'm you're most humble servant."

"Hypocrite!"

Aymar replaced his blade in its sheath, and they both resumed the route, silently. After walking a little way, Bonaventure Chastelart, a qualified chatterbox, broke his abstinence for the second time.

"Permit me, Seineur Aymar de Rochegude, to manifest my astonishment at your alliance with a heretic; in my capacity as a lawyer and adviser, permit me to tell you that it's unseemly and dangerous to marry a Jewess."

"Jew yourself!"

"Jew myself!"

"Yes, donkey-driver that you are! What are you, then, if not a poor Jew?"

---

76. Carnifex was the nickname given to the public executioner in Rome, and hence, by extension, to others of the same profession.

"Me, Bonaventure Chastelart, legitimate son of Claude Chastelart, privileged printer of the Primatial Church of Lyon, and Dame Anne-Pétronille-Maguelonne de Saint-Marcelin, my mother—may God protect them In his bosom!—and younger brother of Pantéléon Chastelart, guardsman of the Chapter of Saint-Paul, a Hebrew, a heretic! Get away, cavalier—you're out of your mind!"

"Less than a faithful Jew, doctor! Look at the source; are we not all reformed and patched-up Jews and pagans, Huguenot-Hebrews of the sect of Jesus of Nazareth, infidels, deserters, renegades of the Mosaic law, of Sabianism,[77] of Sadducism, of polytheism, for the Protestantism of the peasant of Bethlehem? Monstrous as we are, we'd like to raze the rock from which our stream flows. Bastards, we'd like to cut our ancestors' throats. We burn the Hebrews and we kiss their lips; stupidity! We burn them because they're faithful to their law, to their god, and we sing the psalms of their King David around their pyres, shouting *Hosanna in excelsis* to the heavens! A bloody masquerade!"

"Will we be there soon, Seigneur Aymar?"

"Soon."

"What? By Beelzebub, prince of demons! How the devil did you dislodge this swallow from the nest?"

"By chance."

"Chance?"

---

77. The Sabians are named three times in the Quran, along with the Jews and Christians, among the "people of the book," but the reference remains somewhat mysterious. The likelihood is that it refers to the people of Saba or Sheba, referenced several times on the Old Testament, whom some sources credit with beliefs that associated angels with stars and revered the sun; the Magi of the gospels are said by some authorities to have come from there—a notion of which much is made in Gustave Kahn's elaborate Old Testament-based Symbolist fantasy *Le Conte de l'or et du silence* (1898; tr. as *The Tale of Gold and Silence*).

II.
Aro's fa ranson dë l'Angei Blan[78]

O my dove, thou art in the clefts in the rock,
in the secret places of the stairs,
let me see they countenance,
let me hear thy voice; for sweet is thy voice
and thy countenance is comely.[79]

The Bible.

"Yes, every year I come down from Montélimart, my father's abode and my birthplace, to go, out of idleness, to spend a few days in Avignon. One evening, when I was parading my ennui along the rampart, fleeing society and noise, I was unwittingly attracted by the secret charm of harmony, and, awakened with a start, I fell into the midst of a crowd assembled on the bowling green, where the town's elite gather every evening, the fiddlers, the players of lutes, mandolins, hurdy-gurdies, trumpets and buccinas, in order to make concerts of voices and instruments.

"What delightful evenings I spent there beneath and ultra-marine sky speckled with stars, in the cool and serene breeze that played, perfumed and melodious, over our heads, lulled and delighted by choirs of human voices and celestial music! Oh, above all, what rapture, when someone intoned some glorious song, some ballad in the sweet Provençal language; or when, in religious solemnities, on holy days, sacred music was sung, those spiritual hymns, those grave, funereal chants, those majestic psalms, the languorous and sonorous *Stabat*, the sepulchral *Dies irae*, which, although deprived of the organs and mystery of the cathedral, made us shiver with awe, like the solitary contemplation of the immensity.

"As in a carousel, the demoiselles and ladies were seated in a circle in places of honor, their worthy spouses and escorts,

---

78, Perhaps "Measure the ransom of the white angel."

79. *Song of Solomon* 2:14.

posted behind them, entirely dedicated to petty attentions, exchanging forceful courtesies, on the lookout for the slightest gesture of a finger, the slightest blink, sign of satisfaction or pleasure, in order gallantly to applaud the motet or the fiddler who has charmed their beloved.

"Now, one evening, I noticed a young woman nearby, isolated from the ladies, apart from the crowd, leaning on the shoulder of an old man.

"I turned, surprised, and contemplated her.

"From then on, the music no longer affected me; I no longer heard it; perhaps it did not even reach me; the thought of her beauty exorcised it. I cannot describe my rapture; fixed, like a statue whose marble breast had begun to beat, I studied her; she appeared to me like a virgin in an aureole: a virgin painted by Barthélemy Murillo or Diego de Sylva Velásquez. Her beautiful face, in my memory, had no sister; she seemed to belong neither to the beautiful daughters of my mountains, nor the ravishing women of Arles, nor the lively daughters of Marseilles, nor the pretty daughters of Lyon, nor the demoiselles of Paris, nor the blonde Brabantines; she was something Oriental, celestial, unknown! Red-haired, with noble features, tall, graceful, a pale complexion tinted with red, a soft gaze veiled beneath a diaphanous eyelid, grenadine lips. Her costume was simple, but sparkling jewels wound around her hair, her forehead, her ears, her neck, her fingers, and betrayed her fortune.

"The bare-headed, white-bearded old man sitting beside her, leaning on a staff, seemed to be asleep.

"I had been considering her thus for some time when, by chance, her beautiful blue-green eyes strayed in my direction; her two pupils, like two bullets launched by an arquebus, struck me directly in the heart. For the first time, at the sight of a woman, I felt such a commotion that my legs flexed voluptuously, I blushed, I went pale, I was frozen and burning; my whole life, my whole soul, all my blood had flooded into my tumultuous heart; my eyes, with a will of their own, squinted and seemed to gaze into my breast; for the first time, I was subject to the charm of a woman; for the first time, I felt subjugated; for the first time, the love of which I was ignorant, that I held at bay, entered into me; but, like thunder that rushes into a dovecot without being able to find the exit, the love within me could no longer find an exit; my passion will be eternal.

"Returned to myself, having retempered my boldness, I took advantage of the fiddlers' rest and approached the old man.

"'Messire,' I said to him, bowing reverently, 'permit a cavalier to find it unseemly that as noble a demoiselle as this one here should be apart from the serenade of which she would be the glory; if you wish, Messire, I shall open a passage through the crowd in order that you might accompany her without mishap to the ladies' circle.'

"'Monsieur, I cannot take advantage of your generous offer, but I thank you with all my heart.'

"'You are very polite, Messire,' I replied, 'but the demoiselle cannot hear the serenade very well from such a distance.'

"At that moment, the noble red-haired girl nodded her head to thank me; troubled, I stammered a few syllables.

"'Monsieur,' the old man said to me then, 'Dinah, my daughter, is very sensitive to your politeness; I thank you frankly, but that is impossible for us; we are from a foreign hive, and this bee cannot mingle with that wasps'-nest without insult.'

"I withdrew swiftly, internally joyful at my boldness—but I only moved a short distance away, keeping watch so that I might follow them to their dwelling when they left, in order to obtain information about the unknown beauty, to see her on her balcony as I passed by, to penetrate into her home or to get a message to her.

"I lulled myself with her flattering thoughts, arranging all that in my head; I knew her abode; I passed beneath her window; she leaned out; I saluted her with a smile and my hat; I watched for her to go out; I won over her duenna, or, rather, I followed her to church, and as if by hazard, met her by the font; I offered holy water on the tip of my finger to the pretty tip of hers, which bore it to her pretty forehead, which my lips would soon touch too.

"I arranged all that: the declaration of my love; she gave me hers; I was received in her father's house; thus, I swam in a lake of happiness, lost in illusions.

"Occasionally, however, I was tormented by the mysterious meaning of what the old man had said to me: *We are from a foreign hive, and this bee cannot mingle with that wasps'-nest without insult.* I formed a thousand conjectures, which each seemed plausible in turn; from one minute to the next I metamorphosed them; I gave them for a homeland Spain, Bohemia, Bosnia, Venice, Cerigo...I made them Hospodars, Boyars, princes traveling incognito, exiles; then all those interpretations seemed crazy to me. In fact, none of that was any reason to remain aside for fear of insult.

"Then the name of Dinah persecuted me; the name was unknown to me; I had a vague memory of having heard it, but I could not remember when or where.

"A distant noise that made me jump brought me out of all those reveries; I found myself standing up, leaning on a palisade, alone on the deserted rampart; the serenade had finished, the crowd had dispersed. I stamped my foot, and cursed my maladroit distraction; all my happiness vanished; there was no more hope of seeing her again; my passion, born *ex abrupto*, fell the same way.

* * * * * *

"Oh, there is no greater suffering than to encounter a sympathetic being who captivates you, and inclines you to her! One has seen her out walking, at a ball, on a journey, at church; one has darted a glance at her, one has received a blink; one has touched her hand; one has caused her to hide; one is smitten, ravished, enveloped; one has already fashioned a future; there is already love, deeply-rooted love; then, in the time to utter a sigh or to gaze at the sky, that being has flown away like a bird; the apparition is extinct, and one remains devastated, annihilated by the commotion.

"For me, the thought that one will never see again that lightning-flash which has dazzled us, that woman, spontaneously beloved, our touchstone; that two existences made for one another, to be combined, to be happy together in this life and in eternity, are to be parted forever, perhaps to drag themselves out without ever again finding a soul that matches theirs, a mind and heart similarly shaped...for me, that thought is profoundly dolorous.

"I wandered on the rampart for a long time, railing against my fatal luck and the derision of fate, the infernal archer, that had shot a woman at my heart, in order to inflict a mortal wound.

"I wandered, and I filled myself with solitude and calm, often troubled by the image of Dinah, which passed before me repeatedly, which descended upon my forehead and plunged me back into tumultuous tempests, into ascetic delights, into a delirious and voluptuous fever.

"When I got back to my lodgings, the clock was chiming one o'clock in the morning; in my insomnia, mulling over all these things, I remembered that the name of Dinah, which did not seem unknown to me, was in the Holy Bible. I lit my lamp again, and opened my Bible, always placed on the table beside my bed, and, riffling through *Genesis*, I found in chapter XXXIV, *Schechem defileth Dinah.*

"And Dinah the daughter of Leah, which she had bare unto Jacob, went out to see the daughters of the land. And when Shechem the son of Hamor the Hivite, prince of the country, saw her, he took her, and lay with her, and defiled her, etc., etc., etc.[80]

---

80. Borel, only being interested in the verse and not the chapter, omits the rest of the story, but it is not without a certain ironic resonance. Hamor and Jacob discuss the situation calmly, and Jacob agrees to allow Schechem to marry Dinah, and for their two tribes to intermarry, if the Hivites will agree to be circumcised. Hamor agrees, but Jacob's sons mount a sneak attack by night and kill all the males in the city—the Hebrews being, of course, nomads passing through—before taking the women and children away with them: a move of which the Lord, ever-ready in the Old Testament to prefer

"That discovery filled me with joy, and I conjectured that, bearing a Hebrew name, the girl must be a Hebrew. Her Oriental features corroborated that opinion, and by that means I explained the words that her aged father had said to me. Comforted by that discovery, emboldened by hat slight success, I recovered hope of discovering her retreat and swore gravely to dare anything to bring the matter to a conclusion.

"As soon as the sun rose, I traveled through the town. Presuming that they must be strangers passing through, I began by visiting the hostelries; I went to the Croix-d'Or at Saint-Esprit, the Écu de France at Tris-Maures and the Lion d'Argent at Saint-Vidal, asking the landlords everywhere whether they might have in their lodgings an old man with a white beard accompanied by a young woman named Dinah. Everywhere, I received only negative responses. I went to find the rabbi, with no more success.

"Then, without becoming discouraged, I roamed the town; I went to the walkways, the ramparts, the squares, the churches, the synagogue; I did not miss a single serenade, and I visited the surroundings—in vain; I did not obtain the slightest clue.

"After a fortnight of assiduous and difficult research, I gave up. Activity had sustained me; I suddenly fell into ennui and depression; I no longer went out, I stayed in bed half the day, my Holy Bible open beside me—and from time to time, I reread and kissed the page on which the name of Dinah shone.

"Avignon became insipid to me; I hated it; I hated everything; everything seemed to me to be flat or disgusting, and nothing-ness always came to interpose itself between the world and me; I caressed the idea self-annihilation, an idea I had always had at the back of my mind. My worthy hostess advised me to go and spend a few weeks in my father's house, in order to distract myself and pull me out of my malaise, which the good woman attributed to the change in the season.

"So I returned to Montélimart; the ennui followed me. For a

violent over-reaction to tactful diplomacy, does not appear to disapprove.

long time I had had a desire to visit the beautiful city of Lyon, and I set off on the spur of the moment.

III.
Lou gai rĕmĕno l'alo[81]

> I held him, and would not let him go,
> until I had brought him into my mother's house,
> and into the chamber of her that conceived me....
> I would cause thee to drink of spiced wine to
> drink, and the juice of my pomegranate.[82]
>   The Bible.

"I had only been here a few days, where ennui had pursued me, and where my inclination to break with life had become increasingly definite, when, at the corner of the somber and majestic Cathédrale de Saint-Jean, I perceived a young woman in a hurry; I thought I recognized her bearing and drew nearer; it was Dinah! I dared not affirm it, though, not accost her in a cavalier manner.

"I followed her, a few paces behind, calling out several times in a low voice: 'Dinah! Dinah!' She turned round and bowed to me without recognizing me, and I went to her, tremulously.

"'Noble demoiselle,' I said to her, 'do you recall the young man who, on the rampart of Avignon, on the evening of a serenade, spoke to Messire your father, and whom you thanked for his courtesy?'

"'What! It's you?' she said, moved, placing her hand on my arm, lowering her reddened forehead, string at the stones of the parvis.

"'O beautiful Dinah, how happy I am to encounter you! Don't push me away, let me pour out all the suffering that has

---

81. Perhaps "gladness renews worth."

82. Borel probably intended simply to quote *Song of Solomon* 8:2, but confused its beginning with the beginning of 3:4.

accumulated in my heart since the moment I saw you, when I lost all repose! You have caused a sudden love to spring forth within me, a violent passion.

"'I looked out for the end of the serenade in order to follow you to your dwelling, in the hope of being able to confess my love to you some day; I waited in distress for the moment of departure, but you had made such an impact on my heart that I gradually fell into profound cogitation, and when I woke up I was alone on the rampart; I searched for you for a long time, wandering through the town, without success; despairing, a mortal ennui gripped me, and as you see, beautiful lady, I was led to bring it here. Oh, blessed be Heaven, if that is what has granted me the joy of seeing you again! You are, Dinah, he mistress of my life; I am at your knees; if you reject me, you will kill me!"

"'Monsieur, it is not seemly that a young woman should stop like this to chat to a cavalier; don't retain me, I beg you; calm down—see how the passers by are looking at us!'

"'Please, then, let us go into this somber church; there, beneath a dark vault, we can talk of love far from malevolent gazes.'

"'Oh no, Monsieur! I cannot enter that temple, the abode of the enemy of my God; it would hurt my old father too much if he were ever to hear of it.'

"'Who, then, is your God?'

"'The God of Israel!'

"'I had guessed that, for I read your name in *Genesis*. If that is how it is, be my sister, permit me to accompany you, and we can talk.'

"'I put my trust in you, Monsieur.'

"'How long have you lived in Lyon?'

"'I was born here, Monsieur.'

"'Your beauty should have told me that—but when did you leave Avignon?'

"'The day after you saw me at the serenade. Perhaps it is wrong to be so frank, but I cannot lie; at the sight of you I felt touched and assailed by a new sentiment; I had perceived your disturbance and I interpreted your courtesy. When we got up to leave, you were leaning against a palisade; you were so absorbed that we passed close to you and my father bowed to you without you perceiving it; I turned round several times on the way and did not see anyone. Perhaps it's unseemly to confess all that, but it's nevertheless the truth. Your memory agitated me all night. I made every effort to delay my father's departure, in the hope of seeing you again at the serenades, but it was in vain. My father, who deals in precious stones, had come to Avignon on business and found himself imperiously recalled thereby to Lyon. I too have suffered since then!'

"The poor child wiped away a few tears. 'Alas, I could not become accustomed to the thought that told me: *you will never see him again*. However I would be returning to Avignon in a few months, and I hoped....'

"'Oh, Dinah, Dinah, how happy I am! Oh, how much I love you! Oh, how your mind delights me! I adore you, believe me; you are my Rachel, my visible good angel! Dinah, until the moment you appeared to me, I was reputed to be proud and disdainful of women, but I kiss your feet!'

"'Oh, if everything that I experience for you...but tell me, what is your lovely name, so that I might name you too?'

"'Aymar de Rochegude.'

"'Oh, if everything that I experience for you, my Aymar, if everything that I feel is love, believe that I have a great deal of it, of love!'

"During these mutual outpourings, we arrived at the threshold of Dinah's house; then, I asked to arrange a rendezvous in the near future.'

"'Eh! Why?' she said.

"'To see one another and talk of love.'

"'Aymar, there's no need to arrange a rendezvous. You're a distinguished cavalier; you love me; I firmly believe that I love you; come to my father's house whenever you wish; if you wish, let us go up straight away. I shall say to my father, here is the young cavalier who spoke to you on the evening of the serenade on the rampart of Avignon, do you recognize him? I've just met him, a stranger in this city; he loves me very much, I love him too...and my father will bow to you and will love you for love of me.'

"I went up; the worthy old man, Judas, received me benevolently and introduced me to his wife Leah—and since that time, six months ago, I have, so to speak, spent all my leisure time in his house. My love for Dinah has only been increased by a chaste and delightful intimacy, heaping attention and all possible respect on old Judas, who cherishes me, and his Leah, who has made me forget the mother I lost as a child."

IV.
Plouihas dë Marselha[83]

Like rain upon the mown grass,
as showers that water the earth.[84]
The Bible.

At that moment, they turned into a street.

"Maître Bonaventure Chastelart," said Rochegude then, "don't yawn so deeply, I beg you; you'll make a noise, wake the city and bring out the watch."

"Seigneur Aymar, it's just...."

"That's all right, console yourself—it's finished; and besides, we've arrived; here's the Juiverie."

"Jesus Christ! The Juiverie here!" cried the aged lawyer, petrified, making the sign of the cross forcefully.

"Yes, Maître it's really here; look over there, in the corner, at that beautiful house with the overhanging turret, built by your illustrious compatriot Philibert Delorme."

"Philibert Delorme! A sorcerer, wasn't he? An astrologer? Alas, Monseigneur Aymar, cover me a little with your mantle,

---

83. Marseillais rain

84. Psalm 72 (in the A.V.—71 in some versions) verse 5.

I'm hellishly afraid! It seems to me that something has fallen on my head; I've always hear it said that it was perilous to go through Juiveries by night, where it rains cauldrons and crossbow bolts, black cats, mandrakes, bats and Greek fire...."

"Can you believe in such absurdities at your age? A man of law! A doctor! You're pitiful! Maître Bonaventure, on my honor, I can attest that if it rains at night in this quarter, it certainly does not rain mandrakes or black cats!"

V.

Melh ës nocëiar që ëssër unsclat[85]

He that possesseth a good wife, beginneth a possession,
She is like a help unto himself, and a pillar of rest.[86]
The Bible.

The valet who was carrying the lantern ahead of them, stopped half way along the street, next to a large house whose windows were simply glazed with grease-paper on the fifth, sixth, seventh, eighth and ninth stories, doubtless occupied by workmen in golden cloth and silk, who require a soft and pale light. The entrance bay was low and narrow; Aymar ducked under it. The door, of solid wood, whose decoration was outlined in diamond shapes, was ornamented and consolidated by large nails with rounded heads like Milanese breastplates. A carved brass marmoset hung in the middle, serving as a knocker, and the transom window above the stone lintel was fitted with bars.

Aymar de Richegude knocked twice with the marmoset's backside on the door, and a door was immediately heard to grate on its hinges on the second floor, and a soft voice called out: 'It's you, Seigneur Aymar; I'm coming down.'

The stairwell suddenly brightened, and the descending light

---

85. Boissier renders it "Melh es nocëtar që êjfer ufetats"; it is an abridgement of the Biblical proverb cited.

86. *Eccleisaticus* 36:26, echoing a sentiment previously expressed in *Proverbs* 18:22

was reflected through the large windows on to the opposite wall. The door uttered a long groan and opened. Dinah appeared in all her splendor, outlined against the black background of the corridor, dressed in a short brocatelle dress and, as was her custom, laden with gems and jewelry. Her white face was radiant in the obscurity; one might have thought her the angel of the Annunciation. Her small slender hand was carrying an iron candlestick twisted in a spiral, like the serpentine neck of an alchemical retort.

On seeing the young woman, Chastelart, stupefied, opened his eyes wide and took several steps backwards, so great is the power of beauty. Aymar went to her, took her hand, and kissed her forehead over her headband.

"You're late," she said, in a bittersweet tone.

"That's true; I was unavoidably delayed; don't scold me, I beg you. I couldn't come back, as you know, without the notary here."

At that word, Bonaventure Chastelart took off his cap and bowed deeply several times. Then the climbed a small stone spiral stairway, with the aid of a rope serving as a guide, made shiny by friction, like the shaft of a halberd. During the ascent Bonaventure tugged on Aymar's mantle and whispered in his ear: "How beautiful she is, this heretic! Oh, you didn't lie, Rochegude!"

"Father!" cried Dinah, joyfully, from the landing. "It's Aymar and his notary."

They went along a gallery overhanging the courtyard, and into a large room illuminated by a chandelier placed over a gilded wooden candelabrum. The walls were covered with gilded sheepskin hangings, embossed and ridged like the spine of a book. At the back of the room, in a large niche, an inlaid palisander sideboard incrusted with ivory and nacre, crowned with a tabletop in Swiss Griot marble, hollowed out in a scallop like a font, bore an urn overflowing with water, and, to the right and left, large pewter pitchers, bulging like amphorae, like those servant-women still carry today when they go in quest of water during public ceremonies.

Backed up against one of the walls was a glass-fronted display case whose shelves were laden with wooden bowls full of turquoises, amethysts, beryls, onyxes, cornelians, ruby carbuncles, emeralds, aventurines, topazes, sydoines, diamonds, lapis-lazulis, marcasites, cameos and a thousand other stones; against the panes were suspended a number of necklaces of garnet, amber, baroques, coral, etc., etc.—Judas the lapidary's trading stock. He was wearing a black doublet, sunk in his armchair in front of a table covered in Bergamo tapestry, on which a folio Bible garnished with clasps was set, was solemnly reading aloud a passage from *Exodus*.

Leah, his wife, dressed in her most beautiful clothes, was to his left; the brown skin of her neck and hands almost matched the color of the Cap de More silk dress; her eyelashes and chestnut-colored eyebrows, long and bushy, veiled her eyes, which were sparkling as if through a trellis; her crow's-beak nose formed an angular promontory that divided the furnace of her face into two like the blade of a cutlass, but overall, her appearance radiated dignity and affability, and the sound of her soft and mellifluous voice was captivating.

Not far away from her was a group of men and women; their semi-Oriental costume and their characteristic heads coiffed with bastard turbans, conveyed a strong impression of Mesopotamia. They were the relatives and friends of Judas, come to witness the betrothal and the signing of the contract. I do not know whether they were Talmudists or Karaites, but on the other hand, I can affirm that they claimed to belong, in accordance with family tradition, to the tribe of Aaron. When Aymar came in, they bowed and greeted him with "the Lord be with you," to which he responded with a hand-kiss.

Taking off his hat and cape, he said: "Forgive me, my worthy relatives; if I've made you wait, it's the fault of the notary, Maître Bonaventure Chastelart, whom I have the honor of introducing to you. Imperiously forced by my father to return to Montélimart and to leave tomorrow, under threat of disinheritance, as you're not unaware, no respite was possible."

"Judith," said Judas to a serving-woman standing in the doorway, "bring that table and stool closer now, and bring a writing-desk, in order that the lawyer can perform his function."

To her father's right, Dinah smiled knowingly with Rochegude at the embarrassment and panicked expression of Bonaventure, who was fondling a rosary. To reassure him, Rochegude gripped him violently by the arm, feigning a benign expression. "Stupid cowherd," he muttered in his ear, sitting him down at the table as one sits a mannequin down.

"If you're ready, Monsieur Lawyer, you can begin the customary formalities," said Judas. "Interrogate, and we shall respond."

"Monsieur," stammered Maître Bonaventure, taking a parchment from his notebook, "with your son in law, my clerk has prepared the minute of the contract; I request attention; we are about to proceed with the reading.

"Listen:

"Théodebert de Chantemerle, chevalier, Seigneur de Rochecardou, Gorge-de-Loup and other places, Sénéchal de Lyon, know that:

"Before the councilor of the king, notary of Lyon, undersigned,

"Being present, Sieur Carloman, Aymar de Rochegude, in Lyon, where he is resident at the Hôtel de la Cornemuse, Rue des Quatre-Chapeaux, parish of Saint-Nizier, legitimate son of Sieur Tiburce Aymar, Chevalier de Rochegude, resident at the place called Dieulefit, near Montélimart in Dauphiné and the late Madeleine Garnaud, of Rémusat near Nyons; future spouse on the one part;

"And Demoiselle Dinah, legitimate daughter of Israel Judas of Tripoli in Syria, lapidary tradesman in this city, and Dame Leah Baruch of Damascus, living with her father and mother domiciled in the Rue de la Juiverie, parish of Saint-Paul, on the other part.

"Which proceeding, the future groom as major, free and master of his rights, after three respectful and reverential notices given to his father, and after the decease of his mother; to whom and to all he will legitimate the nuptial benediction; and the future bride, with the authority and agreement of the aforesaid sieur and dame, her father and mother, both here present, have promised to take one another in true and legitimate marriage, and to that effect to present themselves at the church...."

"No, no, Monsieur Bonaventure," said Rochegude. "Put, if you please, 'at the synagogue.'"

"At the synagogue...to the devil, if you wish!" murmured the lawyer.

"You are impolite, Monsieur le Notaire Royal, and soiling your duty."

"And to that effect, to present themselves at the synagogue, there to receive the nuptial cur...blessing, on the first invitation of one to the other.

"In favor of which marriage, the aforesaid Sieur Israel Judeas has given and constituted in advance of inheritance to the future spouse of his daughter the sum of fifteen thousand écus, which he has today delivered in coins and currency into the hands of the future spouse, as promised, and in consequence of which, insofar as the future spouse thus authorized is content, he acquits and thanks Sieur Israel Judas.

"In the same favor, the future spouse has constituted in dowry all the wealth and rights that might hereafter...."

"That's all right, that's all right, Maître Chastelart—pass on; we know the obligatory formula."

"Then, ta ta ta ta ta tat a...ah! Here we are....

"Declaring, the future husband that his present property originating from his late mother composes: firstly, two farms and dependencies situated in the said place Rémusat, near Nyons, estimated to be valued at twenty thousand livres; secondly, a country house situated in the same place, judged to be valued at thirty-two thousand livres; thirdly, a house for lease at the sign of the Bras-d'Or, situated in Montélimart, tenanted, valued at nine thousand livres; and, in addition, a cash sum not exceeding five hundred pistoles; and the future wife declaring that she has nothing other than the fifteen thousand écus constituted above.

"Thus agreed reciprocally, accepted and promised to be observed on penalty of all expenses, compensation and interests, by obligation of property, affectation, imposition of dowry and accessories, in the form of the law and custom of this city, and the laws and customs observed there; the parties submitting themselves and renouncing in consequence expressly all other laws and customs that might be contrary thereto, submissions, renunciations and clauses. Made and passed at the said Lyon, in the domicile of the undersigned Sieur Israel Judas, after vespers, on 28 June 1661.

"In the presence of Sieur Abraham Baruch, merchant mercer, brother of Israel Judas, and Sieur Gédéon Tobie, perfumer at Grasse in Provence, who will sign hereunder with the parties.

"Now would you care to come and sign—you first, Monsieur Aymar de Rochegude, then Mademoiselle, and then you, Messieurs."

At that moment, Judith, the serving-woman, brought two enormous bowls to the table filled with sugared almonds, and several baskets, boxes and cases.

When the parents and witnesses had signed, Maître Bonaventure, in accordance with the law and custom, kissed Dinah on both cheeks; she offered him one of the bowls, into which he plunged his cupped hand, and drew out a substantial provision of sugared almonds. Dinah and Aymar threw themselves into the arms of Leah and Judas, who were weeping with joy; then they embraced all their friends; then Judith offered the sugared almonds around the assembly, everyone dipping into them without ceremony and filling their hands. The two spouses offered the wives and daughters of Abraham Baruch and Tobie, their aunts, cousins and friends, boxes of sweetmeats and precious items of clothing, of which they were graciously making them gifts, according to the custom of the city.

When the ceremony was over and the felicitations, protestations of love and eternal amity had been made, the worthy relatives got up in order to retire; it was late.

"Adieu, my friends," Rochegude said to them, "adieu; I'm leaving tomorrow for Montélimart; my father has summoned me tyrannically; I hope to appease him by means of insistences made in person at his knees; I hope to obtain his consent and perhaps return soon with him to celebrate our marriage and our wedding appropriately. May God keep you healthy in body and spirit until then."

"Adieu, Seigneur Aymar! Adieu, my friend! Adieu, cousin! Adieu nephew! Good luck!"

"Adieu!"

"You, Maître Bonaventure, wait for me—we'll leave together."

* * * * * * *

"My good father and mother," Aymar said then, "as I cannot make our betrothal visits with Dinah tomorrow, please give my apologies to our friends, and give them the sugared almonds and presents intended for them. Now, it only remains for me to press you to my heart, as well as my Dinah, whom I love so much!"

"Oh, why it is necessary for you to leave us, Aymar? Say, stay for a few more days!"

"Don't weep, Dinah; I'll come back soon and I shall never leave you again!"

"Stay, stay with me! I have ominous presentiments."

"Folly, my dear child."

"No, I sense something distant, something dolorous, which worries me. Oh, the heavens do not lie is such matters!"

"Console yourself, my dear daughter," said Judas. "What are a few days of waiting? Think of our father Jacob, who, in his uncle Laban's house, waited seven years for Rachel, whom he loved. Unjustly, at the end of seven years, he did not obtain her, and without a murmur, he waited for another seven years; it was only after fourteen years of desires, promises and labors that he received the price of constancy. Have courage, daughter!"

"Courage, my dear!" repeated Leah, who hugged her and kissed her tearful eyes.

"Father," said Aymar, kneeling before Judas, "give me your blessing."

Placing both hands on his son-in-law's head, Judas then read several passages from the Holy Bible, recited a few prayers in Hebrew, and then added in a loud voice: "My son, I bless you in the name of the God of Israel; I bless you like Isaac and Esau; may your posterity be numerous; may your posterity be a people, and may the Almighty, Lord God of Israel, live in you and your posterity! Get up, my son; you will not go astray, for the Lord will protect you and march with you."

Aymar wept; he covered Judas' hands and white beard with kisses, and extracted himself from the arms of Dinah and Leah, who were sobbing.

Aymar could no longer stay there.

"Adieu! Adieu! Let's go, Chastelart; quickly, let's go...."

On the quai, by the light of the lantern carried by the lackey, several écus could be seen shining in Rochegude's hand; then, thanks to the silence, a deep, syncopated, argentine sigh was heard to emanate from Maître Bonaventure Chastelart's purse.

VI.
Langhimën[87]

> Whither is thy beloved gone, O thou fairest
> among women? Whither is thy beloved
> turned aside? that we may seek him with thee.[88]
> *The Bible*.

The end of July drew near; it was about a month since Aymar

---

87. Probably "languishing."

88. *Song of Solomon* 6:1.

de Rochegude had left for Montélimart to go to his father's house in the domain of Dieulefit. He had promised his fiancée to return before long, but nothing announced his imminent return to Dinah. Since his absence she had only received one message in memory of him, one box of Montélimart nougat, a box of larch manna and trinkets, pine-cones from Briançon and a punnet of delicious ring-biscuits from the fair at Sainte-Madeleine de Beaucaire. In the punnet was a note thus conceived:

Aymar de Rochegude to Dinah

My beautiful fiancée, do not be annoyed if I treat you like a child, for I love you like a child. How painful this separation is for me! Of, if you were with me, at least, how this great and primitive nature that surrounds me, which seems today to be dull and insipid, would be animated, would bound like a ram, quiver like a lamb—oh, I would love it, I would understand it better, if your gaze were to open my soul, which is curled up like a hedgehog, if your voice were to expand my heart, if I had your hand in mine, if the mastery of these mountains, going astray is your long red hair, were to inundate me with the nard they exhale! Joyful, we would roam this beautiful country, climbing to the highest peak, and the two of us, under the same cloak, lost in the mist, would see beneath our feet a floor of clouds, and would salute the immensity, and the spirit of the God of Israel, who inhabits high places, would visit us! Forgive me, forgive me, suffering is leading me astray...but is not all that beautiful nevertheless? We would wander all the way from the cave of Balme to Briançon, the eagle's nest, from the bears of Saint-Jean-de-Maurienne to the strong fortress of Viviers, perched like a hat of the summit of a rocky crag.

A mountain-man from Monestier recently sold me a young eagle; I'm training it in order to distract myself;

you won't be annoyed if, in order to pronounce your balsamic name more frequently, I have named it Dinah. My father and all the people who visit me are astonished by that name and interrogate me as to its source; I don't know how to reply to them and call it a whim. These worthy Dauphinois would doubtless rather I had called it Margot.

Since arriving in Dieulefit, I have had several explanatory conversations with my father; these conversations have turned into altercations, and the explanations have not explained anything, as you can imagine. My father is still armored and fortified in his will; nothing can bend his savage firmness. His violent irritability has only increased; however, for some days, doubtless to win me over, he has been feigning a honeyed sweetness that he is not accustomed to distil. On the morning of my arrival I was horribly mistreated; that proud man had taken my three reverential notifications to heart; my persistent determination offended him; he covered me with bile, he blasphemed, and abused me. I remained silent, he was so carried away that when the old man knocked me down and I embraced his knees, he kicked me.

After that fit, in which he expended so much energy, weakness and cold took possession of him, and he often takes to his bed for days on end. He does not want to hear any mention whatsoever of my marriage to you, to a heretic—a Bohemian, as he calls you. To him, the Israelites are heretics and thieves. Not only did he threaten to disinherit me today but, worse still, to have me thrown into a State prison—Pierre-Encise,[89] the Bastille, I don't know, perhaps the Grande-Chartreuse. I've lost almost all hope of bending him, but I shall

---

89. The Château de Pierre-Encise, or Pierre-Scize, sat atop a crag near Lyon at the time when the story is set, but was demolished in 1793.

make a further attempt soon, and whatever happens, I shall soon be with you, blessed or cursed.

Embrace Leah my mother, embrace my father Judas; I need his blessing more than ever. As for you, my Dinah, I adore you, and my soul contemplates you as an arch-saint.

If you find the time to write me a consolation, address that note to me not to Deiulefit, because of my father, but to Montélimart, at the sign of the Bras-d'Or; it will reach me.

This letter filled Dinah with joy and distress; the worthy young woman accused herself of Aymar's misfortunes, and held herself guilty of the ill-treatments and tempests that his love for her was causing him to endure. She could not comprehend that old Rochegude, the father of her fiancé; for her, gentle and devoid of any malice, his cruelty made him appear in her eyes in an inhuman form, with the aspect of an ogre; she could not believe that such barbarity could merge from a human breast. That fortunate child did not know that society perverts everything, that the fanaticism of possession and religion hardens men and makes them bloodthirsty; that the man who is virtuous in his natural state becomes, when civilized, a soldier, a landowner, a priest, a judge or an executioner; she did not know that during her infancy, her grandfather had been burned in the Place de Grève in Paris, and that long before, in order to avoid death, her father, accused of sorcery, had fled that city steeped in human blood.

Six weeks had gone by; Rochegude had not arrived. Poor Dinah grew sadder day by day; her gaiety withered. How hard the waiting seemed! Time stretched behind her and the future darkened in her eyes. She said to herself: *Perhaps, at this moment, Aymar is in a damp cell, calling out to me in a faint voice, only the hoarse echo of a dungeon replying to his moans, and his forehead, when he stands up, is torn by the stalactites of the vault. Or perhaps he has been murdered on the road by bandits....*

These were the rosy thoughts with which she rocked herself; ennui undermined her dully. Once so talkative, she remained idle and taciturn, sitting beside a window of which she was fond. Her melancholy distressed her mother and old Judas, whom she no longer caressed as had been her habit, and whose foreheads she only kissed to moisten them with tears. Weakened by dolor, she ardently sought out everything that irritated her nerves, everything that titillated and awoke her apathy; she loaded herself with the most odorant flowers; she surrounded herself with vases of lilac, jasmine, verbena, roses, lilies and tuberoses; she burned incense and benzoin; she spread around her amber, cinnamon, storax and musk. Often, she was violently agitated, coming and going in the dwelling, her mind seemingly gone astray; sometimes, she even disappeared for hours on end; that absence alarmed the household, they flew about in the city searching for her, in vain; then she came back, calmly.

"I couldn't bear to be enclosed," she said. "I've been to see the sky; I feel better."

At that time of year when everything is reborn, when everything revives, when even the coldest being feels stirred, when one experiences a imperious need for expansion, when the most misanthropic individual casts off his hatred and austerity and wants to be courteous; in that era when a sympathetic sentiment inclines us to love, that young love which even torments those who are unaware of it and throws them into languor and malaise; in that era, Dinah, who, a year before, had had beside her, at her knees, a companion who protected her with his wings, with whom she spent her days in conversations that delighted her, in reading the Bible, in holy confessions and illusory dreams; Dinah, submissive and confident, used to no longer thinking and no longer dreaming about anything but the man whose will she loved, contact with whom had expanded her soul, and whom she needed more than ever; Dinah found herself fatally isolated, lacking the arm that sustained her, the hand that directed her, the mouth that breathed determination, love and hatred to her, and everything; the poor girl, exhausted, collapsed in her distress, and, to cap at all, the dread, the intimate fear of having lost or being fated to lose her beloved, was killing her.

Nothing could draw her out of her cogitation; even so, her sensitive parents tried everything to distract her. They bought her a thousand things for which she had no desire; like a sick child pushing away her toys, she scarcely glanced at the baubles and jewels that would have filled her with delight some time before. Often, they took her on walks through the city, to the Ile-Barbe, the Roche-Taillée, into the woods at Tassin or Roche-Cardon, to the Tour de la Belle-Allemande, along the banks of the Saône and the Rhône—but nothing pleased her; she remained mute beneath her lowered veil.

One day, she asked her mother Leah for permission to write a note to her fiancé, as follows:

> *Aymar, if you love Dinah as Dinah loves you, come immediately, I beg you, if you are still free. If you are no longer free, break your shackles; where you go, I shall go! Or simply tell me where your dungeon is, in order that I might die there with you. Your absence is causing me so much distress, I am so weakened, that I cannot hold my pen, nor any longer collect my thoughts.*
>
> *Come back, my fiancé.*

Six days later, Dinah received this reply:

> *Console yourself, my fiancée, console yourself! I am leaving tomorrow at daybreak. Forgive me for making you suffer so much, but I too have suffered much. To stifle my suffering I have hunted bears in the mountains—and you, to chase away ennui, the bear that stifles you in its laden arms, what have you done? Believing that I would come back any day, I have*

delayed replying to you, I wanted to bring it to you;
I hoped to soften my father, but he is more inflexible
than the Alps. This evening I shall tell him that I am
leaving—can you imagine the squall? Pray to God
that the storm does not break me!

Salutations to Judas and Leah, adieu! In three days,
I shall knock on your door.

VII.
Oustàou Pairolaou[90]

Saying to a stock, Thou art my father;
and to a stone, Thou hast brought me forth.[91]

He putteth his mouth in the dust;
If so there may hope.[92]

The Bible.

In fact, on the same evening that his message departed, after
the meal, Aymar followed his father, who returned to his bedroom, and tremulously, spoke as follows:

"Father, forgive me for troubling you again; you see me
at your feet, don't be angry; remember that, all his life, your
humble son has be submissive; once only, he formed a determination, and that determination is fatal to him. You know that
love cannot be commanded, that true love cannot be torn away;
you know that, because you loved my mother, did you not?"

At that word, Rochegude shuddered, as if afflicted by frightful
memories, and performed frightful contortions in order to set
his face straight.

"Is it my fault," Aymar continued, "if the woman that heaven
has sent me happens to be an Israelite?—if the chosen woman

---

90. Approximately, "To hell with you, paternal house!"

91. *Jeremiah* 2:27

92. *Lamentations* 3:29

belongs to God's chosen people? Is it my fault if she is of the same blood as our Christ? She is beautiful, she is pure, she is virginal, and I adore her! She adores me, and she will adore you too, father! Is there anything like the love of a daughter-in-law? Her joy will cheer up your old age. You are making no reply, but tell me, then, in sum, what daughter-in-law do you want?"

"Never, Monsieur Aymar, will I permit the Christian blood of the Rochegudes to mingle with the impure blood of a Bohemian! A base heretic! Trash!"

"Trash! O, Father, you are very unjust! Look, read the contract, for she is my fiancée. Look, read the contract, which awaits nothing but your signature—you see, she is not penniless, this child, she is rich, if it's gold that you want...."

Rochegude tore it from his hands. "Damnation! What an infernal pact!"

And, without looking at it, he ripped it up and threw the pieces in Aymar's face.

"There—there's your betrothal! We'll see, wretch, whether you'll dishonor your family!"

"Father, you strike me because you know that I will not strike you; however, I'm young and strong; I have blood that is boiling; I have a heart that is hammering in my breast! Look, old man, I could break you as I break this door!"

And the door, broken down, fell before the impact with a frightful racket.

Rochegude, overwhelmed and livid, fell back in his armchair.

"Enough, enough, Father! All this is killing me! You are rock, I am iron! I'm leaving tomorrow. Adieu!"

"You shan't leave, do you hear!"

"I'm leaving, Father; but Heaven and Earth, what is there about this union that is so fatal? Tell me what makes you so furious?"

"A Bohemian! A damned soul! The blood of the Rochegudes is Christian!"

"Oh, my God, you sing very loudly about your Christian blood—what does it matter to you whether it's Christian or

Moorish? You're not so very religious, you don't have so much faith! I'm sure that you don't believe in God. Is it because you don't believe in Him, in God?"

At these words, Rochegude suddenly stood up; gripped by a demonic fury, he grabbed a knife by the blade and, with his blood-stained hand, hammered the hilt on the table-top.

"Get out, get out, brigand! I command you!" And with his other hand, seizing his son by the hair, he dragged him along the floor, along the corridor, and threw him down the stairs.

VIII.
Bënëzets los maldisors dë vos[93]

Their roar is like that of the lion.[94]
And the foundations of the thresholds shook.[95]
The Bible.

The next day, at dawn, Aymar came down. The grooms, accompanied by his black horse and the filly that he intended for Dinah, and several mules laden with valises, were already waiting.

Woken up by the whinnying of the horses, Rochegude hurriedly opened is bedroom window, slamming the shutters against the wall, and, stupefied, shouted at Aymar: "You shan't leave, or I'll disinherit and curse you!"

"I'm leaving, Father; as for the rest, do as you will; my other father, out there, will bless me."

"You shan't leave, I tell you!"

Rochegude disappeared from the window.

Aymar and his caravan set off; they were scarcely half way along the avenue when Rochegude reappeared on the perron, half-naked, with an arquebus in his hand.

---

93. Approximately, "Blessed are your curses."

94. *Isaiah* 5:29

95. *Isaiah* 6:4

"Stop, parricide! Stop, I curse you! May the lighting strike you down! May Hell swallow you up! Stop, I tell you! I curse you and expel you! It's your father who is cursing you, and Heaven is witness to it! You shan't leave!"

He stamped on the stone slab and struck the pillars of the porch with his head; the house shuddered; it was frightful to see. Aymar, silently, was still drawing away. When he reached the bend in the avenue, losing hope of binging him back, Rochegude redoubled his fury.

"Get out, get out, parricide, monster, forever!"

And he took aim with his arquebus. A detonation rang out; Aymar uttered a cry, and Rochegude fell down, stiff, on the steps of the porch.

IX.
Bourdëscâdo[96]

> For I am languishing of love.[97]
> *The Bible*.

Since Dinah had received Aymar's letter she had been less anxious, but no less agitated; the next day, in the evening, she said to her father: "I'm going out to visit my friend Elisabeth; I'll be back soon." It was a foolish lie, for she was little disposed to society, to conversation; in order to think at her ease and to see the heavens, as she said, alone, she went, imprudently to wander along the banks of the Saône.

Her future would arrive in two or three days. What beautiful dreams would she not have, further stimulated by solitude!

A little beyond the Ile-Barbe, a ferryman was sitting in the prow of his *bèche*, a kind of boat sheltered by sails or awnings, like a gondola.

---

96. Caprice.

97. *Song of Solomon* 2:5 (The A.V. has "sick" but other versions have "languishing," which is probably more accurate.)

Dinah was gripped by a sudden whim.

"Boatman," she said, drawing near, "I would like to sail on this beautiful water, but I'm alone."

"What does that matter, beautiful lady?"

"Boatman, here's an écu for my passage, and here is my purse, in order that you might respect a sick young woman."

The boatman took the écu and the purse; Dinah leapt into the bèche, and disappeared under the awning.

The boat was already moving away.

Suddenly, a soft symphony became audible, in the distance, gliding over the surface of the water, and another bèche appeared, forcefully rowed, from which inextinguishable bursts of laughter often emerged. It was laden with young men and women who had come o make music and frolic in the cool of the evening; they were rowing toward Dinah's boat, and passed very close to it, leaning over to see beneath the silent awning—but the ferryman hastened to row upstream, and the indiscreet persons went on downstream without having seen anything.

Dinah's bèche was still going upstream, still drawing further away, although night had fallen, and she only asked the boatman to sail for an hour at the most.

And the boatman quit his bench, and slid under the awning. A cry escaped the bèche, which disappeared over the horizon.

X.
Escumergamën[98]

And the hair of thine head like
purple; the king is held in the galleries.[99]

How beautiful are thy feet with slippers
O prince's daughter! the joints of thy
thighs are like jewels, the work of the hands of a

---

98. Excommunication.

99. *Song of Solomon* 7:5.

cunning workman....
Thy two breasts are like
two young roes that are twins.[100]
The Bible.

"Why, what are you doing, man? Stay on your bench and row in the current. Let's go back down; you can see that it's already late. Don't come near me!"

"You're beautiful, Mademoiselle!"

"You're mad!"

"It's you who've put this madness in my head."

"Get back—don't touch me. What do you want!"

"Nothing, except what Monsieur le Sénéschal wanted from my sister three months ago."

"Monsieur le Sénéschal—you're slandering him."

"I'm slandering him...it's my sister's belly that's slandering him. Oh, what soft hands! I've not touched many as soft as that. What a pleasure to be caressed by white and dainty hands. A lovely foot...and the leg, let's see!"

"Help, help! Let me, go, lout!"

"So beautiful, so beautiful, the donzelle...let's not shout ourselves hoarse. Oh, the leg's divine!"

"Help! Murder!"

"Murder—not yet; you get to work too quickly. Come on, calm down; let me kiss those beautiful eyes; be good, child, no one wants to hurt you; let me kiss that beautiful neck...."

"Oh, might I die...Hey! Help! Murder!"

"You're wasting your time; no one will come. Besides, can't I make you shut up? I've got a supply of ropes and material for gags."

"Traitor! Coward! Kill me!"

"Don't get frightened for so little; I'm used to this, myself; what one obtains willingly is of no value to me; it's rape I like! So, in the last war against Germany I enrolled voluntarily, and

---

100. *Song of Solomon* 7:1 and 7:3.

God knows, I sowed more Frenchmen than I killed Germans! You can fight all you like, beauty, it'll do no good. I'm not afraid, I tell you; I'm used to this; I rape a girl the way you play the spinet, and I'll kill you, if necessary, as you embroider a ruff."

"Oh, my poor fiancée!"

"Aha! We have a fiancée, it appears! Very good! The night's serene, let's chat. You're betrothed, my lovely virgin? Your fiancé will be overtaken; it's not always the fisherman who eats the shad; that's the way it is in this world; one can't count on anything; Guillot digs, and it's Charlot who fertilizes.[101] Oh, how charming you are, noble lady! How I love you! What joy to hug you in my arms! Me, Jean Ponthu, a ferryman, an oarsman—a noble lady? Oh, if you wanted to love me! Look at the beautiful rings! Pretty and pricey, aren't they? The same hand as my Marion. God be blessed! Let go of them, I'll give them to her on your behalf...."

"You'll break my fingers!"

"Often, when I was a soldier, on sentry-duty at night, I reflected, and I said to myself: We peasants, our sisters, our daughters and our wives are always for Messieurs the seigneurs, the nobles, the bourgeois; they're the ones who violate our women, and we simpletons never do anything to their wives, their daughters—that's not just. I also said to myself: why, then, are we so poor and they so rich? Oh, of course, that I was never able to explain to myself; it's not just, is it? To form a fellow and make him malevolent, there's nothing like a war.

"Charming necklace, fine pearls! My Marion has exactly the same neck as you. God be blessed! That'll work out well. I'll give them to get on your behalf, won't I?

"I'm truly sorry to strip such pretty ears; let me kiss them to take the pain away! But my Marion has no pendants suitable for the next fashion, and you can understand...come on, don't cry; I'll give them to her on your behalf too. But with such a simple costume, now, you can't keep those gold pins in your hair; I'll

---

101. "Charlot" was the nickname of Charles Sansom, the executioner on the Terror, who operated the guillotine.

have to let your hair down. Oh, you're a hundred times more beautiful unkempt!

"Now, at least, we have nothing more to lose...."

"Help! Help! Let me go, I beg you, or kill me straight away."

"Are we still struggling? Curse you! Give me those little hands so I can tie them."

"Murder! Will no one come, then?"

"Shut up—here's a bandage to calm you down; come on, lift your head so I can tie this gag."

"Mercy, mercy! Let me go in the name of God! Oh, let me go! What do you want, money? What do you want? You'll have it. Oh, you're hurting me too much, executioner, brigand! Aiee! Aiee! I'm doomed...."

Then, nothing more was heard in the boat but dull moans, stifled cries and croaks, which died away.

About an hour later, Jean Ponthu, the boatman, emerged from beneath the awning, dragging Dinah by the hair; at the moment when he threw her into the Saône, her gag came loose, and in a broken voice, she called Aymar's name.

And Jean Ponthu, at the prow of his boat, a harpoon in his hand, leaned over, forcing Dinah's body underwater again and again, every time it rose to the surface.

XI.

Dòou[102]

The dead praise not the Lord.[103]

My strength is dried up like a potsherd; and
my tongue cleaveth to my jaws; and
thou has brought me into the dust of death.[104]
The Bible.

---

102. Mourning, or dolor.

103. *Psalm* 115:17.

104. *Psalm* 22:15.

All night long, they searched for Dinah in the city.

At daybreak, peasants who were bringing their milk and produce to the city perceived, while crossing the stone bridge, the cadaver of a young woman, caught by her long red hair on the stones and reefs that brush the surface of the Saône at that point.

Jean Ponthu, the boatman, picked her up in his boat and brought her to the bank at the place known as La Morte qui Trompe; people gathered around her, full of regret, contemplating her fatal beauty; her two little hands, bruised, were tied behind her back with coarse rope.

Suddenly, a voice from the crowd exclaimed: "Don't you recognize her? It's Dinah, the red-haired! Dinah the beautiful Jewess! The daughter of Judas the lapidary, who lives back there, in the Juiverie."

All day long, there was a crowd in the house of Israel Judas. Dinah lay exposed on her bed, dressed in her best clothes and adorned with her jewels, in accordance with the Hebrew ritual. Leah, her poor mother, dying, was seated at the foot of the bed, uttering howls. Judas, leaning on his elbows in his armchair, his doublet ripped and his head covered in ashes, mute, devoured his dolor.

A rabbi prayed.

XII.
Goudoumar! Goullamas![105]

Who is the man who wraps a sentence
in words without science?[106]
The Bible.

---

105. Idler! Ruffian!

106. Borel's version of this quotation scores no hits on Google, so it might be misquoted; I can find no obvious English equivalent, although the sentiment and style are similar to *Ecclesiasticus*, so I have translated Borel's version.

At midday, at the town hall, under the vestibule, at the door of an alderman's office, a suntanned and thickset man wearing the costume of the captains of the port, was raging and struggling with servants who were trying to force him back.

"Hey, you fellows, what's all the noise at the door?" shouted a voice from inside.

"Messire, it's a captain, a bostman, trying to force an entry in site of your orders!"

"Eh? Yes, damn it, it's Jean Ponthu the ferryman. I've been made to wait for two hours; I could have walked all the way to Geneva by now, damn it!"

Then, distributing a few blows with his fists, Jean Ponthu shoved the servants away, threw the door open, and hurtled into the office.

"Monsieur Boatman, you're a peasant, a bumpkin! For making such a racket in this house, you deserve to be sent to lie down in the cellar."

"Monseigneur...."

All right, what do you want?"

"I've come to report of a drowned person I fished out this morning at the stone bridge, and demand the two-pistole reward."

"Has the cadaver been recognized?"

"Yes, Messire; it's a young woman named Dinah, child of Israel Judas, a lapidary."

"A Jewess?"

"Yes, Messire, a heretic, a huguenot...a Jewess...."

"A Jewess! You're going to fish out Jews, bumpkin! And you have the effrontery, after that, to come and demand a reward? Hey, servants! Hey, Martin! Hey, Lefabre! Throw this idler, this ruffian, out for me!

"Who fishes out a heretic, Monsieur Boatman, fishes out a dog."

XIII.
Golgotha

And he buried him in a valley in the land
of Moab, over against Beth-peor: but no man
knoweth of his sepulchre unto this day.[107]
The Bible.

At about two o'clock in the morning, a white coffin, carried
by four men and followed by a sparse procession, went silently
through the city.

At intervals, a few window-frames were heard creaking, the
grating of window-catches and door-knobs, and a few wrapped-
up heads leaned out over the street. They were good bourgeois
or old women who, woken up by the footsteps, had run to their
windows to see what was happening.

"What is it, my spouse?"

"A heretic burial, if I'm not mistaken; I think I can see a
white coffin."

"It's a young woman, for sure, poor thing—so soon!"

"Fortunate is one who dies before having known the world!"

Then those good bourgeois uttered profound sighs, and
closed their windows.

"Maître Bonaventure Chastelart, isn't that a procession of
Huguenots passing by?"

"No, neighbor, for there are no torches or lanterns, and
besides, this isn't the route to the hospital; it's nothing, except
some bitch of a Jewess being dragged to the Madeleine or to
Béchevilain."

As soon as day broke, a caravan of riders appeared beyond
the plain on the left bank of the Rhône; a young man was at the
head, accompanied by a few smart riders; servants and mules
laden with valises brought up the rear.

Having arrived at a field known as the Madeleine, the burial

---

107. *Deuteronomy* 34:6.

ground of executed criminals, the Golgotha of the Israelites, the rider prancing in the lead said to an old man digging a grave: "Good man, what time is it now?"

"About three o'clock; you're at the gates of the city."

"Thank you my good man—but for whom is the grave that you're digging so hurriedly this morning?"

"Seigneur, it's to bury a beautiful child found in the Saône yesterday."

"Very young?"

"Seventeen years old, Seigneur."

"But this field, my good man, isn't holy ground, is it?"

"That's true, Seigneur, but this is the cemetery of murderers and Jew."

"Israelites! Do you know the name of the young woman?"

"If I'm not mistaken, it's Dinah, the daughter of Israel Judas, lapidary."

"Dinah! Hellfire! My fiancée!!!"

"Moreover, Seigneur, here's the procession advancing, over there; do you see the white coffin?"

Aymar remained bleak and cold momentarily; then he called to one of his horsemen: "Carle, my friend, soon you shall take my cloak and carried it to my father, as Joseph's bloody cloak was taken to his father Jacob ; you shall say to him that you have seen my fiancée; for there she is, advancing. Look!"

He threw his purse to the gravedigger. "And you, old man, broaden that ditch!" Then he cried to the heavens, in a resounding voice: "Dinah! Israel! Eternity!"

And he discharged the pistols from his saddle into his head.

PASSEREAU,
THE STUDENT
(PARIS)

...............................The wall
Sustains him; to see him, one would surely think him
One stone more, on the Gothic stones,
Where lanterns dance like fantastic specters.
He waits....[108]

Alfred de Musset

..............................and that she die, as
It is true that she will cause the death of a man.

Alfred de Musset

Amours, scourge of the world, execrable folly,
You whom a tie so frail to sensuality binds,
When by so many other knots you hold to dolor,
If eye, by the eyes of a woman without heart,
You can enter my belly and poison my heart,
As from a wound one wrenches a blade,
Rather than a coward seen to be cured out it,

---

108. From "Don Paez," from which the second quotation also comes;
that poem, along with the third citation, from a poem generally known by
its first line, "Amour fléau du monde, exécrable folie," was reprinted in
de Musset's *Premières poésies* (1838), but Borel must have seen them in
periodicals or in manuscript. He must also have seen the Gérard de Nerval
item in manuscript; this appears to be its only publication.

I shall wrench it out, though I must die of it.
Alfred de Musset

And how should the gold be, Mademoiselle? Should
it be stained with blood or stained with tears?
Should it be stolen in gross with a dagger, or in detail,
with a charge, a place, or a shop?
Gérard

I.
Carabins[109]

One believes it, the other does not. Albert's discoveries in Estelle's home. The Vicomte de Bagneux immoral in the cause of hygiene. He dines at the expense of the nobility. Another controversy, the same thesis. Philogène. Inventory of the two carabins.

"Fortunately, my dear Passereau, I don't believe in the virtue of women. Otherwise, on my honor, I'd have had a cardboard nose and have grown very fat."

"What a student you are, my dear Albert!"

"Already, I'd had a few distant suspicions; my virgin didn't seem to me so very immaculate; her respectable mother reminded me of a stonemason; and then again, I've noticed that the frontal or coronal or her skull is underdeveloped or depressed, that the occipital distance of her ears is enormous, and that her cerebellum, the indubitable seat of physical love, as you know, forms an extraordinary protuberance. She has, besides, eyes cleft in the manner of antique Venuses, and open, bow-shaped nostrils—an infallible sign of lust.

"So, this morning, at seven o'clock, after I'd drummed for a long time on the door, she opened up, alarmed, and threw

---

109. "*Carabin*" is a familiar term for a medical student; I have left it untranslated here because it figures in a significant play on words later in the story.

herself into my arms and covered my face with caresses; all that seemed to me suspiciously like a blindfold with which she was trying to cover my eyes. On going in, the scent of biped game gripped my olfactory sense. 'Damn it, my beauty, what brush have you been browning? There's a masculine odor here?'

"'What are you saying, friend? It's nothing, the musty air of the night, perhaps. I'll open the windows.'

"'And that half-smoked cigar? You smoke cigars? Since when have you been a Spaniard?'

"'It was my brother, yesterday evening, who forgot it.'

"'Oh, your brother—he's precocious, smoking in the crib—what a libertine! To pass directly from the teat to the cigar—bravo!'

"'My older brother, I tell you!'

"'Oh, very well—but you're carrying a walking-stick with a golden handle now? The fashion's out of date!'

"'It's my father's stick, which he left behind yesterday.'

"'It appears that the entire family called in yesterday? Russian boots! Your poor father doubtless left these behind too, yesterday, and went home barefoot? Poor fellow!'

"At that last thrust, the noble girl threw herself at my knees, weeping, kissing my hands, and crying: 'Oh, forgive me! Listen to me, I beg you! My dear, I'll tell you everything; don't be angry!'

"'I'm not angry, Madame; I'm quite calm and composed—so why are you crying? Your little brother smokes, your father has forgotten his cane and his boots, all that's quite natural; why should I get angry? No, believe me, I'm calm, quite calm!'

"'How cruel you are, Albert! Please don't push me away without hearing me out. If you knew! I was pure when I was free of need. If you knew how far hunger and misery pushes you....'

"'And sloth, Madame.

"'You're cruel, Albert.'

"At that moment, there was a mighty sneeze in a nearby closet.

"'Tell me, my lovely she-wolf, is that your father, who left that sneeze here yesterday? Please, have pity on him—he's cold, he'll catch a chill. Open up, then!'

"'Albert, Albert, I beg you, don't make a fuss in the house; they'll send me away; I'll be taken for one of *them*. Please, don't make a scene!'"

"'Calm down señora; have no fear of a scene; when I make a drama, I choose my hero. But that dear collaborator must be cold; it's impolite, let me open the door. Monsieur Adventurer, come in, please, so that I won't cause you any inconvenience! To stay there stark naked, in a cold room, in epizootic weather! Monsieur, that's how one catches cholera!'

"'By what right, Monsieur Carabin, do you come to disturb honest folk at dawn?'

"'At dawn...rosy-fingered; Monsieur is making poetry...a trifle classical, alas. By what right, you ask? I was about to ask you that. But, at any rate, you're very fortunate to get out of this Tour de Nesle alive.

"'My God! What do you mean?'

"'Nothing.'

"'Albert, you're a villain to treat me like this!'

"'My beauty, you're rather foul-mouthed this morning. Now, then, Monsieur intruder, get dressed without fear. Just now, you asked me who I was; first, tell me who I am, and I'll tell both of you what you are. Our trinity doesn't have a very holy appearance, and all three of us, although fundamentally quite honest, seem to be rather nasty individuals: you, a night-prowler, Madame a prostitute and me, what at court is called a courtier and in Shakespeare a Pandarus. But to reassure you, with respect to myself, don't believe any of it; I'm like Lindor, a simple bachelor,[110] Albert de Romorantin, my family is well-known. I thought that Madame had some modesty in her face, I brought her love, but I was mistaken; it's money that's needed, isn't it?'

---

110. In Pierre Beaumarchais' *Le Barbier de Séville* (1775).

"The brave unknown was only a short fellow, ugly and going grey, scarcely terrible in appearance, and, take my word for it, very well-dressed.

"'My dear young man,' he said to me then, 'I like your frankness; your manners are distinguished; I can see that you come from a good family. Although in the right, you've treated me well; let's be friends.' He murmured in my ear: "I, myself, am the Vicomte de Bagneux. Yesterday, I met Madame and followed her, and went up to her. I would not have done, old as I am, if my doctor, Dr. Lisfranc,[111] had not specially prescribed coitus to dissipate an oppression of sanguine congestions.'

"'Dr. Lisfranc, my professor of clinical medicine! Oh, bravo! Madame, I'll thank him on your behalf; it's him, you see, who is sending you such a noble clientele. So, Monsieur, you prefer amour to the waters at Barège?'

"'Yes, in this season. But my dear student, like me, you're still hungry; will you have breakfast with me at the Palais-Royal? I make the offer wholeheartedly.'

"'I can refuse nothing to a gallant man, Monsieur; I shall be your table-companion.'

"Estelle was weeping.

"'Let's leave right away, my young friend.'

"'But have you paid Madame? On public bridges one does not pay; with women, it's the other way around; it's the common ones that one pays.'

"'Albert, you're vile!'

"'Adieu, my little concubine; I won't hold this adventure against you,' the Vicomte said to Estelle, protectively.

"'Adieu, Rosebud!' I said to her in my turn; 'adieu, stainless virgin, angel of candor and frankness; adieu, timid adolescent; adieu, *belle de nuit*!'

"'Laugh, trample me underfoot, Albert! I'm guilty—but be generous; you'll come back this evening, won't you? I'll tell you everything; I'll tell you why..."

111. Jacques Lisfranc de St. Martin (1790-1847) was a noted surgeon and gynecologist.

"'A plague on it!'

"'Come back, Albert, I beg you!'

"'My angel, when I have some money, tell me your tariff.'

"Then, Estelle fell unconscious. We left.

"What a delightful breakfast I had with that gallant man! I'm still intoxicated by it; I can still feel my mind disturbed by the Spanish wine."

"Albert, you address yourself to any woman that comes along; you go looking for love on the street—and then you complain?"

"No, no, I'm not complaining, my dear Passereau!"

"I not surprised by your poor opinion of women if you judge them all by that standard. It's exactly as if one assessed the beautiful climate of France by the rainy skies of Paris."

"No, no, it's not by means of matters of detail that my intelligence weighs up their intrinsic value, it's by general studies; I know what I'm taking about. I've known, like you, pyramidal virtuousness; I know the cloth of which virtue is made; I know the warp and the weft of it; I've reduced it to lint."

"If I thought that you believed all that, I'd be offended, but you're talking nonsense—or, at least, it's your breakfast that's talking. Then again, its fashionable to play the rake; it's an old custom to slander women, so one slanders them. Charles IX hated cats antipathetically, so, courtiers, valets, all the way down to the meanest bourgeois, in order to give themselves a regal air, an inclination, a dash of courtly style, felt ill at the sight of a tomcat. So, cats are traitors, infidels, murderers—what do I know? as the adage says, which has become as popular as Captain Guilheri or Marlborough. Henri III detested the female sex, he required catamites! Quickly, everyone who is anyone also requires catamites—all and sundry, all the way down to the street-porter, who on Sundays, has his own and cries out against women; but Henri III is already a long way away, and old. Slandering women, like madrigals, is obsolete—it reeks of the provincial, you see?"

"O illusions, illusions! My poor Passereau, you're a novice; poor boy, it hurts me to see it. The merest beggar-woman you see, you immediately make into a star, a pearl, a flower! You purify her, you sanctify her. You really are very amusing. O illusions, illusions!"

"If they're illusions, I implore you not to take them away from me; that would kill me. What is life without them? A squeezed sponge, a skeleton laid bare, a dolorous nothingness."

"Foolishness!"

"You see? It's the first liaisons at the beginning of life that give permanent direction to our heart and our thoughts. You despise women because you've only known despicable women, or those who have appeared to you as such. Heaven has willed that I encounter everywhere on my path none but choice souls, full of glory and virtue; I judge the unknown by the known. If I'm mistaken, is that a bad thing? Allow me my error; but frankly, look, tell me: do you believe that my Philogène is not a simple and naïve person, a devoted friend, a faithful lover? Oh, I'd put my hand in the fire...."

"No, no, Passereau, don't put anything in the fire! How long have you been attached to Philogène?"

"About two months."

"Good—I'll give you another month, and you can tell me your news. That's the usual duration: three months."

"Albert, you're offending me!"

"Adieu, Passereau—in a month!"

* * * * * * *

This entire conversation, word for word, had taken place while two students were descending the Rue Saint-Jacques. They were not Montaigu capettes[112] but two spirited young men, similarly dressed, with large books under their arms, emerging from the amphitheater.

One of them, Passereau, the orthodox one, had a calm and

---

112. The students of the Collège de Montaigu, part of the Faculté des Arts at the Université de Paris were known familiarly as "capettes" because of the distinctive capes they wore.

dreamy expression, and wore a costume imitative of German students: long hair like Clodion le Chevelu,[113] a small cap, a turned-down collar, a fine and short black frock-coat, spurs and a Nuremburg pipe. The other, the loquacious Albert, expansive and gesticulating, wore his grey hat titled over his ear, a red scarf round his neck, a long black velvet surcoat with metal buttons; his flower-like mouth and his swaying gait gave him the appearance, the attitude and the bold and graceful style that is known as "swagger," which is possessed to a marvelous degree by Andalusian *majos*.[114]

II.
Mariette

Passereau encounters a salamander. The sala-mander's moral; he proves that women doom young men by making them acrobats. Mariette the soubrette. Passereau is genteel. Coarse scholastic jokes. Initial suspicions. Colonel Vogtland's message. Altercation with an excited courier. Another moral.

The two students separated abruptly in that fashion; for opposite reasons, both of them felt pity in their hearts, and considered one another reciprocally as mad; each of them went his own way, with a tear in his eye for his friend's blindness; they were both sincere—a rare thing in this day and age.

On the quai, Passereau leapt into a cab.

"Where to, Monsieur?"

"Rue de Ménilmontant."

"Damn! That's a long way."

"Not as far as Saint-Jacques de Compostelle."

"Or Notre-Dame-du-Pilier."

---

113. A fifth-century Frankish king, the first of the Merovingians.

114. Spaniards of the lower classes who dressed flashily, in a traditional style deliberately contrasted with the "Frenchified" progressive elite, in order to put on airs.

Then, cracking his whip to get the horses moving, the coachman began singing lines from the bolero in *Contrabandista*:

> *Tengo yo un caballo bayo*
> *Que se muere por la yegua*

Immediately, Passereau supplied the next two:

> *Y yo como soy su amo*
> *Me muero por la mozuela.*[115]

The coachman was surprised by the reply.

"Are you Spanish, Señor?"

"No."

"You certainly look it."

"People often say that."

Passereau had a hint of exoticism and a southern complexion. The bourgeois guard even thought his appearance dangerous to a monarchy, and in time of civil disturbance he had been arrested several times for the crime of walking and wearing an illegal suntan.

"At least, Señor, you've lived in Spain, and you speak Castilian."

"Neither one nor the other."

"Whoever has not seen Spain is blind, and whoever has seen it is blinded. Señor, have you the desire to make a journey there?"

"I long to do so, my good man, but I dare not; I'm afraid of losing the rest of my reason there, of killing the love of my homeland. I sense that after having been the guest of Cordoba, Seville and Grenada, I would no longer be able to live anywhere else. Epaña! España! Espanña! Like the tarantula, your bite drives one mad! But you, my friend, you're Spanish, and you've

---

115. These words are from a popular song, but they do not appear to have any connection with "El Contrabandista," by the Spanish tenor Miguel García,

left Spain?"

"No, Señor, I'm Don Martínez of Cuba."

This Martínez was the incombustible man who had been exhibited in an oven some time before in the Jardín de Tivoli. Having promptly excited the curiosity of the city, he had had to live; the poor fellow had become a cab-driver—and Passereau marveled at having encountered the famous salamander in such a bad way.

"Pardon my indiscretion, *Señor Estudiante*, but you seem to be as pensive and sad as a man in love. Your face is imprinted with a chagrin more profound than that of the *caballero desa-morado*. It breaks my heart to see you thus."

"Amour! Amour! *Me muero por la Mozuela!*"

"Take care, my dear young man, take care! Listen to me: the advice of a wretch is sometimes worth following.

"Be as fragile, as fickle and as perfidious as a woman; don't put too much into love—you'll doom yourself! Don't let that passion take the highest place in your heart—you'll doom your-self! Don't build it on the ruins of others—you'll doom your-self! Don't abnegate for its sake anything that might charm you and attach you to life; at the first shock, you'll fall flat.

"Women aren't worth the sacrifice. Love as you sing, as you mount a horse, as you gamble, as you read, but no more. Don't count on them for anything stable, noble and pure; you'll be too bitterly disappointed.

"Forgive me for saying all this to you; it's not to deprive you of your youthful illusions and make you old and blasé, it's to save you from many stumbling-blocks, many pitfalls. In this case, the advice of a wretch is often worthy of being heard and followed, especially when the wretch in question has been made wretched by those in whom you are investing your sole faith and your life; one makes one's own destiny.

"Like you, I believed, I gave myself, I doomed myself! I was once young and brilliant, like you: take care! They're the ones who made me an exile, an acrobat and a servant."

"Oh, have no fear of that for me, my good man; when love,

the sole cable that still moors my boat to the bank, is broken, it will all be over; I shall kill myself!" Then Passereau cried: "Stop, friend! Stop! We're going past the house: this is it, here, at this door." He slipped an écu into the hand of the incombustible man and leapt out of the cab.

"*¡Viva Dios! Señor Estudiante, es V. m. d. muy dadivoso, muy liberal! Dois os guarde muchos años. Caballero,* you'll be sure to remember Martinez the *Calesero* and the number of his cab?"

"Yes, yes!"

The aristocratic student went into the indicated house, and Martinez, very jovial, turned round, singing a bizarre verse half in Castilian and half Gitano.

> *Cuando mi cabalo entró en Cadiz*
> *Entró con capa y sombrero,*
> *Saleron a recibirlo*
> *Los perros del matadero.*
> *Ay jaleo! Muchachas,*
> *Quien mi compra un jilo negro.*
> *Mi caballo esta cansado...*
> *Yo me voy corriendo.*

With the gravity of a senator or an usher complimented by the tribunal, Passereau went upstairs, head bowed.

"Oh, it's you, handsome student!"

"Bonjour, my little Mariette."

"Bonjour."

"Your mistress has gone out?"

"Is not my mistress yours too, a little? Say our mistress. She's just gone out; you're out of luck."

"Where has she gone at this hour?"

"To the riding-school, for her lesson."

"The beauty rides? I don't know."

"She has a lovely seat, it's said."

"You're laughing, you bad girl! Do you always play the

comedy soubrette like this?"

"Anyway, my friend, she'll undoubtedly be back soon; yesterday's lesson was a long one; I presume that today's will be short. Come in and wait for her in the boudoir."

"All right; but come and keep me company; only my own, I get very bored in a boudoir—and besides, it's anticanonical. Come along then, coquette—are you afraid?"

"You're a medical student."

"Medical students are well known for their philogyny. I've never eaten a woman alive."

"Pooh!"

"Sit down closer, I beg you. Good! Let's chat. I've been fond of you for a long time, you know."

"An honor without profit—Madame has the enjoyment of that amour."

"You see, Mariette, after Europe, Asia, Africa, America, Oceania and Philogène, your mistress, it's you, the seventh continent of the world, that I like best."

"An honor without profit; the seventh continent of the world is greatly in need of a Christopher Columbus."

"Shameless hussy! Then let me kiss your beautiful shoulder, your ivory shoulder! And your breasts—a true Parnassus with a double peak, but a Romantic Parnassus."

"Monsieur, 'it's in vain that a reckless man at Parnassus....'"

"What, Mademoiselle, you know our anti-phlogistic Boileau![116] But let go—what are you afraid of, puerility? My good friend, don't you know how much I love your mistress? Know, then, that when I love a woman, when she has received my love, that I have received her faith, and that is why Philogène is faithful to me."

"Or is taking her lesson at the riding-school."

"I keep for her the strict fidelity that she keeps for me."

116. Nicolas Boileau-Despréaux (1636-1771) was nicknamed "the lawgiver of Parnassus" because of his elaborate pontificating on the arts, and was a doyen of the Classicist school to which the Romantic Movement formed in opposition.

"Oh, that's not reassuring. O my honor! O my virtue! Help! Let me go! Monsieur Passereau, I'm going out for a moment. If someone rings, will you open the door and ask them to wait."

"I'll open the door, even if it's thunder in person."

As son as he was alone, the student's physiognomy suddenly changed; it became grave and somber again, as was its custom, but even graver and more somber; doubtless the malicious but playful remarks that Mariette had made about her mistress had cut him to the quick, and had awakened a suspicion in his confident mind in spite of him. No tomb had ever contained a more dismal body than that boudoir.

Suddenly, wrenching himself out of that immobile concentration, that internal life, seemingly using his hand to chase away some invisible thing that was obsessing him, the phantom got up—and his face suddenly lit up, like a hooded lantern suddenly opened wide in the darkness. Then he rushed into the drawing room, ran to a miniature of a woman attached to the mirror, and covered it with kisses.

Having strode back and forth on he parquet for a long time, he finally stopped at the piano, started playing frantically and singing, in a low voice, the *Estudiantina*:

> *Estudiante soy señora,*
> *Estudiante y no me pesa,*
> *Por que de la Estudiantina*
> *Sale toda la nobleza.*
> *Ay sí, ay no*
> *Morena te quiero yo,*
> *Any no, ay sí*
> *Morena muero por ti!*
>
> *¿Rosita del mes de mayo*
> *Quien te ha quitado el color?*
> *Un estudiante pulido,*
> *Con un besito de amor.*
> *Ay sí, ay no*

Morena te quiero yo
Ay no, ay sí
Morena muero por ti!

Con los estudiantes, madre!
No quiero ir a paseo,
Porque al medio del camino
Suelen tender el manteo.
Ay sí, ay no
Morena te quiero yo
Ay no, ay sí
Morena muero por ti!

Boom! Boom! Boom!

"*Carajo!* What churl's breaking down the door like that? What are you making that din for, man? Can't you see the door-bell?"

"Monsieur, I've been ringing it for ten minutes."

"Damn! I didn't hear it, my friend."

"Personally, I could hear you singing in Latin very clearly. Is it you, Monsieur, who are Mademoiselle Philogène? There's a letter for her, from Colonel Vogtland."

"From Colonel Vogtland? Give it to me!"

"I have strict instructions only to give it to her."

"Drunkard!"

"Drunkard? It's possible—but I'm French, from the département of Calvados; I'm not decorated, but I have the honor. To hell with the Prussians! That's how it is!"

"Go away, clown."

"Oh, don't play the dressmaker here. No bluff, or I go back to the tobacconist's!"

"Go away!"

"What I say is that it's by way of a pledge; only, try to have a little more circumspection in your words, and don't forget the tip."

"A tip? Wretch! To go put more color in your stomach, or

turn your intestines to parchment? Go away—you're drunk."

III.
Fickle as the Waves.

Doubt. Anguish. Passion. Indiscretion. More doubt! Poor Passereau has mistaken a kept woman for an angelic maiden. He was the lover of the heart and Vogtland the paymaster. Torture. Limpidity is only mud. Abomination.

Behold Passereau alone, death in his soul and the letter in his hand: what is he to do? Doubt and suspicion assail him; all is lost!

Trust is like an old building, it collapses as soon as one takes an ax to it. Who is Colonel Vogtland? What is his connection with Philogène? Why this message?

After long indecision, a long struggle, in order to escape his anguish, he will break the seal of that letter, which either contains the condemnation without appeal or the solemn acquittal of his ignominiously-suspected mistress, crushed beneath the weight of an infamous accusation in the secret tribunal of his heart.

"Me, break this seal? No, I'm mad!" he cries. "Once opened, what will I do if Philogène emerges from it covered in glory? I'll have made myself vile in her eyes, jealous, indiscreet and treacherous—for it's a treason to break a seal, in order to leap into a prudish confidence with boots and spurs. Yes, but what if I'm mistaken? Who will tell me? Who will tell me that I'm not the great dupe of a profligate woman? Must I wait until someone shouts it at me in the street? Until I hear laughter in doorways when I pass by with her on my arm? Until I hear murmurs around me: 'That's today's student—I preferred the one before last—it's shameful, a well-bred young man going out in broad daylight with such a whore! Ugh!' Oh, that would be atrocious! I need to know what's what; I need to know what I can believe in!

"Let's see...but no! Isn't it madness to want to get to the

bottom of it? Who digs into things, digs his grave. For if this letter forbids me to have love and esteem for that woman, if it enjoins me, in a loud voice, to trample her underfoot, to hate her...oh, what a frightful awakening! I'd die of it! For I need my Philogène, I need my love, for my life! It's all the oil in my lamp; to spill it would snuff it out! It would kill me!

"Passereau, Passereau, how ungrateful and cruel you are to that woman! Why accuse her, why soil her—why? Do you know what this note contains No! By what right, then...?

"Passion is leading me astray.

"Oh no, for sure, that sweet, good, naïve friend, that candid child, who incessantly overwhelms me with love and promises, whom I heap with attention, with joy, with happiness, and to whom I have dedicated my youth, my life, to whom I've sworn eternal fidelity—oh no, for sure, she couldn't, she wouldn't dare deceive me! No, no, Philogène, you're pure and faithful!"

Then Passereau, going to a window, caused the letter to yawn beneath his fingers, and paraded his inflamed eye, his avid gaze, inside.

At every word he deciphered, he stamped his foot and uttered profound groans.

"Great God! Presentiments are your voice, then, for your voice alone never lies! Horror, horror! Oh, Philogène, it's atrocious! Me, who, this very morning, would have answered for you with my head and my life, who would have called God a liar if God had accused you! Oh, it's abominable! Oh, it's vile! But take care! No one knows what remains in my heart, when love is no longer there. Take care!

"All well and good, Monsieur le Colonel; all well and good, Monsieur Vogtland; I'll be there too, at the rendezvous! All three of us will be there!"

Exhausted, he let himself fall upon the sofa and, with his head hidden in his hands, he wept hot tears.

Word for word, this is what the fatal letter contained:

My dear Philogène,

A mutiny of the non-commissioned officers in my regiment has recalled me urgently to Versailles; don't expect me tonight. It won't be possible for me to return for two or three days. So, on Sunday, be at the Tuileries at five o'clock, under the chestnut-trees by the marble boar; as soon as I get down from the carriage I'll run to join you there, and we'll go to dinner together. Three days without seeing you is a long time, and very cruel, but duty is duty! Love me, as I love you.
Adieu! I cover your entire body with kisses,

Vogtland.

Is it possible to find anything less ambiguous and more overwhelming? After the anguish of doubt, Passereau rediscovered conviction. He was convinced!

But all that suffering was not enough; it was not enough to know that the woman he had surrounded with such delicate attentions and on whom he had lavished the purest love, was deceitful, base and vile. He was destined, that day, to go from one fall to a more terrible one, to lose everything, forever, irredeemably. The woman he had thought chaste, innocent, modest; the woman she had only approached tremulously; the woman whose virginity he had thought it a crime to take, a crime to have troubled the limpidity of her beautiful soul, had finally appeared to his eyes in all her hideousness: libertine, filthy, lascivious and foul!

Wanting to leave her a note, and rummaging in a drawer in search of an inkwell, he discovered—Heavens, I'm ashamed to say it—morocco bound, gilded and illuminated, an Arétin![117]

I shall leave you to imagine his consternation. He was

117. One of the works of "Pierre l'Arétin"—i.e. Pietro Aretino (1492-1556), a famous licentious satirist generally credited with being the inventor of literate pornography, probably his brothel-set *Dialogues.*

crushed. His lips, drawn back swollen and slack, expressed the most profound disgust, and his breast, oppressed, uttered etching hiccups.

At that moment, Mariette returned, and Passereau suppressed his dolor.

"Madame hasn't come back yet?"

"No, my dear."

"Riding pleases her..."

"She's very fond of it."

"Alas, your laughter is strained—you're very chagrined, very agitated; believe me, my ear master, if you're suffering, don't suffer for her. You poor young man, if you only knew...but has someone been here while I was gone?"

"No...oh, except that someone brought this letter on behalf of Colonel Vogtland."

"From Colonel Vogtland! I'm no longer astonished to see you so disturbed. Poor young man, you've been grossly deceived!"

"Adieu, adieu, Mariette!"

"Have courage, I beg you—you're breaking my heart. Shall I tell her that you came?"

"Yes, but nothing more!"

Ashamed, he slipped out of the house furtively, like a lecher leaving a brothel.

On the boulevard, at the cab-stand, he found Martinez again, threw his arms around him and kissed his cheeks, to the great astonishment of the passers-by.

"Oh, my friend, you were right. Fickle as the waves! Let's go, let's go! Whip, whip, flat out! I need to stun myself."

IV.
Albert Preaches

Our student is decidedly splenetic. Splenalgia. He creates an artificial climate, sun and punch. His imagination attaches no dread to the approach or the

*consequences of death, nor gives him an artificial sen-
sibility. Ratiocination. Aretology. He goes to sleep.*

Having arrived home, Passereau fell back into a cold and
mute torpor. Habitually, his handsome face bore the imprint of
a profound but benevolent melancholy, but no longer: his eyes,
having become haggard, are engulfed by furrowed brows; his
mouth, in a rictus of agonized laughter, is closed by jaws that
are clenched and interlocked; his muscles are tense; he comes
and he goes, his hooked fingers clutching and breaking everything they encounter; he is bowed down and gathered within
himself like a wounded wild beast; his head, hanging down,
rocks incessantly from one shoulder to the other, like the head
of a presbyopic eagle seeking to catch sight of prospective prey;
his entire expression is grim and infernal.

Suddenly, he opens the windows; leans out precipitately
and brutally closes the shutters, recloses the windows and the
interior blinds—now that he is in complete darkness, he bursts
out in joy. Then he lights lamps, candles, chandeliers, torches,
makes up an enormous fire in the grate in spite of the heat, and
rings. One of the domestics comes running.

"Laurent, bring up a bowl, sugar, lemons, tea and five or six
bottles of rum or brandy—and go right away to the home of my
friend Albert, to ask him to come here immediately. Simply tell
him that it's the day of my oblivion."

The domestic did not seem in the least astonished by all the
preparations, the illumination or the haste; he did everything he
had been instructed to do, as if it were an everyday, ordinary
service.

Indeed, all that was nothing new; Passereau had a thousand
eccentricities and this was the one he repeated most frequently.
Of nervous temperament, impressionable and irritable, as soon
as the atmosphere was not uplifting, the sky serene, the sun
bright and hot, he suffered profoundly. What he needed was
a warm climate, pure air, burning sunlight—Marseilles, Nice,
Antibes, a Spanish sun, an Italian life! So, chagrined at being

constrained to live in the foggy, damp, cold, dirty, noxious and clammy capital city, he was only waiting to receive his degree to abandon it forever; his dream was to go abroad, to take up residence in Colombia or Panama.

Thus, on rainy, cloudy and dull days, when the north wind blew, when there was fog or drizzle, he fell into a depression, he sighed vaguely, wept and sank into ennui, a desperate apathy; his sole refrain was: "Life is exceedingly bitter, and the grave serene—down with life!"

It was then that he summoned oblivion with horn and halloo. "There are only three things one can do," he said, "at such a time, all three of which lead to oblivion: get dead drunk, sleep dreamlessly or kill oneself. Let's get drunk and go to sleep; to kill oneself requires more effort than I'm disposed to make just now; we'll see about that later. I no longer want this stupid daylight; let's close the windows and the shutters. Fire! Light! Tobacco! Punch! Laurent, stock me up with food and come to see me from time to time. As soon as the sun reappears, and life can be beautiful, come and let me know, and open my windows."

Sometimes, the bad weather having dragged on, he remained thus cloistered for a month, perpetually surrounded by lamps and torches, inundated with splendid artificial daylight, reading, sometimes writing, but most often drunk and asleep. His door was closed, except to Albert, who, quite gladly, came to imprison himself with him, not moved by the same delirium, the same suffering, the same desolation, but for the originality of the fact, to experience life against the grain for a while and parody the rectilinear bourgeoisie—and above all, lured by the punch and cigarettes, in which Albert had a religious faith, a profound conviction and a very distinguished consideration.

Passereau's "days of oblivion" were not always the effect of fog, rain and black weather; often, as in this case, they were provoked by ennui, frustration and chagrin.

Suddenly, precipitate footsteps, roulades and bursts of laughter on the staircase announced Albert's arrival.

"Bonjour, my old Passereau, so we're having a 'day of

oblivion' are we? I sensed it his morning in your somber expression; in sum, it suits me quite well, for, to be frank, although it's might habit to take everything lightly, I'm still upset by this morning's adventure; I won't be sorry to submerge myself for a while."

"Oh, my poor Albert, if your adventure of this morning is weighing you down, mine this afternoon is killing me!"

"What do you mean?"

"You gave me a month, didn't you? Thanks! I'll give you back thirty days."

"Oh, a delightful burlesque! What do you think about the virtue of women now? What do you think of your saintly Philogène? Delightful, delightful! Tell me about the farce."

"Alas! Let's not talk about it—you're hurting me. Pour me some punch, and cheers!"

"You know, Passereau, you're not very gallant. You might have waited for me instead of drinking alone; that's nearly a bowl that you've swilled alone like a anchorite."

"Life is very bitter and the grave serene. Drink, drink! Pour, I beg you; I still have my reason, I'm still thinking, I'm suffering! Pour, then, Albert!"

"It would grieve me, my friend, word of honor, if I were capable of grief, to see you taking things to heart so. What is it, after all? A nasty, vulgar, trite misadventure! You want to love absolutely—forget it, I beg you; everywhere, you'll find nothing but despicable creatures; everywhere, under an enamel of candor, a vile, coarse clay; young deceptive, unfaithful, sordid mistresses; old, adulterous and spiteful wives. Never go prowling around women to weave sentiment, but only for joyful or sanitary reasons, and then only when nature shoves you in the back."

"Albert, in the aridity of your soul, who wouldn't recognize a doctor? Take up your scalpel, talk muscles and phlebotomy, or shut up—you make me feel pity."

"And besides, you see, reasoning logically, it's absurd to demand fidelity and constancy of a woman; it's absurd to appeal for an impossible virtue that is utterly antipathetic to her constitution. It's in the nature of woman to be fickle, flighty, intoxicated, inconstant—she has to be, it's necessary, and that's all right. It's necessary that she not weigh herself down, analyze, think, be over-subtle; it's necessary that she be always and forever intoxicated, drawn from one thing to another, passing lightly over the past sufferings of her wretched condition, and for her not to glimpse the abjection into which society has driven her."

"Life is very bitter and the grave serene! Pour the drink, Albert, poor—I'm finally tottering; pour, I can feel reality fading away."

"You'll always be unhappy if you're unable to stop at superficialities, if you always want to dig and dig. The excavations of thought and reason are deadly; they're always followed by cave-ins. One can't live and think; it's necessary to renounce one or the other. Who could bear existence if, like you, they were eternally thinking? For it requires so little to drive one to death: to look at the sky, a star, and wonder what it is: then our misery, our baseness, our intelligence, flat and limited, appear in all their splendor. Once feels pity for oneself, and disgust; weary and ashamed of oneself—the self of which one was stupidly proud—one summons oblivion to one's aid, more incomprehensible still...."

"It's necessary to arrange oneself in such a manner that everything flows over one, as over a suit of armor. It's necessary to take everything cheerfully; it's necessary to laugh."

"For pity's sake!"

"It's necessary to laugh at everything, to flit from flower to flower, from pleasure to pleasure, from joy to joy...."

"To begin with, what is a joy, and a pleasure? I don't know."

"It's necessary to satisfy one's whim."

"I'll satisfy it!"

"Gamble, spend, lust, lie, be insouciant, idle, a charlatan."

"Punch, Albert, punch! Pour, then! Enough morals! Believe me, death resides in my bosom; I'm not cut out for life."

"But isn't it a pity to see a young man, one of the most brilliant in his career, endowed with a superior intelligence, whose mind can embrace the world and the sciences, debasing himself, crouching down, brutalizing himself, annihilating himself, because of the treachery of a girl. Isn't it pitiful? So wake up, Passereau!"

"Death resides in my bosom; I'm not cut out for life, I tell you."

"Is there any shortage of girls, to take your revenge? Is there any shortage of places on earth, if you're sick of this one? Go away, travel, see everything, hear everything, touch everything, taste everything—and if, in your journey, you've found nothing that attracts you, no sky that agrees with you, no creature that charms you and captivates you, if you haven't found a beautiful beach on which to pitch your tent, come back—only then will it be time to seek oblivion; you'll be doing the right thing, and I'll applaud you!"

"Life is very bitter and the grave serene! Pour, Albert! Punch! Punch! Let me sleep! Another glass of oblivion. Tell me, do I still have my tenacious reason?"

"Not in human eyes."

"Finally!"

Then Passereau dragged himself, as best he could, to his bed, and fell upon it heavily. Albert finished off the bowl they had started and left, striding in zigzags, and holding himself as rigid and perpendicular as the tower of Pisa or the steeple of Saint-Severin.

V.
Incongruity.

Awakening. Good King Dagobert put his trousers on backwards.[118] *What an infamous thing an umbrella is!* De torrente in via bibet.[119] Su majestad christianisme el verdugo.[120] *Absurdities! More absurdities. Yet more absurdities. Always absurdities!*

The next morning, very early, a few candles were still burning in a sinister fashion. Pale and decomposed, Passereau was cursing and swearing on his bed, hanging on his bell-pull.

"Damn it! The swine isn't coming up! If you need an aubade, I'll give you one! Is he dead, damn it? Am I the bellringer for the dead? God's justice! The bumpkin's making love in the arms of some slut!"

And crying out like a fanatic, he yanked the bell-pull: *Ding! Ding! Ding!*—so hard that the copper wire snapped, leaving the string dangling from his hand like the stump of an épée in the hand of a champion.

"My God, Monsieur Passereau, you're very impatient this morning!"

"God's truth, Laurent, you'll have me damned—I've been ringing since three o'clock. What were you doing—waiting for the resurrection? Quickly, get my clothes ready; I need to go out."

"I wouldn't have thought you'd be up so early after last night's ceremony. The weather's very bad—it's raining cats and dogs; you can't go out."

---

118. There is a lewd French popular song about the Merovingian king Dagobert being in such a hurry to get out of a woman's bedroom that he puts his trousers of backwards.

119. A line from G. F. Handel's *Dixit Dominus* (1707), based on *Psalm* 110. It corresponds to the words "he shall drink of the brook," but the reference is, as will become obvious, ironic.

120. Roughly, "His Christian Majesty the executioner."

"My clothes, I tell you; I need to go out, even if the weather's bad enough to put mythology to shame."

Laurent was obliged to dress Passereau; he was so absorbed and preoccupied that he could not see what he was doing.

"I beg your pardon, Monsieur, but like your head, your trousers seem to me to be the wrong way round."

"It's a royal and Merovingian distraction!"

"Alas, my dear Master, you're troubling me; your expression is even sadder and more anxious than ever. You're in a black mood."

"The deepest."

"Will you be back for dinner, Monsieur?"

"I don't know."

"I swear to you that it's raining hard enough to give the universe pleurisy."

"I hope it dies of it!"

"Wait a minute—at least take a carriage or an umbrella."

"An umbrella! You insult me, Laurent. An umbrella! The sublimated comfort of civilization, a talking blazon, an incarnation , quintessence and symbol of our epoch! An umbrella! A miserable transubstantiation of the cape and the épée! An umbrella! You insult me, Laurent! Adieu!"

Buffeted by a gusting wind and uninterrupted rain, a genuine drenching stock-clearance of the heavens, there goes our medical student, skirting the cloister of a house on he edge of the narrow and deserted Ruelle de Saint-Jean or Saint-Nicolas, below the Boulevard Saint-Martin. The poor devil was streaming with water, like a tipped-up chamber-pot. He had crossed the city— him, such a hydrophobe!—with his head bowed, paying no attention to the douches showering him. Passers-by burst out laughing on seeing him patrolling thus, with the compunction and impassivity of a dervish, but he did not hear anything; with a firm tread he marched through the torrents and rivers that were in his path, even if he had to wade hip-deep, and sometimes, he declaimed fervently the well-known lines from *Hernani*:

Oh, when jealous love boils in our heads,
When our hearts swell and fill with tempests
What does it matter that a cloud in the sky
Can hurl storms and lightning at us as we go?

After a rather long conversation at the door, it was finally opened to him.

"What does Monsieur want?"

"El Señor Verdugo."

"Pardon?"

"Oh, sorry. Is Monsieur Sanson at home?"[121]

"Yes, he's eating breakfast. Come in."

"Monsieur, Accept my regards."

"I'm at your service. What urgent business brings you to me in such a storm?"

"Urgent, as you say."

"Let's see!"

"I beg your pardon for my boldness in taking the liberty of coming to disturb you at home, and to request a service within the dependence of your functions.

"Within the dependence of my functions? I only render cruel ones."

"Cruel to the cowardly, gentle to the strong."

"Indeed."

"I've come to ask you, although it's very demanding on my part, being entirely unknown to you—at any rate, I'm ready to pay the costs and expenses that are due to you."

"Explain yourself?"

"I've come to ask you humbly, I would be very obliged for the condescension, to do me the honor and favor of guillotining me."

"What's that?"

---

121. This would be Henri Sanson (1767-1840), the fifth of the six Sansons whose dynasty of executioners outlasted kings, republics, and an empire; he inherited the position from his famous father Charles in 1793, just in time to catch the end of the Terror, and held it for 47 years thereafter.

"I would like you to guillotine me."

"That's taking a joke too far, young man. Have you come to insult me in my own home?"

"Far from it; listen to me, I beg you; the step I'm taking coming here is grave and serious."

"If I didn't fear being impolite, I'd tell you straight out that you seem to me to be demented."

"I would seem so to many others, Monsieur but I swear by all your esophagotomies that I'm sane and in full possession of my faculties—it's just that the service I'm asking of you is not customary—which is to say, not within the customs of the crowd, and whoever does not do exactly what the crowd does is a madman."

"You're honest, I see. I'd certainly like to believe that you have no intention of insulting me, nor of reminding me of my fatal mission, which I've put out of my mind. I'd like to believe that you aren't demented."

"You do me justice."

"Are you not an artist? By your costume...."

"I am if you are, for we are colleagues, to some extent; my studies are not without numerous relationships with yours; like you, I'm a surgeon, but you're my master in amputation; my operations are less solemn and less sure than yours, and that's what brings me to you."

"You do me honor."

"No, for between you and me there is the distance and the connection of a thread to a distaff; I operate naively with my hands, while you, Monsieur, amputate mechanically, on an industrial scale."

"You do me honor. But in sum, what can I do to help you?"

"I would like you, as I've already taken the liberty of telling you, to guillotine me."

"Come on, let's be serious—no more of that, it's a poor joke."

"Please believe that it's the unique and serious reason for my visit."

"An original joke!"

"Without further exordium, this is the situation. For a long time I've wanted to cut short my existence, which wearies me and importunes me, but I was stubbornly deluded by a vestige of hope; I continually put it off. Finally, a wretched street-porter of human miseries, I snapped under the burden, and have come to set it down."

"You, weary of life so soon! Why, my friend?"

"Life is facultative; one can tolerate it in certain conditions—on the condition of happiness—and one can, certainly, with every right, cut it short when it brings us suffering; existence was imposed upon me against me will, just as baptism was imposed upon me; I have abjured the baptism; today, I want to reclaim oblivion."

"Are you alone, devoid of relatives?"

"I have too many of them."

"Are you devoid of fortune?"

"The golden calf is not my god."

"Have you no love for science?"

"Science is merely false semblance; science is vain."

"Have you no passion, then, no lover?"

"I have lost both, forever."

One doesn't give up on love at twenty, and the loss of a lover, great though it might be, is not irreparable."

"I'm world-weary."

"Your eyes shine and your heart beats; you're not that."

"I've seen everything clearly."

"Even love?"

"Love! But what is love, then? It's poeticized for the usage of fools. A gross periodic need, a shrill cry of nature, eternal nature that reproduces and multiplies, a brutal penchant, a carnal intersection of sex-organs, a spasm! Nothing more! Passion, tenderness, honor and sentiment all come down to that."

"What odious language!"

"Yesterday, I did not talk like this; yesterday, I was still deluded, but many veils have fallen from my eyes since yesterday: no one was fuller of illusions and beliefs than me, no one was more sentimental than me. The greater and more beautiful the dream has been, the more dolorous the dull awakening is. Yesterday, I was sensitive, today I'm ferocious. I loved a woman with all the force of my being. I believed that she had love for me, but she was playing with me. I thought her honest, but she was vile and base. I thought her naïve, angelic and pure, but she's a whore! O rage! And love alone, love for that woman, retained me in this world!"

"I understand your chagrin, but all of that is nothing very serious. It's one of the thousand adventures of a young man that has befallen you; don't get the habit of killing yourself every time. I don't see anything in it that could drive you to suicide. I know that a disappointment is often very painful, but a young man as strong and intelligent as you, ought to overcome the greatest adversities. This is merely childish, and if we are to live again after the life of this world, you'll certainly be very ashamed when you've found existence and composure again, to have sacrificed yourself for something so petty and trivial."

"As I told you just now, it's not only since this catastrophe that I've resolved to quit life; love alone was holding me back from the accomplishment of my design. I don't even say that if I had been more fortunate, that if I had found a worthy and faithful woman, then my project might not have faded away eventually—but today, everything has changed, and I've sworn to have done with it; an oath is irrevocable."

"You can see that I was right to think you demented."

"Demented! Tell me, then, you who have your share of reason, what are we doing in this world? What's the point? Why are we here? What are we prideful wretches, except passive means of reproduction and destruction?"

"You are demented!"

"But all that is merely a digression—let's get back to the object of my visit. I beg you, once again, therefore, to grant my request: I'll pay all your expenses in full."

"What request? What, exactly, do you want?"

"Not much—I simply want you to guillotine me."

"Never my friend—that's pure extravagance. Even if I wanted to, I couldn't, alas. May God preserve me from ever inflicting the slightest scratch on you."

"Why is that? Don't you have the right and the liberty to do whatever seems appropriate to you? Society has given you an instrument; are you not its ultimate musician? Can it forbid you to do a favor for a friend?"

"It's true that society has made me heir to a scaffold—or, rather, that my father bequeathed me a guillotine as his entire movable and immovable patrimony, but society has said to me: you shall only play that instrument for those we send to you."

"It's society that has sent me."

"No it isn't."

"Yes, it's my disgust for society."

"You've come directly to me, my dear chap, and that's not the right way. You've taken the high road instead of the winding track. Go back, and come via the gendarmes, the cells, the jailers and the judges."

"You're determined not to do me this favor? You're not very obliging to me. But good God, I'm not asking that you do it in broad daylight, in the heart of Paris, in the middle of the Grève; this is a private affair, a domestic matter—here, in a corner of your garden, or wherever you wish—it doesn't matter. I'm accommodating, you see."

"No, it's impossible—to kill an innocent man!"

"But isn't that common practice?"

"I'm not a murderer."

"How cruel you are to refuse something that costs you so little!"

"I'm not a murderer!"

"Perhaps I've offended you, but I didn't mean to; you're not a cut-throat, I know; your humanity and philanthropy are renowned."

"If you sincerely desire to die, suicide is easy, with any weapon that comes to hand—a pistol, your scalpel...."

"No, no, I won't like that—there's not sufficient guarantee of success; the arm might flinch and strike awkwardly; one might disfigure oneself, butcher oneself—in sum, miss the mark, as they say."

"This is becoming annoying."

"But your means is so quick and so sure; I beg you, in compensation for the many men whose necks you've been obliged to sever, I implore you, decapitate me amicably."

"I can't."

"But that's absurd."

"Don't be insulting!"

"All right, if you don't want to do it of your own free will, you'll be obliged to kill me! If it's necessary to go via the gendarmes and judges, that's the way I'll go!"

"Then I shall be your humble servant."

"You don't want to—that's all right. Why not? Because I'm innocent—a fine invalidation! After all, if it's only a crime that's required, that's easy and simple. All right! We've no lack of Kotzebues in France, its Karl Sands that are in short supply!"[122] Glory to Karl Sand! Monsieur executor of noble works, until we meet again, in a month at the most...be ready, have your blade sharpened by the cutler, I don't want anything to go wrong."

"God keep you from me, young man!"

"If France has its bland writers sold abroad, its bland detractors of its young generation, its Kotzebues....it shall also have its avenger, its Karl Sand.

"Glory to Sand!!!"

VI.
Further Incongruity

Passereau writes to Philogène. Petition to the Chambre. He proposes the establishment of a factory.

---

122. The conservative German dramatist August Kotzebue was murdered in 1819 by a student named Karl Sand, which provided the excuse for the statesman Klemens von Metternich to issue the repressive Carlsbad Decrees, which clamped down on academic freedom.

The advantage the government will obtain from the new monopoly. Is Passereau demented, or still in possession of his reason? A problem to resolve.

"Laurent, put this letter in the post. Will it get there before five o'clock?"

"No, Monsieur, it's too late."

"Have it taken by a messenger, then."

"'To Mademoiselle...Mademoiselle Philogène, Rue de Ménilmontant.' Mademoiselle Philogène! I deduced correctly from your manner—you're in love, my dear master!"

"Brilliant! Very much in love. Look, send this at the same time to the Chambre des Communes—I mean Députés—for delivery to the secretariat."

"Also urgent?"

"Very urgent."

In the first, Passereau requested Philogène not to go out after her meal, his intention being to visit her at six o'clock in the evening.

The other was a petition to the Chambre, of which this was the substance:

TO MESSIEURS LES DÉPUTÉS

Messieurs,

Please do not find it impudent that a young cabin-boy like me should take the liberty of addressing, from the depths of the hold, a very humble item of advice to the old pilots of the three-master of the representative government.

At a time when the nation is in penury and the treasury in the third stage of phthisis, at a time when the delightful tax-payers have sold everything, all the way down their braces, to pay taxes, surtaxes, countertaxes, retaxes, supertaxes, archtaxes, customs duties, counter-duties, tallies and retallies, capitations, archcapitations and humiliations; at a moment when your indebted monarchy and your pear-shaped sovereign are shivering in shirt-sleeves, it is the duty of every good citizen to come to their aid, either by means of gifts and voluntary paraguantes[123] or by industrious advice. Not yet being of age, it is by the latter and unique means that I may try to run to your aid.

"Help yourself, and the heavens will help you."

I therefore want to propose a new tax, which will not completely ruin the nation; a new duty that will not weigh more heavily upon the classes of pure race, hidalgic and archiepis-copalian, than the rabble; a new duty that will not prevent the populace from eating something with its bread, when it has any; a new and very moral duty; a phenomenal duty, levied not on dice or lotteries, nor suet, nor prostitutes, nor tobacco, nor judges, nor the living, nor the dead; in sum, a new duty only speculating on the moribund. It is necessary, as far as possible, to impose taxes on luxury items.

For some years, suicide, inoculated into our customs, has become common practice; a few malevolent individuals, doubt-less Carlists or republicans, have attributed its rapid increase to the misfortunes of the times. They are imbeciles! As I said, therefore, suicide has become very fashionable, almost as fash-ionable as in the third century of the Christian Era. Like dueling, suicide is incorrigible; instead of letting it go entirely to waste, it seemed to me that it would be wiser to make it a milk-cow, and to draw a creamy revenue from it.

This, then, in brief, is what I propose. The government should establish, in Paris and every departmental capital, a large factory powered by water or steam, in order to kill, by a gentle and agreeable method, after the fashion of the guillotine, people weary of life who wish to commit suicide. If the body and the head were to fall into a bottomless basket and be imme-diately borne away by the current of a river, it would avoid the expense of funeral directors and gravediggers. In dry regions, one could adapt the apparatus of the windmill. The machine

---

123. Tips.

would be supervised and operated by the resident executioner of the locality, as a cure supervises his parish, without an increase in salary.

According to calculations made and checked, ten people per day, on average, commit suicide in each département, which makes 3,650 a year, and 3,660 for leap years; in sum, for France, an annual total of 302,950 in ordinary years and 303,570 in leap years. Assume that the usual price to be paid is set at 100 francs—for one can have private cabinets for aristocrats, which would carry a higher price, like nuptial blessings in a church. 302,950 at 100 francs per head would produce 30,295,000 francs—a very attractive and plump return, which would be a great relief to the public treasury.

This establishment would satisfy all social requirements with regard to the salubrity, the morality and the needs of the State. Firstly, with regard to salubrity, because the vital air would to longer be vitiated by the putrid miasmas and pestilential exhalations emanating from the bodies of suicides strewn and putrefying on the roads; typhus would thus be warded off; secondly, with regard to amenity, because citizens would no longer be exposed to the risk of bumping their heads on the legs of people hanged from the trees in walkways and public gardens, or being crushed by the fall of those plunging from widows; thirdly with regard to the would-be suicides, because they would have the certain guarantee of the comfortable and convenient success of their attempts, and because the country would be preserved from hideous and crippled individuals disfigured by unsuccessful attempts; fourthly, morality would benefit therefrom, firstly, because it would be done legally and in the most profound secrecy, and what is more, suicide, becoming a bourgeois and industrial affair, would promptly fall into desuetude; as witness actors, who have been in decline ever since they became citizens and not pariahs outside society and its laws; fifthly, with regard to the needs of the State, because it would pour enormous sums into its leaky coffers.

Civilization, Messieurs—as the eloquent *Constitutionnel*,

your newssheet, says—marches in giant strides; and it is France, Messieurs, which is the drum-major of that civilization with seven-league boots. It is therefore up to France to set the world an example of initiative in all social improvements, in all progress and all philanthropic establishments; and it is up to you, Messieurs, the representatives of that glorious France, the lanterns of this Age of Enlightenment—as the *Constitutionnel*, your newssheet, says—to welcome this important project generously. By doing so, you will pour abundance into the treasury, and joy into the hearts of suicides, who will no longer be reduced, as I am myself today, to disemboweling themelves ignobly with a knife, blowing their brains out with an arquebus, or asphyxiating themselves with their window-fastenings.

I have the honor of being, Messieurs, with all the considerations that are due to you. Your very humble and very submissive admirer

Passereau Student of Medicine,
7 Rue Saint-Dominique d'Enfer

The Petitions Committee will doubtless make its report on this in one of its imminent sessions. It will be very regrettable if it is not taken under consideration, and if the Chamber does not put it to the vote.

VII.
Oh! That's Nasty!

Passereau visits Philogène. Passereau dissimulates and banters. They go for a walk among market-gardens. Passsereau, as if by chance, encounters the house of his foster-father and takes Philogène into an unkempt garden. Is there anything sweeter than solitude? Passereau allows a glimpse of his suspicions, and Philogène protests. He dissimulates and banters. They moment of the crime draws near; let us pray to God! Under the lime-trees. Notice, if you please, that this is not a romance to out-do Jean-Jacques and Richardson.[124]

Exactly at the appointed hour, Passereau arrived. On opening the door to him, Mariette exclaimed, with a surprised expression: "Why, it's you my handsome student! Alas, even though it gives me great pleasure to see you, I thought you were a man of heart, and I hoped very much that you would not set foot here again. Do you love her, then, in spite of everything? You can't extricate yourself, then?"

"I hope, at least, my friend, that you haven't said anything about me that could have made her suspect the slightest change in me with respect to her?"

"Nothing!"

"You haven't told her that I was here when the colonel's note arrived?"

"No, I wouldn't do that."

"Is she in?"

"I ought to say no. My God, how little nobility you have in your soul! Or how you must grieve to be so unfortunately smitten with ardent love for a...you're deceived, and you're not unaware of it!"

"In accusing me thus, do you know the oath I have sworn? Do you know what I have in my heart? Reserve your reproaches, Mariette."

"Come in—she's in her boudoir."

Philogène, having left the table, was lying on her sofa, ruminating her dinner, sated and replete, like a cow that has eaten too much clover.

---

124. Jean-Jacques Rousseau's philosophical love story *Julie; ou la nouvelle Héloise* (1761) was one of the century's great best-sellers, and an important precursor of French Romanticism; its emphasis on authenticity is echoed and parodied in Passreau's sentiments. Its epistolary form echoed that of the novels of Samuel Richardson, including *Pamela; or, Virtue Rewarded* (1740), which were enormously popular in France and scathingly parodied by the Marquis de Sade.

"Oh, there you are, Monsieur Flighty—you're going to clip your wings! For three gigantic days, your lover has not see you."

"You call me flighty very cheaply, my dear; when I come no one's here; Madame is out riding, or in town."

"Is riding a bad thing? You seem to be offering me a reproach."

"Far from it."

"Come here then, so that I can kiss your forehead; let's make peace—come on, then! Poor friend, it seems to have been an eternity...."

"You don't only study equitation at the riding-school, do you? You must have theoretical treatises.

"Yes, I think I have...."

"How high do you jump? What position to you adopt?"

"Why aren't you addressing me as *tu* today? That hurts me; it seems that you're annoyed."

"Annoyed! By what?"

"How do I know?"

"Are you not always the same for me?[125] Are you not always good, loving and sincere?"

"Always! You'd wound me by doubting it."

"Me, doubt you? You wound me in your turn."

"How happy I am—I can see that you still love me. I love you too, my Passereau."

"How could I not adore you? A beautiful body, a beautiful heart! Could I love anyone worthier than you? Oh, no—as God knows!"

"How generous you are, my darling—your words uplift me."

"Happy—exceedingly happy—is the honorable young man who whom Heaven sends, as it has to me a pure and faithful woman!"

"Happy—exceedingly happy—is the pure woman to whom Heaven sends a noble and gentle soul!"

"Life must be easy and delightful for them."

"You're smiling to yourself, Passereau."

125. Passereau reverts to addressing Philogène as tu rather than vous at this point.

"Can't you see that it's intoxication? You're laughing, my beauty."

"Can't you see that it's joy? Don't push me away like that, my love; how cold and sad you are in my company today, you who are so free with caresses—and such loving caresses!"

"What do you want me to do?"

"I'm not asking for anything, Passereau, but I can scarcely kiss you on the cheek. When I touch your lips you recoil, and your eyes fix up no me and frighten me! Are you ill? Are you in pain?"

"Yes, I'm in pain."

"Poor love! Would you like some tea?"

"No, I need to breathe and walk; let's go out."

"It's dark—it's very late."

"So much the better."

"I don't feel like it."

"As you wish, then."

"No, no—don't get annoyed; I'll do anything you want."

They went out. Passereau, mute, took his mistress by the arm, as a contrite husband takes his wife's arm when the honeymoon is over.

"But why are you determined to go this way, along ugly and deserted streets? Let's go along the Boulevard Beaumarchais instead."

"My dear, I need solitude and darkness."

"Where are you taking me through these market-gardens? The Chemin des Amandiers leads to the cemetery—are you taking me to the grave?"

"I'm very fond the calm of this quarter, where I spent my childhood with the wife of a market-gardener, my foster-mother.[126] Look, do you see that kind of hut over there to the right? It's my foster-father's palace. I haven't shaken his hand

---

126. It was customary at the time for the children of aristocrats to be handed-over to proletarian wet nurses in order to spare their mothers the tiresome obligation of breast-feeding, sometimes creating a curious relationship with the foster-family that was capable of lasting a lifetime.

for some time. What serene memories all this awakes in me! If it weren't so late, I'd go in to embrace him, but these good people without vices and ambition go to bed with the sun and get up with it, in contrast with the corruption that desires long nights to be abridged and hides during the day like the owl. Look at these beautiful gardens, these flourishing vegetable-plots—all this is theirs. Look, over there—the avenue where I took my first steps. Here's a field, almost uncultivated; once it was a rich nursery; it belongs to a young collier. Here's a gap in the hedge—let's go in and walk beneath those lime-trees for a while."

"What a strange idea! Aren't you afraid that we'll be mistaken for nocturnal thieves?"

"Have no fear, my love, no one around here is awake. Besides, I'm known in the neighborhood and to the owner of the field, where I often come to take solitary walks in the spring."

"How dark it is; if I weren't with you, Passereau, I'd be scared!"

"Child!"

"How easy it would be to cut someone's throat in this deserted quarter!"

"Wouldn't it?"

"Who would come to your aid? You could cry out all you liked."

"Crying out would be a waste of time."

"Passereau, shall we take that path through the raspberry-bushes?"

"No, no—let's go into the limes."

"Passereau, you're making me trot like a mule. I'm very tired."

"Let's sit down. Do you know any greater happiness than for two people to be alone in a deserted spot, especially at night? Not to hear anything in the darkness that surrounds you; to have nothing but brushwood and tones around you; and in that profound silence, to listen to the palpitations of the heart that responds to the beating of your own, a heart that only beats for you! In the midst of all that bleak and indifferent nature, to press in your arms a being all on fire, for whom one has forgotten all others, who intoxicates you with the kisses of her bitter mouth and condemns all others! Who puts you to sleep with her magnetic caresses!"

"Oh, Passereau, it makes one swoon! I was ignorant of all the charms of the silence of the fields; it's the first time that I've talked about love with the man I love under the heavens. You know, we shall always hold one another imprisoned—oh, how much better that is than four walls!"

"If we grow old, faithful to one another, when we are near the grave, with what joy we shall count this night among our beautiful memories, for our liaison is not a matter of a day!"

"Union, constancy for life!"

"Before long, my uncle, my guardian, will give me an account of my wealth and emancipate me; as soon as I am free, my beauty, we shall go to ask the law to unite us, and if my guardian wants to enquire as to your dowry, I shall enumerate your virtues."

"How you fill me with joy! What generosity to a poor woman who can only love you! Oh, may that day come so. I long for us to live together. Don't hug me like that, Passereau, I'm dying—you'll kill me!"

"Kill you, beautiful homicide! It would be a great pity."

"Yes—for it's a rare thing for a woman to love you for yourself, and only you/"

"Like you, you mean?"

"Spare my modesty."

"For it's a rare thing, a woman as sincere, naïve and faithful as you."

"You're making me blush."

"Take care—one only blushes out of modesty or shame."

"My God! How abruptly you're treating me this evening. What brutal politeness, what reserve! When I kiss you, or when I caress you, it's as if I were touching you with a red hot iron; you flinch. Perhaps you have something against me? Could I have hurt you, or displeased you, my love? You must speak; you must tell me what is in your heart; let your chagrin out; I'm your friend; you mustn't hide anything from me—I'll console you."

"Poison and treacle at the same time!"

"What do you mean? You know that you're hiding something from me; I'm causing you to suffer, annoying you. My God, what a mystery! Speak to me, speak to me, I beg you! Tell me what I've done; I'll put it right, even if it kills me! You have something against me? Someone has slandered me—people are so perverse!"

"Yes, it's true, my love, not that I believe it—someone has slandered you. Wicked people have blackened you; they've said that you're deceiving me, that you're joyfully unfaithful to me. But I affirm that I don't believe it, that it's a infamous lie!"

"Very infamous! You must have little confidence in me, you must hold me in wretched esteem, for a few spoken words to change you so much and so suddenly in my regard, and throw you into such distress."

"I've been told that you're fickle, but I assure you that it doesn't trouble me at all."

"That's not very liberal on your part. People could say the most admissible or the most shameful things about you, and I wouldn't even hear them. You don't trust me, Passereau!"

"Yes, yes, my beauty; I appreciate you."

"Me, your friend, deceive you! Never! I love you; I love you more than anything. Passereau, you're my God! We're bound to one another by an oath more sacred than all the oaths made before humans—and I would betray that oath? Me! Can you believe that, Passereau? Ingrate! Unjust! You make me angry! What have I done, then? I'm a woman of honor, Passereau, know that! But what infamous person could have accused me of infamy? Me, cloistered, retiring, only using the liberty that you generously leave me. No, no, Passereau, believe me—I'm worthy of you, I'm innocent! I take Heaven as my witness! Clear in my conscience, I shall not seek to wash away this dirty slander. Do you know how I love you, do you understood the extent of my love for you? I love you so much—so much! Rather than betray my duty and my faith, rather than betray you, I would kill myself!"

"Yes, better death than ignominy."

"Oh, you're frightening me. Don't look at me like that! Your eyes are rolling like the eyes of a tiger in the darkness."

"Would you like to come with me, my love? I have a strong desire to go on a journey—I'm bored with Paris."

"When?"

"As soon as possible. We can leave tomorrow, if you wish. Let's go to Geneva."

"Tomorrow, Sunday? I can't."

"Why, what's keeping you here?"

"Nothing, except that I promised to go to dinner with a relative; if I miss it, he'll be very upset."

"Let's go on Monday, or during the week."

"No, my friend, I'm very sorry, but I still can't; I've promised relatives to spend a few days with them, near Paris. I can't get out of it on any pretext whatsoever."

"You don't want to?"

"I can't. Your face is becoming terrible, Passereau! Why are you squeezing my neck like that? You're hurting me; you're doing me harm!"

"Forgive me, forgive me—I forgot myself. It was a spasm. I'm in pain; I'm thirsty!"

"Let's go back to the house, I beg you. If you were to fall unconscious, what could I do for you here? What difficulties I'd be in!"

"Hold on, my love, before leaving, to make me feel better, go pick me a few fruits from those espaliers covering the wall over there, at the end of the path through the raspberries; you'll give me great pleasure."

"My God, Passereau, how you're trembling as you speak to me—you're in a great deal of pain, then?"

"Yes!"

"This path, do you mean?"

"Yes, go straight ahead, and have no fear."

Scarcely had Philogène taken a few paces than she disappeared into the darkness. Passereau lay down on the ground, putting his ear to the ground, listening in frightful anxiety.

Suddenly, Philogène uttered a heart-rending scream, and there was a dull sound, like that of a human body falling, a loud splash, and groans that seemed subterranean. Then Passereau got up, with the convulsions of a man possessed by a demon, and precipitated himself into the path through the raspberries at top speed.

As he drew closer, the cries became more distinct: "Help! Help!"

Abruptly, he stopped, knelt down at leaned over a large well, at ground level. The water, far below, was agitated; from time to time, something white appeared at the surface, and exhausted plaints escaped.

"Help, help, Passereau—I'm drowning!"

Bent over, silent, he listened without responding, as one leans over a balcony listening to a distant melody. The moans gradually died away.

Then, in a loud voice, further amplified by the echo of the well, Passereau howled: "You want help, my beauty? That's all right—wait! I'll go tell Colonel Vogtland to bring you an Arétin!"

Philogène replied with a frightful strangled plaint. She was still floating on the surface, tearing at the ruined wall with her fingernails.

Then Passereau, with a great effort, detached the broken stones of the well-head, one by one, and dropped them on top of her.

Everything became silent again—and, as bleak as a funereal vision, he went back and forth beneath the lime-trees all night.

VIII.
A Perfectly Natural Ending

A chapter that might seem superfluous, which the reader could have been spared—when I say "the reader" I'm speaking hypothetically, for it would be presumptuous of me to think that I might have even one, even if it were a Russian. Without one, though, the story of Passereau would have been immoral; it is always necessary for a crime to receive a punishment.

The little red-haired man had sounded half past five on the clock of the Château des Tuileries, for the little red-haired man reappeared a little while ago with the new host and his master mason. Passereau was walking through the wood of chestnut trees; to kill time, he had gazed on two or three very indigestible great newspapers. Our handsome student was getting considerably annoyed in that damnable place, continually assailed by various schismatics and forced to endure the declarations of love of those bourgeois of Gomorrah. Finally, he saw a man running in all haste toward the pedestal of the marble boar, then going around and around it, craning his neck and looking in every direction with a sullen and nonplussed expression.

The individual in question, tall and stout, enveloped in a blue overcoat, ornamented by an insignificant face cut in two by an enormous moustache, was carrying spurs, which he clinked impatiently, and a long riding-crop, with which he caressed the bones of his legs. Having studied him momentarily and looked him up and down like a horse at a fair, Passereau approached him and bowed.

"Are you waiting for someone, Monsieur?"

"What does that matter to you, young man?"

"It matters a great deal."

"You're exercising a scarcely honorable profession, Monsieur—do you think I didn't see you spying on me just now?"

"You're waiting for a woman, aren't you?"

"No, Monsieur, a hermaphrodite."

"You're at odds with the dear heart."

"Puny wretch!"

"It's true, Monsieur, that my corpulence is no match for yours, and that on a butcher's scales you'd weigh more than me, but your coarse voice and your big bones don't frighten me. Believe me, the sole domination is that of intelligence, and yours, Monsieur, seems to me to be ill-formed."

"What is this twittering?"

"Admit it; there's no shame in it—you're waiting for a woman, Mademoiselle Philogène, but you'll wait in vain, saving a miracle, and this world's age of miracles is past. She won't come; I assure you of that, on my head and my blood."

"In any case, you won't prevent it!"

"Don't swear anything, Monsieur le Colonel Vogtland."

"Who told you my name? Triple damn! This is beyond me."

"You only expected to find one marble boar here, and you've found two, one of them alive, and ready to give you a good fight."

"No, Monsieur, I've only found one boar, and one pig."

"You'll give me choice of weapons."

"You have a point of honor too? Everything's mixed up. You're playing the soldier; my child, you do better to play the ironmonger. You're lucky and unlucky—you'd have a rude apprenticeship with me!"

"Enough of that patronizing tone—you make me feel pity, swordsman as you are."

"Triple damn! The shopkeeper's rebellious!"

"Don't come near me, Monsieur le Carabinier—you reek of the stables!"

"Puny wretch! If I weren't holding myself in cheek, I'd give you a slap with my boot."

"Look at me hard—do you think I'm trembling? One man's as good as another; don't you know what will can do? Your emperor, whose soles you kissed, quivering, like me, has left you in the lurch. Oh, we're no longer in the times when the mercenary lorded it over the world and boxed the citizen's ears, the times when one took one's hat off to a recruit or a sentinel. You'll fight me!"

"If you want, I'll fight—which is to say, literal translation, I'll kill you."

"Who knows? There are bad barbers who cut the face. Tomorrow morning, what meeting-place? Boulogne or Montmartre?"

"Montmartre."

"What time?"

"Your choice."

"Eight o'clock."

"So be it. Although one man's as good as another, as you so elegantly put it, I don't like anonymity. Would it be possible to know who you are?"

"Passeareau."

"Your estate?"

"Student."

"Triple damn! Shoddy goods!"

"If we weren't fighting to the death, I'll bring my medical bag and offer you my services to patch you up, but if, by chance, you'd like me, after your death, to open you up and embalm you, please regard me, honorifically, as your devoted servant."

"Monsieur is a physician? We're colleagues."

"I am that to many people."

"Monsieur is a *carabin?*"

"Monsieur is a *carabinier?*"

"But triple damn it, the donzelle isn't going to come?"

"I presume not."

"Perhaps I was wrong to get angry so soon? Perhaps you were sent by Philogène to tell me that she couldn't get to the rendezvous? Perhaps she's ill?"

"Very ill."

"Perhaps you're her doctor?"

"Yes, her doctor."

"I offer you a thousand apologies for having treated you so badly. I didn't know...."

"Tomorrow morning, at eight o'clock, at Montmartre!"

"But please, tell me, how is she? What's happened to her? Is she in great danger?"

"What weapon will you bring?"

"Answer me, I beg you—you're cruel, you, her doctor! For an insult offered unwittingly, for an insult for which I've apologized—answer me, if she in danger of dying? Is she in agony? I must run...answer me, then! If you only knew how much I love her...!"

"If you only knew how much I loved her!"

"She's my mistress."[127]

"She's my mistress!"

"Her, Philogène?"

"Her, Philogène."

"Triple damn!"

"Great God!"

"I'm flabbergasted!"

"I'm amazed. Having intercepted your agreeable pullet, I've come, in her stead, to ask you by what right, since she's been mine for three months, my only love, you've intruded in my amours?"

"Tell me, first, since I've been keeping her for two years, by what right you're intruding on mine?"

"What! You were keeping her?"

"Yes, and very costly it's been."

"Oh, the slut! I did well..."

---

127. This is, of course, a fortunate confirmation, from the viewpoint of the story's morality. Suppose that the incriminating letter had, in fact, been forged by the envious Mariette during her temporary absence, and that Philogène had been completely innocent. Passereau, who did not wait for a conclusive falsification of that hypothesis before murdering poor Philogène, would have seemed a perfect idiot if that had turned out to be the case—or, to be strictly accurate, an even more perfect idiot than he actually seems. Not, of course, hat a nice girl like Mariette would ever have dreamt of doing any such thing....

"What have you done?"

"Nothing."

"Swear to me, for I need to know where I stand, that you've been her happy lover for three months."

"I swear it by Christ! But swear to me, too, that you've been her happy keeper for two years."

"I swear it by Martin Luther!"

"Calumny!"

"You're the liar!"

"I don't say that you haven't attempted the climb, but you've been dismissed."

"I don't say that you haven't stormed the breach, but you certainly had no reward for your siege."

"What weapon shall we choose, definitely?"

"You definitely want to fight? Surely, to avenge yourself for her rigor?"

"No, for her favors."

"Peasant!"

"Dandy! Do you think, then, that you can snatch my beloved from my arms with impunity? Oh, you're much mistaken, Monsieur the belated Céladon![128] You've come to sow tares in my field. You've come, no doubt, to solicit love with gold. The woman is mine; I shall keep her; I want her; I need her; I shall defend her against her aggressor; I shall maintain her! Death to whoever comes, like you, to poach on my land! You'll fight, Monsieur le Colonel!"

"I'll kill you."

"We know your ill-famed reputation. But as I can't handle a sword and am also myopic and can't fire a pistol, I beg you to submit yourself to hazard!

"As you wish—all the more so as I don't like murder and it would be murdering you. However courageous you might be, the fight would be unequal; what could you do against an infallible skill? Hazard alone can balance the odds; I refer myself

128. The shepherd lover of the eponymous heroine of Honoré d'Urfé's vast pastoral romance *L'Astrée* (1607-27).

to hazard. But reflect, my dear friend; I don't like to go to the dueling-ground for a trivial reason; I'll tell you, frankly, that I have no vehement desire for vengeance; I don't hate you, and if you would care simply to assure me that you'll renounce forever any pursuit of live regarding Pihlogène and troubling my possession, I'll accept your word of honor—for I can see that you're a man of honor. All will be said and done. Will you?"

"You're joking—never! We're two riders for one mare; let the survivor have her. You shan't criticize me later; like you, I have an immutable will, and don't expect any mercy—I shall be ferocious."

"Let the survivor have her! Would you care to fire at point-blank range, with one pistol loaded and the other not?"

"I don't like that."

"Heads or tails?"

"Too childish."

"Do you know any gambling games?"

"No."

"Me neither—so the chances are equal. Let's bet our lives."

"Bravo! But on what?"

"Draughts or dominoes?"

"So be it. Let's go to the nearest café."

"No, tomorrow."

"Tomorrow, tomorrow! One shouldn't put off this sort of affair."

"I have to go to dinner."

"I can't let you go; I'll stay with you. You're going to maltreat Philogène. Let's settle the quarrel right away."

"I have to go to dinner."

"Let's go to dinner—where are you going? I'll go with you."

"The first-class restaurant over there, on the corner of the Rue Castiglione. Is that all right with you?"

"Thank you—we'll each pay our share."

With that, our student and our soldier—or our soldier and our student; I leave everyone the choice of giving precedence to whoever seems appropriate, according to their taste and predilection—headed along the Rue de Rivoli. Has a better-matched married couple ever been seen going into a catering establishment to "have a ball?" One big-boned, of hyperbolic stature, who would have been able to serve, praise God, in the observatory of the late Mathieu Lemsberg,[129] a killer by the sword, that's the husband on the one hand. One small, child-like and pretty, who would have made a charming doctor for the employment of women, a killer by Broussais;[130] that's the husband on the other hand. As if for a fine party, they enclosed themselves in a very private room—I'm sure that evil thoughts came to the waiter's mind—which shows us that it's necessary not to judge by appearances. Let us avoid reckless judgments; it's easy to mistake, as in this instance, people who are intent on cutting one another's throats for people who are intent on embracing one another.

"This meal, for one of us, will be the last—the last supper," said Passereau then. "It ought to be copious, with no regard for the sumptuary regulations of the late, very constant Henri II, who doubtless overstepped the mark many a time in honor of Madame Diane,[131] and with more solid reasons, we can certainly infringe them in honor of Madame la Mort."

"I understand; you want, as we say in the barracks to have 'a good chew'—that suits me well enough; I agree! To prepare yourself for the great action to follow, to procure aplomb and audacity, you want to saltpeter the brain—that's very wise! It's what I did on my first campaign; when the day promised to be hot, I fortified myself with an intense armor of sparkling cham-

---

129. A little-known physician cited disapprovingly in a few eighteenth-century textbooks, who apparently recommended that patients should not be bled during rainy weather—although the recommendation would probably have done some good, albeit by accident, had the orthodox been willing to follow it..

130. The physician and pathologist François-Joseph-Victor Broussais (1772-1838), who worked for many years at the Val-de-Grâce, but was a convert to phrenology in later life

131. Henri II's mistress Diane de Poitiers.

pagne."

"No, it's not for that, for I'm resigned to quitting life; I'd even be sorry if I happened to win."

"Me too."

"And I'll ask you, if things come out in your favor, not to show me any mercy and to kill me without remorse."

"Me too. For life, as you rightly say, is beginning to weigh upon me constitutionally. A trooper without a war is the desolation of desolations; he's a physician without an epidemic; a Coitier under Louis XI.

"Will you please, spare us that barbarism, and leave Maître Coictier his *c*?"

"Coictier! Oh, but of course, that's a barbarism! My dear friend, it's necessary to have a tinplate mouth to pronounce that so cruelly Gallic name. Besides which, in his five-act tragedy in French verse, Casimir Delavigne invariable says Coitier."[132]

"A fine authority, your rhymer from Le Havre de Grâce!"

"Shut up, damn it! You're insulting me in the person of that nursling cherished by nine sisters, the nine Muses, the Pierides!"

Alas for the honor of the corps, it was high time the carabinier finished his feast; his voluble and prolix conversation was becoming almost as clear as Victor Cousin,[133] almost as scholarly as Raoul Rochette,[134] almost as Chinese as Rémusat,[135]

132. The variant spellings of the name of the French physician Jacques Coitier, Coictier, Coytier. Cotier or Coctier (1430-1506) created an enduring controversy among the writers of medical textbooks; Victor Hugo plumped for Coictier in *Notre-Dame de Paris* (1831), which obviously settled the matter once and for all as far as the members of the Romantic Movement were concerned.

133. The philosopher Victor Cousin (1792-1867) was a significant advocate of "common sense realism," in opposition to the German idealism favoured by most Romantics.

134. Raoul Rochette (1790-1854) was still rather obscure when *Champavert* was written, but subsequently built a significant reputation as a historian while working as a curator at the Bibliothèque Nationale.

135. The Comte de Rémusat (1797-1875) spent his childhood at the heart of the Imperial court but developed more liberal views; although Borel

almost as English as le Guizot,[136] almost as chronological as Roger de Beauvoir,[137] almost as artistic as de Lécluse,[138] and for immortality in silk stockings, it was pure scribbling.

He had, in the language of the factory, stuffed his torso inordinately.

The fact is that he had a truly academic capacity, and save for the representatives oft the people, there is hardly anyone but a camel who could have entered the lists with him with any chance—and in the state in which he was, he could have undertaken a desert crossing in perfect security—I won't say the Sahara because I hate pleonasm; that's a buffoonery common in the Asiatic society of Paris; it's as well when one makes Oriental jokes to give notice of the fact; it's as well, in such a flower-bed, to advertise risible locations.

In a corner of the booth they called the cemetery, the carabin and the carabinier had piled up the defunct bottles, and God knows how contagious the mortality had been.

There they go! There they go! Through the streets, the alleyways, the dead ends, the squares, the intersections, cluttered with vehicles and pedestrians. There they go! There they go! Through the mud, the roadways, the sewers, the boundaries, the gutters, the streetwalkers. There they go! They're going forth, colleague and companion, and one might think them a road-mender and a member of the Académie des Inscriptions

---

would have known him as a journalist, he went on to become a significant Republican Statesman until he was exiled in 1851.

136. François le Guizot (1787-1874) effectively became a negative image of Rémusat in political terms; a leading player in the July Revolution of 1830, he published two volumes of a massive history of the English Revolution in the 1820s, but only finished after being exiled in 1848.

137. Roger de Beauvoir was the pseudonym of Roger de Bully (1806-1866), whom Borel would have known as a flamboyant dandy and friend of Alexandre Dumas, whose fiction was in a similar swashbuckling historical vein.

138. Presumably Fleury de Lécluse (1774-1845), with whose work as a grammarian and translator of Plutarch Borel would have been familiar.

going to deliver a learned lecture, there they go, as it were, like "Orchestra" and "Pilaster."

Speaking of Orestes and Pylades, would you like a recipe for a highly successful farce? Firstly, it's necessary to mention those classical friends at least thirteen times; secondly, to mention acupuncture at least once; thirdly, to mention the honor of France and Napoléon at least three times; fourthly, not to forget two or three blunders regarding the Romantics, and especially not to omit making them say that Jean Racine is a guttersnipe and to make jokes about those vagabonds Goethe and Chat-qu'expire;[139] fifthly to extol Molière and Corneille, whom one must, above all, not have read, in order to make them into a cloak with the aid of which one can pass through the barrière of the public, like those veal-calves one sneaks in fraudulently by dressing them in a smock and cap. The whole in the French of Monsieur Drouineau[140] and with the rhyming couplets of the old Marquis de Chabannes—if I say the Marquis de Chabannes,[141] it's because I know he's no swordsman, and as I don't like dueling, which doesn't mean that I don't like eating, I'm choosing the least possibly dangerous personality and would never, like Boileau, push audacity so far as to call a cat a cat.

Having arrived at the Café de la Régence, they rapidly demanded a game of dominoes; the fatal moment had come! God—for there is no chance, even in dominoes—was about to decide, in his wisdom, which of the two should die: the carabin

---

139. A tortured pun on the name of Chateaubriand, perhaps comprehensible if one renders it the second part of the name aub'riant [suggestive of "cheerful dawn"]

140. Gustave Drouineau (1798-1878) achieved great success in 1829 with the best-seller *Ernest ou le travers de siècle*, in spite of its extraordinary length. Borel was not to know that his success would be meteoric, and that he would end up creating his own religious sect in despair.

141. French history is replete with glorious Seigneurs de Chabannes, but the one Borel has in mind is Jean-Frédéric de Chabannes, Marquis de Curton (1762-1832), who was fond of issuing bombastic proclamations calling for the "regeneration" of France during the 1820s, often including samples of his awful poetry.

or the carabinier.

Vogtland was sometimes as arrogant as a corporal instructor, and sometimes rather expansive.

"Double six, twelve, 1812—that's exactly the year in which I had the advantage of losing my venerable father."

"No silliness, Colonel; let's play seriously," growled Passereau, "and above all, don't play dominoes upside-down."

Our student was thoughtful and intense, wrapped up in himself, like a certain contemporary poet, or a little guinea-pig feeling the cold.

A gallery of bourgeois surrounded their table and took an interest in their game. If those worthy people had had any suspicion of what was at stake, they would certainly have been terribly fearful, and would have taken their umbrellas—or somebody else's—and fled at top speed, unless they were edematous or gouty.

Vogtland, like a companion of duty, used to drinking by the liter, who happens to have gone into a café while on a spree, was swallowing his seventeenth cup when the game ended to his advantage. At that conclusion, Passereau smiled agreeably.

"Come on, let's get on with it," he said, "I'm in a hurry to get it over."

"What kind of death would you prefer?"

"Blow my brains out."

"All right. I'll go to my house in the Rue de Rohan to get my pistols. Walk slowly and I'll catch up with you. Where are you going—the Champs-Élysées?"

Vogtland soon reappeared; silently, they went along the great avenue and went through the Barrière de l'Étoile . A few houses further on than the tavern of the Neapolitan Graziano, where one can eat excellent macaroni, they turned off the road and went down into the fields below the causeway. It was pitch dark. There, having gone along a cloister wall for some distance, Passereau said: "Let's stop here. This will do, it seems to me."

"You think so?"

"Yes."

"Are you ready?"

"Yes, Monsieur: arm yourself. Above all, no delicacy: if you fire into the air, you're a coward."

"Have no fear; I won't miss."

"Aim at my head and my heart, please."

"With pleasure; but lean on the wall in order not to recoil, and count to three. I'll fire on three."

"One, two...wait! We've bet our lives for a woman?"

"Yes."

"She belongs to the survivor?"

"Yes!"

"Listen carefully to what I'm going to tell you, and do it, I beg you: the last wish of a dying man is sacred."

"I'll do it."

"Tomorrow morning, go to the Rue des Amandiers-Popincourt; at the entrance, on the right, you'll see a field terminated by an avenue of lime-trees, enclosed by a wall made of animal bones and a living hedge. Climb over the hedge, and then take a long path through raspberry bushes, and at the very end of that path you'll find a well at ground level."

"And then?"

"Then lean over and look into its depths. Now do your duty, here's the signal: one, two, three!"

CHAMPAVERT,
THE LYCANTHROPE
(PARIS)

For society is nothing but a fetid marsh
Whose bed alone, undoubtedly, is pure and limpid,
But where that which is dirtiest, most
Venomous and stinking, always rises to the top!
And that's a pity! It's a real heap of yellow
Grass, dry reeds spread out in sheaves,
Putrid stems, split mushrooms rotting,
Thorny bushes, tangled in all directions,
Green mire, foamy and swarming with insects,
Toads and worms, which infectious wrinkles
Furrow, all strewn with drowned animals,
Whose bellies appear, black and gross.

Gérard[142]

I.
Testament

To Jean-Louis, laborer

I shall die alone, my dear Jean-Louis, I shall die alone!
However, I have received and made a promise. A man has said

---

142. This poem does not appear to have been published elsewhere during
Gérard de Nerval's lifetime.

to me: "You are weary of life, you hate it determinedly; when you are ready, we shall flee it together. I'm ready, Jean-Louis, I tell you; already I'm bracing myself for the heap—and you, are you ready? Be ready, simple as I am, I believe in an oath! Men change their minds. However, you cannot have forgotten so soon, and besides, I've often reminded you of that night, when, after having wandered for a long time in the forest, appreciating all things at their price, distilling, analyzing and dissecting life, passions, society, laws, the past and the future, breaking the deceptive optical glass and the artificial lamp illuminating it, we were sickened with disgust before so many lies and miseries. Then, if you care to remember, we wept; yes, you wept! Your hand clasped mine, and we swore an oath. If I remind you of all that it's not because I want, notwithstanding, to urge you to make the leap—no, it's simply so that you will no longer criticize a resolution that was once yours. Alas, your new fate has undoubtedly altered your ideas; that, doubtless, is what binds you to life, like an oyster to a rock. You have left the stupid profession that your father imposed on you; employed, you have deserted your employment and renounced smiles and ministerial tips; depraved as you are, manual laborer! You have been so vulgar, as they say, driven by the instinct of the hunting-dog to leave the city where the enchanter dwells—as the impudent sycophants say, the foxes eating the cheese of an ignorant, haughty bourgeoisie, which shows off its wattle like a turkey—in order to return to the field from which your ancestor departed to cringe in the city. You have been so vulgar, as they say, so crazy as to prefer the coarse smock, laced-up trousers and loincloth to the vice-like waistcoat and asphyxiating frock-coat, wound by a captain, to the cravat like a yoke, to boots soaped with talc and icy, ephemeral gloves; a costume of ease, in which one is comfortably swaddled, provided that one does not use either one's hands or one's feet, that one does not turn one's head, that one does not lean either forwards or backwards, or kneel down, or sit down. You have exchanged the great village for the village, the spectacle of the vaudeville for that of nature, the streets lined from top to bottom with boutiques, swarming with fiacres and tumbrils, for deserted roads, rustically bordered by living hedges and forests; there, there is nothing to gossip about, no posters in shop windows, nor jugglers on the sidewalk, nor sirens exhaling eau-de-vie, nothing urban! A man, left to himself, solitary and silent, is reduced to thinking.

You're happy now, happy, a happy ploughman—what a scandal! Perhaps happiness can prostitute itself thus! Go, then, tell that to the wife of the three-star banker, who is going stale up there on her balcony. "Ugh!" she would say, her gorge rising and spitting. "Ugh! A happy ploughman! A dimwit!" For myself, without flattery, I understand you well enough, you and your happiness, if happiness it is. Happiness—what a derisory word! I've never encountered any man brazen enough to admit to being happy.

Once, perhaps, I too dreamed of the life that you have realized; then, I believed in the fields of the Bucolics, the peasants of the Idylls, in Favart's[143] villagers, the shepherdesses of Boucher's transoms. I said to myself, if felicity is not resident in the city, surely it finds a refuge in the fields. I thought then that if one were to have clogs on one's feet, a smock, a straw hat, that if one got up with the sun, and wielded a coulter, if one hoed or watered a field, if one followed a laden she-ass, if one ate cabbages, beans and pork, and roosted like a chicken at dusk, one would be happy, very delicately happy. I thought...but I no longer think that....

However, if I were to remain any longer among or apart from human beings, it is what you have chosen that I would choose; I would become a rustic, like you, but even more primitive, wilder; I would eat chestnut bread in the mountains of the Vivarais; I would become a bear-hunter in the Pyrenees, a charcoal-burner in the Ardennes or a woodcutter in the Alps. But today, that's not enough. What's the point, when I'd wear away my vigor in stupid labor, wielding an ax, a pick or a pile-driver? What's the

---

143. The dramatist Charles Favart (1710-1792), highly successful as director of the Opéra-Comique.

point, when my heart would become as stony as my hands? It's no longer brutalization I need, it's oblivion! But you no longer want oblivion; you want to live—so live, and I'll die alone.

So much for the promise you made me, and which you're breaking.

And so much for mine, which I'm also forswearing.

Mine is an oath sworn to a woman, to a strong woman; one day, both exhausted, locked together, entwined, my face hidden in her blonde hair, which my mouth was chewing, and with which I wanted to veil myself, we were delving deep into the past, talking about our misfortunes—or amours, I mean, for our amours had been terrible, for my love is fatal; I'm as deadly as a gibbet. Poor girl, what did I do to you? Oh, how you suffered because of me! I've been very unjust!

Let the impostors come, then, that I might strangle them! The knaves who sing of love, who garland it, who trumpet it, who make it into a chubby-cheeked child, plump with enjoyments—let them come, the impostors, that I might strangle them! To sing of love! For me, amour is hatred, moans, cries, shame, mourning, iron, tears, blood, cadavers, bones, remorse—I've known no other kind! So come on, rosy pastorals, sing of love! A derision. A bitter sham.

So, that poor woman, punctuating her phrases with heart-rending kisses, says to me, gravely and thoughtfully—for Flava is a strong woman, I repeat, a woman who surpasses all others: "Champavert, promise to grant me what I'm about to ask of you."

"My dear, I can't make such a promise."

"Oh, I beg you, promise me."

"No, I can't."

"How fearful you are—do you dread that I'll reveal a desire that will be fatal for you? Oh, you're not generous; I you see, would make you a promise blindly; that's because I love you! There's nothing in the world that I wouldn't do for you, if you said that you wanted it. Oh, it's just like a man...."

"My love, there's nothing in the world that I wouldn't do for you either, you know that full well. Speak—have I ever refused you anything?"

"I want you, Champavert, to swear to me that you will never kill yourself alone—never! On the day when you're weary of life, quickly, come find me, and simply say to me: 'I want to end it.' I will get up immediately, and we'll go out, and we'll kill ourselves while we embrace."

I swore it. She kissed me twenty times over my heart. I didn't demand the same oath from her; she would have said to me: 'Right now'—and the bushel of my disgusts was not complete; one pin still attached me to life. I knew her to be resolute; she had been nursing that plan for a long time; thinking that she might carry it out at any moment, she carried her last will and testament on her person, so that no one would be accused of her murder. I've hesitated for a long time, I've been indecisive for a long time, so I should go to inform her of my belated decision and say to her: "Flava, I'm finally ready' Get up, come with me, and we'll kill ourselves."

I'd take so much pleasure in perishing with her; she's well worthy of it! Nevertheless, I don't want to, and I won't do it. The world is so stupid, it would say that we had...that I had killed myself for love. No, no, I don't want that; the world is so stupid, it's incapable of believing that life might be a burden of which a robust man might rid himself; it's incapable of believing in a thirst for oblivion, nor that one might find existence repugnant; it has to materialize everything in terms of cause and effect; an idea, so far as the world in concerned, is impalpable; it needs to gauge and cube everything, even its God! When it learns of the end of a suicide, it immediately goes in search of rustic, visible causes—quickly, it's because of a woman, a passion, gambling losses, domestic dishonor, mental alienation. No, no, I won't inform her; I'll die alone. I don't want anyone to say that Flava and Champavert killed one another for love, for some unfortunate, frustrated intrigue, driven to despair. It's not out of despair—I've never hoped. No, no, I don't want that.

Am I insane, alas, insane, not to want the world on which

I spit, which I despise, which I shove away with my foot, to accuse me of dying for love—weakness! Well, when I'm annihilated, what will the gross conjectures of men make of me? Their gossip won't disturb my dung-heap. But no, it's more powerful than me; I can't overcome that imbecility; weak as I am, I'll suffer from that thought until the hour sounds. No, I won't inform her; no, I'll kill myself alone.

Jean-Louis, Jean-Louis, you, you can live, since you've encountered felicity, you can live! Oh, may fate protect me from dragging you down the staircase with me into the cistern of death. Your plumage is still sticky with the moribund illusions that we impaled together, one by one; I thought you were an unblinking falcon ready to take flight for oblivion, but the world is still your chaperone. Perhaps you're waiting for an interval of peace, of rest, at the end of the quarry! What you lacked in your youth you hope to see fall upon you in decrepitude? You can't believe that existence can only be that, nothing but what you know; if it's not only that, you say to yourself, if there's no epoch of bliss, no season of pure joy, which redeems all opprobrium, how have so many people dragged heir carapaces to the end? How have thy consented to vegetate, perpetually and miserably, to patrol the stagnant pond of society until extinction? How? It's because, like you, the crowd hopes; like you, it still believes that it is on the point of attaining its vanished dream, its mad desire; it's because, like the cat that wants to seize what is in the depths of a mirror, at the moment that it leaps, radiantly upon its prey, its claws merely collide with and scrape the glass; stupefied, but not enlightened, it persists, and lies in wait, lured as before. But you, who have passed behind the mirror, who have scratched the silvering with your fingernails, who know that it is nothing but reflective glass and tinplate, alluringly, are you still lying in wait?

The world is a theater: posters in large letters, emphatic titles, hooking the crowd that immediately gets up, washes, combs its side-whiskers, puts on its ruff and is dominical coat, curls its hair, puts on its calico dress, and there it goes, umbrella in hand, brisk, joyful, desirous; it arrives, it pays; for the crowd always pays, each for the seat of his choice, or, rather, according to the qualification he has been awarded, in the vast amphitheater, the aristocracy bolted into its barred cabins, the rabble remaining in the mercy-seats. The curtain goes up, ears are pricked and necks crane; the crowd listens; for the crowd always listens; for the crowd the illusion is always complete; it is reality; the crowd identifies itself, it laughs it weeps, it conceives hatreds, amours; it howls, whistles, applauds; in vain, sometimes, its senses that it is being abused and arms itself with its opera-glasses; it is myopic, nothing can destroy its illusion and its faith, which the actors exploit so gallantly.

But you, Jean-Louis, who have penetrated into the wings, you, who have seen the other side of the palace, the flat sky, and touched the backcloth; you, who have seen the kings at close range, and naked, charlatans padded with straw; you, who have seem the carcasses of the duennas through the ocher and the plaster with which they are smeared; you, who have bedded the female lead, so innocent and virginal on stage, whose mouth reeks of the pharmacy; you, who know that the genovines[144] are only fakes; you, for whom the kings, soldiers, nobles, beauties and servants are nothing but crapulous mummers who play honor, glory and justice according to their allotted roles; Pharisees who, far from the eyes of the amphitheater, drag themselves through debauchery and bathe in turpitude; you, Jean-Louis, who are no longer fascinated, washed clean of error, will you listen to the farce all the way to the end? Will you remain in the theater mob until the end, a benevolent, open-mouthed spectator of that ignoble pantomime? Oh, Jean-Louis, you will have fallen so far from grace!

I don't hold it against you, because you're holding on to life now; certainly, you have the right to live, since the scaffold has no claim on you; you can carry your head proudly on your

144. Genovines were gold coins of extraordinarily high value issued in Genoa, which became legendary, and hence very popular in theatrical melodrama.

shoulders; it's no longer a seditious head today, the furnace no longer contains anything but iron mash; you can carry it stubbornly, that pacific head, with the privilege of the king and the authorization of Monsieur le Maire. Besides which, don't you live in the fields? And the fields are attached to existence. In truth, what could be more attractive? There are some cows; there, a hayrick; there, a croaking pond; there, threshers in a barn; there, a braying donkey; there, splashing mud; there, a field of beets. What could be more absorbing? It has an irresistible charm; I feel it. Only one thing would perhaps please me less: the monotony, the sempiternal physiognomy of nature; always rain and sun, sun and rain, always spring and autumn, heat and cold; always, and forever. Nothing is more tedious than fixity, than an immovable cycle, a perpetual almanac. Every year, green trees and green trees forever: Fontainebleau! Who will deliver us from green trees? How it dulls my mind! Why not more variety? Why do the leaves not take on all the colors of the rainbow by turns? Fontainebleau! How stupid that greenery is!

I don't hold it against you, Jean-Louis that you're clinging to life—no, but that you claim "not to understand the reasons that are driving me so abruptly to suicide!" It's you, Jean-Louis, who are asking me that? Fatality! What has changed you so? What can have refreshed your heart to such an extent, while mine is steeped in bitterness? "Abruptly." Can you really say that? You're not unaware, though, that the thought of death is the oldest of my thoughts; you're not unaware that, of every three desires, two have always been for oblivion; you're not unaware that you have applauded that yourself. It's too late now, I've taken offense; but everything that you could say to me would be in vain, I'll finish...but I love you too much not to redoubt your criticism; at least a friend won't vituperate against me; at least you can say: he did the right thing; he was brave; he killed himself.

II.
Edura

That statement completed, Champavert put it in an envelope, wrote the address: *To Jean-Louis, laborer, at the chapel in Vaudragon*; and sealed it; then he got up, calmly, as if relieved, drank a mug of tea, lit a Virginia cigarette, sat on the window-sill, smoking and staring vaguely into space. When the cigarette was finished, he went back into the room, and, making a circuit of the walls, kissed the portraits of his companions one by one, and, one by one, smashed them on the floor; then, with a mocking laugh, shrugging his shoulders disdainfully, he tore up all his books and threw them into the fire; and, arming himself with a hatchet appended to a trophy, one after another, he hacked up all the items of furniture contained in his lodgings. The floor was covered with debris, and the flames in the fireplace spread into the room. His sick heart palpitated with joy; he did not want to leave anything behind that might be useful—nothing; he did not want people, after his death, to divide up what he had possessed with laughter on their lips, for anyone after his death to love an object that he had loved, for anyone else to walk in the sunlight in his cast-offs. If he had had any money he would have thrown it in the water or buried it, so profound was his aversion for people, so much did he abhor inheritance. He was not the kind of man to have trees planted on his grave in order to shelter the weary traveler from the midday heat; he would rather have had a pitfall trap hollowed out to swallow up stray carriage-passengers or pedestrians lost in the long grass.

Satisfied with his devastation, he sat down on the ruins, as the architect Fontaine sat down on the rubble of Saint-Germain-l'Auxerre, and, opening a half-burned chest, he took out a small enameled box, lifted it to his lips intoxicatedly, and covered it with kisses.

"Edura! Edura! My first and most terrible love! My Warens!"[145]

---

145. Françoise-Louise Warens was the benefactress and mistress of Jean-Jacques Rousseau, who was thirteen years her junior and referred to her in

he repeated, his forehead red and his hands clenched, crushing and cracking the box in fingers bathed with the large tears that were falling from his eyes.

"Edura! My beautiful Edura! Woman, woman, how fatal you have been to me! If you had wanted to, you could have made something great of me; I feel all too keenly that I was predestined for it, given nothing but a word, a single word! You never pronounced it, that word, vile woman! You've done me harm! You've doomed me; you could have made me a lion; the good in my heart might have grown under your caresses; your voice, your soft speech, your kisses could have exorcised the venom that is overflowing within me; suffering has made me a ferocious wolf. Look, how I break this trinket that came to me from you!

And, hurling the enamel box on the ground, he stamped his heel upon it, and pulverized it.

"Die, die, all memory of her! Of her, who caused hatred to enter my heart; of her, who steeped my youth in bile when she could have made it so beautiful, so sublime! It's you, Edura, it's you who have embittered me, you who have expelled the generosity from my head, the sensitivity from my breast, who have worn me out and worn me down by torture and desire. It's you who have caused me to hate everything, you have doomed me when my life was open to so rich a future; it's you who have planted the seed of death in my bosom, the misery that has fertilized it.

"O inconceivable passion! Amour, amour who can explain you? Edura, O my Edura! Don't believe, after all, that I hate you. I shall always love you madly; I still quiver at your name, as before. I love you, and it's you who have killed me, you who have turned me toward oblivion. You have done me so much harm, and I love you so much! And yet you are no more to me than a confused memory; the years have passed quickly, and have made a young man of me; but you, they have aged,

---

his Confessions as his "maman."

tarnished and faded; you're no more than a gold button, a hollow willow bending over. Cavaliers no longer look at you; you no longer have a heart; you're no longer a queen. If, therefore, you had wanted to pluck my love—an immortal amaranth, which has not withered—it would still ornament you. A mother, you would have a passionate child in your arms; my blood, my warm kisses, would remind you of the life that has fled; you would have had an obliging support until the end; my youth would have overshadowed your age, and my arm would punish any mocker who lifted your veil.

"What has become of all those handsome dandies—what have they become? They can scarcely recall your name. True mounted Cossacks, the men to which you surrendered yourself, have all discarded you, in their nomad passion; they collected you as loot in passing. Poor woman! Insensate! Where, then, are the friends you prepared for the return? Suffer, suffer now; it's only just that I should be avenged, I've suffered so much. Now, perhaps, your cheeks, which no kiss will revive, are moist with tears; you languish in solitude, and that unaccustomed solitude will undermine you; perhaps diminish you—what abasement! Making pretty faces at young men who reject you and turn their backs on you. When you want to talk about love, people laugh. Suffer, suffer for a long time, that I might be well avenged! Inconceivable passion, I love you still; I feel it here; I can't hide it from myself; I love you, and I hate you profoundly; and yet, if you came to take my hand, if you came to whisper to me the word that you have always known, if you came to tell me that you loved me, as before...for you did love me, I'm sure of it; I'm sure that you have stifled your love for me, that you have rejected mine, because to love, to be loved by an obscure child was not what your prideful spirit wanted, and I still love you as violently; and yet, I tell you, if you came to me, I would reject you; for I love you today for what you once were, and not for what you are. If you threw yourself at my knees, I would be pitiless; I would strike you; if you clung to me, I would drag you away, coldly; I would be avenged!"

Then, leaning on his elbows, silently, poor Champavert wept bitterly.

"It's the first step in life that decides life; pour vinegar into the sweetest wine, and it will become vinegar," he murmured, picking up the debris of the enamel box, which he kissed and put in his purse.

Suddenly, he got up, jammed his hat down on his head, went out and locked his door.

"Here's my key," he said, as he went past the concierge's lodge. "I'm leaving for a voyage to distant parts. If anyone asks for me, please tell them that I've left the city for a long time."

"Are you going to Spain, which you love so much?"

"Further."

"Algeria?"

"Further."

He went out.

III.
Flava

That evening, a friend met him in the Rue Jean-Jacques Rousseau, as he was coming out of the post office.

At about eight o'clock, in the Chemin des Rosiers on the heights of Montmartre, he rang at a red gate.

A young woman opened it: her blonde hair floating over her white dress; her pale complexion and her anxious gaze, her languorous but disengaged gait, her hollow bosom and bowed head testified mournfully that suffering, like a thunderbolt, had ravaged and was ravaging that beautiful, broken, deflowered creature.

On seeing Champavert she uttered an exclamation of surprise. "You, my savage, at this hour—what chance brings you here?"

"Friend, if I've come, it's not a matter of chance; it's expressly to see you."

"At least permit me to doubt, Champavert."

"Bad girl—you're trying to wound me. Are you alone?"

"Yes."

"Entirely alone?"

"Yes."

"Your father?"

"He's gone down to the city."

"That's lucky! I can see you and talk to you at leisure, without his wide eyes and big ears spying."

"What has changed you thus, my Champavert? What sun has melted the ice of your heart? Oh, truly, it's a fine thing, after two months of absence, to come and play the lover."

"Flava, I'm not playing; I am to you what I've always been. I accept your reproaches, I know that in appearance, I might merit them; I'm not very assiduous, it's true, but you still reign in my heart; you reign like the fatherland in the heart of an exile; you reign like life in the heart of a man condemned. Absence does not destroy love, you know. I'm not very assiduous, it's true, but what do you want me to do here more frequently? Suffer! Always kept out of sight, like a political prisoner, I can't even squeeze your hand, whisper in your ear; our gazes can scarcely meet; it hurts me too much; I can't bear it. How many times have I been tempted to strike your father, your jailers, to take your arm and tell you that we should flee! Oh, if you were free, or if we could at least indulge in pleasant conversation, you wouldn't complain about the infrequency of my visits."

"But what does it matter, since the mere sight of you restores so much courage to my heart? Oh, it's cruel, Champavert, to hate a woman so, and then to spring from the ground like a demon, two or three times a year, to come to tell her lies, to tell her that you love her—oh, it's cruel, Champavert!"

"Flava, you're treating me harshly, you're taking pleasure in tormenting me! Is it necessary, then, always to renew my avowals of love, as at the start? Always to be making further proclamations? You should at least know me after the six years we've been linked together. If I'm not assiduous, am I not a faithful lover? I know that you have the right to doubt me, that once, when very young, I was wicked, but has my constancy not redeemed all that? I love you, Flava; I love you profoundly and forever. Would you like another oath? I love you, Flava, and I swear to you on the body...."

"Silence! Silence, Champavert! Don't invoke his shade!"

"Don't weep, Flava! Don't weep, good mother; your tears have hollowed out your cheeks sufficiently, your tears are bitter on my lips; don't weep, good mother! He's happier than we are; he is not."

"Happier than we are, he is not.... That's the truth, Champavert; how I love that thought! Oh, tell me, are you ready?"

"No, my beauty, let's wait a while; perhaps better days will arise for us; so young still, we have a long future! Wait a while, we've drunk absinthe before the feast, let's await, after the mourning of the night, the dawn and the dew."

"Champavert, when a tree has been struck by lightning, no spring can redeem it; it is withered at the root, until a wood-cutter chops it down with his ax. Champavert, shall we wait for the stroke of the ax of death, the belated woodcutter? That would be cowardly!"

"It's reckless to prejudge the future, my beauty, let's rid ourselves of this somberness; let's be less elegiac, please."

"That's right, at leisure, jest! You're grimacing, Champavert; your laughter isn't laughter that comes from the heart, it's the laughter of torment. You gave yourself away just now."

During this conversation, in a shady arbor, the moon had risen above the horizon and its rays, piercing the vacillating foliage of the chestnut-trees, sowed the sand with nacre and the darkness with silver fireflies. The nightingale was not yet singing its nocturne, and nothing could be heard in the immensity except the amorous sound of their voices, rising up like the sigh of a Gnomide.[146]

---

146. A female gnome.

IV.
Damnation

"The plain is dark and solitary; get up, my love, and go down to the orchard; come and walk down there, near the cistern; it's been a long time since I knelt on that ground; perhaps the holly shading his mortuary crib has been cropped? Let's go see."

"Oh no, the holly is green and busy and the grass long and beautiful; my tears are a fecund rain, and I water them every night."

"You go down to the well every night?"

"Yes, every night! When everyone in the house is asleep, I get up and go down to say my prayer over his grave. When I've prayed abundantly and wept copiously beneath the heavens, I feel calmer. Nature seems to forgive me my crime; I seem to hear in the universal silence a voice coming from the stars, which cries to me: 'Your crime is not your own, weak child of the earth; it is humankind's and society's! May its blood fall back upon them and it! I go back in before dawn, and then enjoy a more peaceful sleep, devoid of frightful dreams."

"Mystery woman! Why have you never mentioned these nocturnal visits to me? I would have been there myself; I would have come to pray and weep with you."

"Don't do that, Champavert, above all, don't do that—you'll doom me! Several times, my suspicious father has followed me, I'm sure of it; I've seen him, there, hidden behind the wall of the cistern, listening to me; we'd give ourselves away. So I've been very careful to whisper my prayers, for fear that he might understand why I'm praying. He's asked me several times, with a knowing smile, whether I might be a sleepwalker; I pretended not to understand, and, without being disconcerted, I replied that I might well be."

They were almost at the bottom of the steep path that led down to the well; the moon had disappeared, the sky was black; a few lightning flashes were visible on the horizon, like phosphoric gleams. Flava was leaning on Champavert's arm; he was clutching a branch of verbena in his hand.

"Is there any odor sweeter than Indian verbena? Do you like flowers, Flava?"

"Very much."

"For you to love flowers, Flava, is self-love! Do you like perfumes?"

"Very much."

"For myself, I love them madly. It's said that it ill befits a man, but what do I care? I'm no more effeminate for it. If I let myself go, I'd fill my lodgings with balsamic plants, charge myself with scents like a little mistress. When I'm depressed, a branch of odorant honeysuckle is a great consolation for me.

"Many cavaliers mount a guard beneath a beauty's balcony; personally, I'd climb up for a flower; many cavaliers make long journeys to talk of love; I'd go to Spain for a bergamot, to the Orient for benzoin; many cavaliers sell their cloak in order to gamble away the price; personally, I'd trade mine for a phial of attar of roses.

"But for me, Flava, above all, you are the most odorant phial, the sweetest reseda, the most precious Arabic balm. So, for you, I'd do more than watch beneath a balcony; I'd do more than undertake a pilgrimage, I'd do more than deprive myself of my cloak; if you demanded it, I'd live!"

"You're giving yourself away again, Champavert—are you ready? Tell me, I beg you: remember your promise!"

"Oh, not that; I mean that if I were decided on oblivion, and you wanted me to live, I would live."

"Champavert, you're blaspheming in speaking thus of oblivion; you're making me infernally ill! Look, then, at the furrowed sky, that plain, those hills, that majestic nature! Look at me! And after that, believe in oblivion if you can!"

"Like you, Flava, I once loved poems and phrases."

"Alas, if we aren't to be reborn happy for eternity, it would be very atrocious! A life of suffering and misery, and nothing afterwards?"

"Oblivion."

"Oh! You don't believe that!"

"Yes, I believe it. It's out of cowardice that humans recoil before oblivion; they fashion a future life according to their whim, lull themselves and intoxicate themselves with the lie that they have made for themselves, and, content with that discovery, when they die, like madmen on the bed of iron, with a foolish laugh on their faces, they say to you: 'Adieu! Au revoir! I'm leaving for a better world; we'll meet again up there!' And then, with an even more foolish laugh, their heirs, with joy in their hearts, reply: 'Adieu! Bon voyage! We'll be joining you before long, prepare our reservations in the hostelry of paradise.'

"Well, no! Idiots that you are, you're going where all things go, to oblivion! And it's face to face with death, with one foot in grave, cowards, that I tell you that! I don't want another life; I've had enough of living; it's oblivion that I'm summoning!"

"Shut up, shut up, Champavert, don't blaspheme so—if you know how frightful your gaze is! But what, then, my love will be the recompense for the unfortunates tortured down here?"

"Who will compensate the horse for its sweat, the forest for the ax, the saw and the fire? Undoubtedly, there's also another life for horses and oaks? A paradise!"

"You're raving, Champavert, shut up! God can hear you; don't you fear his thunder?"

"If there's a God who launches thunderbolts, I defy him! Let him launch his lightning at me, then, this powerful God who has everything, I defy him! Here, I spit at the heavens! Look over there, do you see that poor lightning fading away on the horizon? One would think that it were afraid of me. Oh, quite frankly, your God isn't susceptible to a point of honor. If I were God, if I had thunderbolts in my hand, oh, I wouldn't allow myself to be insulted, defied by an insect, an earthworm!

"Anyway, you Christians, you've hanged your God—and you've done well, for, if there were a God, he'd warrant hanging."

"Oh, let me flee; the earth is opening up beneath your feet! Satan, you fill me with horror! Leave me, Champavert; I haven't made any pact; shut up, I beg you; I'll die if you blaspheme any more! Must I kiss your feet?"

"Until now, I've maintained my composure, but so many miseries have enraged me! Oh, if I held humankind as I'm holding you, I'd strangle it! If it had but one life, I'd strike it with this dagger, I'd annihilate it! If I held your God, I'd strike him as I'm striking this tree! If I held my mother, my mother who gave me life, I'd disembowel her! There's nothing more infamous than a mother! Oh, if only she'd strangled me in her entrails, as you did to our son.... Horror! I'm raving.....

"Atrocious world! It's necessary, then, that a girl kill her son, else she loses her honor! Flava, you're an honorable daughter, you have massacred yours! You're a virgin, Flava! Horror! Get away from this grave, that I might tear the earth with my fingernails; I want to see my son again; I want to see him again in my final hour!"

"Don't disturb his sacred tomb!"

"Sacred! I tell you that I want to see my son again in my final hour! Let me dig up this grave."

The rain was falling in waves, the thunder roaring, and when the lightning-flashes hurled their sheets of flame over the plain, Flava could be seen, disheveled, her white dress like a shroud, lying beneath the holly bushes. Champavert, on his knees on the ground, was digging in the sand with his fingernails and his dagger. Suddenly, he stood up, holding a skeleton laden with rags in his fist.

"Flava! Flava!" he cried. "Look, look! Look, then, at your son; look, that's what eternity is! Look!"

"You're making me suffer so much, Champavert, kill me! All this for one crime, one alone—oh, it's too much!"

"Law! Virtue! Honor! You're satisfied—here, take back your prey! Barbaric words, you wanted it—here, look, this is your work—yours! Are you content with your victim? Are you content with your victims? Bastard! It's very brazen of you, to have wanted to be born without royal authorization, without banns! Eh! The law, eh? Honor?

"Don't weep, Flava. What is it, anyway? Nothing: an infanticide. Many timid virgins are on their third, many virtuous women count their springs by murders, Barbaric law! Ferocious prejudice! Infamous honor! Men! Society! Here! Take your prey! I return it to you!"

As he howled those final words, Champavert hurled the cadaver away, which, rolling down the steep slope, fell on to the stones of the road and shattered.

"Champavert, Champavert, finish me!" croaked Flava, could and dying. "Are you ready now?"

"Yes."

"Strike me, that I might die first! Look, strike here—it's my heart! Adieu!!!"

"To oblivion!!!"

On that last word, Champavert knelt down, put the point of the dagger to Flava's breast and, propping the hilt against his own breast, let himself fall heavily upon her, hugging her in his arms; the blade went in coldly, and Flava uttered a scream of death that made the quarries roar.

Champavert extracted the blade from the wound, rose to his feet, and, head bowed, went down the hill and disappeared into the fog and the rain.

V.

De Profundis

The next day, at dawn, a haulier heard a crack under the wheel of his cart; it was the fleshy skeleton of a child.

A peasant found the cadaver of a woman, with a hole in her heart, near the well.

And on the Buttes de Monfaulcon, a knacker, whistling his song and rolling up his sleeves, perceived, lying on a pile of horse-dung, a man covered in blood. His head, tipped back and dipped in the mire, only allowed the sight of a long black beard. There was a large knife buried in his breast, like a stake.

ABOUT THE TRANSLATOR

BRIAN STABLEFORD has translated more than a hundred volumes of French prose into English. His principal interests are the French Romantic Movement and its Decadent/Symbolist aftermath, with particular reference to the evolution of the *conte cruel*, and the evolution of the *roman scientifique* from its origins in the eighteen-century *conte philosophique* to the aftermath of the Great War of 1914-18.

www.ingramcontent.com/pod-product-compliance
Lightning Source LLC
Chambersburg PA
CBHW021240260626
47155CB00004BA/1239